Gaby pushed Cross away, and to her surprise, he allowed the distance. He even stepped back to give her room. "What is it?" he asked again.

"Something's wrong."

"Okay." He turned a full circle, searching the area. He held his body in the deceptively relaxed pose of someone who knew how to kick serious ass.

Moderating her strained breathing, keeping her thoughts calm and free, Gaby took her time scanning the area. She detected the commonplace turbulence of humans out on this muggy, electric night—but not the red-hot evil she sought . . .

Until she again faced Cross.

It lurked *behind* him, in the playground.

Stepping around the detective, Gaby strode determinedly toward the evil, and sensed it taking flight, evading her, running from her.

Like a candle, once snuffed, only a wisp of smoke remained as a reminder of the flame. Gaby wanted to follow, to hunt the malignant corruption and chase it to ground, but damn it, Cross stood there, watching her, waiting.

Because she couldn't risk him or her secrets, knowing that with him observing her every move she *couldn't* proceed, she cast him a quelling glare.

"Fascinating," he said, without a speck of humor. "Now tell me what the hell is going on."

SERVANT
THE AWAKENING

L. L. FOSTER

BERKLEY BOOKS, NEW YORK

THE BERKLEY PUBLISHING GROUP
Published by the Penguin Group
Penguin Group (USA) Inc.
375 Hudson Street, New York, New York 10014, USA
Penguin Group (Canada), 90 Eglinton Avenue East, Suite 700, Toronto, Ontario M4P 2Y3, Canada
(a division of Pearson Penguin Canada Inc.)
Penguin Books Ltd., 80 Strand, London WC2R 0RL, England
Penguin Group Ireland, 25 St. Stephen's Green, Dublin 2, Ireland (a division of Penguin Books Ltd.)
Penguin Group (Australia), 250 Camberwell Road, Camberwell, Victoria 3124, Australia
(a division of Pearson Australia Group Pty. Ltd.)
Penguin Books India Pvt. Ltd., 11 Community Centre, Panchsheel Park, New Delhi—110 017, India
Penguin Group (NZ), 67 Apollo Drive, Rosedale, North Shore 0632, New Zealand
(a division of Pearson New Zealand Ltd.)
Penguin Books (South Africa) (Pty.) Ltd., 24 Sturdee Avenue, Rosebank, Johannesburg 2196,
South Africa

Penguin Books Ltd., Registered Offices: 80 Strand, London WC2R 0RL, England

This is a work of fiction. Names, characters, places, and incidents either are the product of the author's imagination or are used fictitiously, and any resemblance to actual persons, living or dead, business establishments, events, or locales is entirely coincidental. The publisher does not have any control over and does not assume any responsibility for author or third-party websites or their content.

SERVANT: THE AWAKENING

A Berkley Book / published by arrangement with the author

PRINTING HISTORY
Berkley edition / October 2007

Copyright © 2007 by Lori Foster.
Excerpt from *Servant: The Acceptance* by L. L. Foster copyright © 2008 by Lori Foster.
Stepback illustration by John Blumen.
Cover design by Rita Frangie.
Interior text design by Laura K. Corless.

ISBN: 978-0-425-21874-7

BERKLEY®
Berkley Books are published by The Berkley Publishing Group,
a division of Penguin Group (USA) Inc.,
375 Hudson Street, New York, New York 10014.
BERKLEY® is a registered trademark of Penguin Group (USA) Inc.
The "B" design is a trademark belonging to Penguin Group (USA) Inc.

PRINTED IN THE UNITED STATES OF AMERICA

10 9 8 7 6 5 4 3 2 1

Chapter 1

"Be very, very still now. Don't move."

Gray eyes, faded from years of living, cloudy with dementia, gave only a blank stare.

So amusing, the lack of mental acuity. "Yes, I know you hear me, even if you do look hollow and empty. But I suppose it's okay that you don't understand everything happening. Better, even." Humor tilted the corners of the physician's mouth. "It makes my job that much easier."

The personality of this human shell was long gone, eaten away by neglect, age, and disease. There could be no soul, not in something so pathetic and uncomprehending. Now the frail, emancipated body would serve a higher calling. Science would benefit. The extent of possibilities learned had no boundaries.

Exciting, that's what it was. Challenging and, though some would never admit it, honorable.

The overhead light glinted on the heavy-duty steel wire

snips. Proper surgical tools would be better, but they were costly and not easy to steal. The fewer chances taken, the better.

For the sake of science, a carpenter's tools would have to do.

Carefully, the physician guided one gangling finger into the jaws of the snips. Not too far, just deep enough to remove the very tip.

The fingerprint.

Evidence of any life. Of any background.

Such precautions were necessary in the event the discarded bodies, the ones that couldn't hold up under the trials, were ever found. There could be no evidence to trace, no way to be implicated.

Ready.

One breath. Two. *Squeeze.*

Brittle bone crunched, severed, between the razor-sharp blades; shock stilled the subject, and a second later, a tearing, agonizing scream bounded around the cavernous room, stirring the others to rail and groan in helpless fear.

Disturbed by the ballyhoo, the doctor glanced around at each of them. They might be incoherent and utterly useless to functioning society, but they still perceived the trials awaiting them.

Fortunately, they'd come to this remote location drugged almost comatose, and before the hallucinogens and painkillers wore off, they'd been strapped down securely with crude, makeshift restraints.

Those same straps kept this body still, and no one was around to hear the eerie wails of agony. No one who mattered.

The next finger found the same fate.

Warm blood pooled onto the rickety table and stained the rough linens. Sterilized stitching took place after every two or three removals. Boring, tedious work, but necessary to stop the blood flow and assist in healing.

Effective experimentation could not be done on a dead body.

"Now." Smiling, the doctor looked down to find the body unnaturally still. Pain had carried the patient to the oblivion of unconsciousness. Annoyance replaced the amusement; every great doctor appreciated an attentive audience to witness strokes of brilliance.

But perhaps it was better this way. There'd be no more need for small talk. No need to soothe.

On to business.

The right hand still waited.

The crimson sunrise spilled into the cramped but tidy room, bringing with it the monotony of responsibility and the taint of rancid malevolence. Funny, how people always assumed evil lurked in the shadowy night, that it wore a face of frightening proportions, that it could—in any way—be predictable.

With the nine-millimeter resting in her hand, her finger curved around the trigger, Gabrielle Cody lay unmoving. The knife strapped to her back dug into her spine with reassuring familiarity. Even in sleep, her muscles stayed taut, her body prepared.

Today, her twenty-first birthday, dawned no different from any other. Had she really hoped to have a respite from the grueling duty?

The sounds of birds awakening, cars driving by, and the relentless, rhythmic beating of her heart swarmed her mind. She wished she could deny the morning. She wished she could be reborn as someone else, someone . . . normal.

But no matter how Gabrielle strained and resisted, she

couldn't deny the pull. With each second that ticked past, the clawing from within swelled, screaming louder inside her head, making her guts churn and her blood rush hot until the walls of her chest burned like fire. With a tearing groan and a stiffening of her legs, she narrowed her eyes and did her best to focus on the cracked and stained ceiling.

Leave me alone.

The silent command resonated within her head, just like the inexorable draw that refused to be ignored.

Battling it brought a light sweat to her skin, leaving her naked body slick. Her breath soughed in and out. The lumpy mattress took on the appeal of hard gravel, urging her to start the day.

Resistance was futile.

"Fuck it." Gabrielle thrust herself off the bed in a rush of acceptance. Her bare feet padded in hollow silence across the floor to the open window, where she stared at the hazy sunrise swimming on the horizon. The mid-June day would torture with heat and humidity—perfect for her birthday.

As long as it didn't storm, she could function. But if black clouds moved in and the thunder began to belch and bluster . . . Just thinking of it made her palms damp and her throat tight. Shit. She might as well fear the dark or the occasional spider while she was at it.

She snorted, scrubbed at her tired eyes, and surveyed everything within her range of sight.

As usual, her attention landed on the playground first, surrounded by a sturdy chain-link fence that couldn't stop a damn thing and would offer no protection from the real threats. By midmorning, laughing, innocent children would be at play with an excess of noise and excitement.

The now-abandoned elementary school drew her notice next. Once, long ago, it taught dreams and encouraged illusions. They'd put up the fence to keep the kids in, ignorant and oblivious to the true dangers lurking beneath a veneer of social acceptability.

All along the road, traffic multiplied in a scorched wave of colors and sounds and exhaust fumes. It hadn't rained in weeks and brittle tree leaves rustled under the encouragement of a hot, restless breeze.

Gaby drew a breath—and held it.

Somewhere out there, somewhere that no one could see or suspect, horrible things waited, taunting her senses, painfully pricking her nerves, making her vision slide within. She knew it. She always knew it.

She fucking *hated* it.

Wrenching away from the window, she unbuckled the knife strap from around her waist and carried it, with the heavy gun, into the bathroom. In her efficiency apartment, it was the only closed room. A single large room housed everything else: her bed, her hot plate, an old rickety desk and a minuscule dresser, a microwave and small refrigerator.

After setting the weapons aside, she double-bolted the special door she'd installed for her peace of mind, and then turned on the shower. The original door and flimsy lock hadn't taken much more than a single punch before giving way. Now, when the rush of water impaired her perceptions, it'd require a talented locksmith or a true behemoth to break in.

Whenever circumstances like sleeping or bathing left her vulnerable, Gaby did all she could to protect herself. The shower, with its old rattling pipes, made more noise than most. At times, it sounded like the demons from hell were trying to crawl through the walls.

Some would call her specialized precautions paranoid.

But then, most had no idea that crazed demons *did* crawl the earth.

Death didn't frighten her. No, there were times when Gaby prayed for death to take her.

Those prayers went unanswered.

What she didn't want, what she couldn't bear to contemplate, was unending torment. She could handle pain; she always had. But if the pain had no end . . .

Locking her teeth, Gaby stepped under the tepid spray and let the water hit her face, trickle down her body. It didn't dispel the truth of what she had to do, what she put off doing. It didn't ease her muscles or alleviate the agony that became a part of her, more so with every passing moment.

It only removed the sweat and took the sting out of her eyes.

Lingering in the shower, she cleaned her teeth while straining her ears to hear any sound of intrusion. Ten minutes later, clean and dry, she combed back her short dark hair and dressed in a way that wouldn't draw attention. Birthday or not, she could no longer deny her God-appointed duty.

Closing her eyes and relaxing her mind allowed her to drop her resistance, leaving her open to the summons.

Like the spike of a frozen ice pick, it struck her nape, then slowly, raggedly, scraped down her spine and straight into her soul.

Her muscles jerked and twitched, and her mouth opened on a gasp as the pain dug deep, expanding to invade her every nerve ending. She didn't shy away from the agony; she knew it would do no good. As an incentive, the physical misery would remain until she finished the job.

In her practiced way, Gaby evened her breathing, accepting, embracing the pain so it could revitalize her, heightening her awareness and honing her instincts to razor sharpness.

Today someone—some*thing*—would die.

She knew, because she'd kill it.

But not with the gun. Gun blasts made too much noise and drew too much attention. What Gaby had to do, no one would understand.

So no one could know.

She locked the weapon away in a special box that fit into her bedsprings. Eventually, someone would invade this sanctum, and then she'd have to move on. Until then, she did everything in her power to appear as a normal being.

Mustering a pretense of indifference, harboring her knife beneath her loose dark T-shirt and frayed jeans, Gaby left her apartment and went down the long, dark, narrow stairwell. Her footfalls caused a hollow echo in the dilapidated building while her mind moved ahead to her duties, where she'd start and how she'd finish.

Before she could leave the aged brick building, Morty Vance, her landlord and the owner of a kitschy comic book store next door, stepped out of his apartment.

"Gaby."

Urgency sizzled and snapped, but she kept her voice even, her façade one of normalcy, when normalcy remained so far out of her reach.

"Mort." It wasn't easy, but she somehow managed to lighten the intensity of her scowl. Mort wasn't a bad guy. The gray aura of difficulty and depression clung to him, but there were no reds or browns to indicate the presence of evil. "I was just—"

"Going to join me for breakfast." Knowing her weaknesses, he held a chipped ceramic mug filled with fragrant, steaming coffee toward her nose. "Scrambled eggs are fresh off the stove. Come in and eat."

Food. At his mention, her stomach rumbled in hollow

need. How the hell did she constantly forget food? Father Mullond, rest his soul, had chastised her again and again for not refueling.

Thanks to her less-than-healthy eating habits, she weighed only one-twenty, which looked odd considering she stood six feet tall. But that sometimes worked to her advantage. Despite the lankiness of her limbs, omnipotent strength surged through her. Along with fluid muscles, she possessed awesome speed and deadly accuracy.

The devil's tools, but a gift from God.

Or so Father Mullond insisted.

Gaby had few female curves to get in the way of her duty. In no way, shape, or form could she ever be labeled as a typical woman. Hell, she barely passed as typically human.

Morty, the dumbshit, didn't seem to notice or care.

Gaby wasn't psychic, not in the entertainment-perfect, romantic way average people liked to perceive special abilities. Her *talent*, as Father Mullond had dared to call it, proved more basic than that. She knew jack about summoning past lives or interpreting the musings of ghosts or whatever other melodrama supposed-psychics dished out.

She perceived the intention of the mentally sick, the innately wicked, the crazed fiends that scuttled over the surface of the earth, pretending to be like everyone else, fooling most, but not her.

When instructed, she took care of them.

Morty wasn't evil, so she didn't bother dwelling on him. But she'd have to be a real dope to be oblivious to his infatuation.

Sick bastard.

What did she have to draw male attention? Not a damn thing, which, she supposed, proved Mort's desperation for female company. Or maybe any company.

She glanced at the mug, at his pathetically hopeful grin, and gave up with a shrug. "Yeah, sure. Why not?"

Fueling her body made her stronger, so it'd be easier to carry on. Each summons left her so depleted, so weak and vulnerable, just surviving became a chore. A little nourishment first wouldn't hurt.

Besides, she had some time before anything major happened. It meant she'd have to rush to reach her destination, wherever that destination might be, but she'd spent most of her life rushing from one ghastly abomination to another.

Her cheap rubber flip-flops slapped the scarred wooden floor as she crossed the hall and took the coffee. The hem of her loose-fitting jeans kicked up dust motes, sending them afloat in the gray, stagnant air. And still, Morty watched her with transparent idolatry.

After a deep drink that burned her throat and felt like heaven as it hit her empty stomach, Gaby followed Mort into his rooms.

She'd met Morty Vance three years ago after a particularly grueling destruction had left her too exposed to stay in her past residence. Thanks to Morty and his comic book store, she had a job to support herself while fulfilling her duty.

She lived too wired, and a lot too cautious, to tolerate nosy neighbors. The room above Morty's apartment suited her, and having the connecting comic book store next door proved convenient. No one, not even Morty, knew what she did to support herself, or about her calling. But Morty had seen her going up the stairs covered in sweat, sometimes spattered with blood, often bruised and worse.

As per their initial agreement before she rented from him, and despite his personal interest, Mort respected her privacy.

Whenever he'd come upon her in those situations, he'd

offered assistance that she had to refuse. He'd offered protection, which she knew he couldn't give.

He offered . . . friendship.

And damn it, she'd never had a friend. So, just as she couldn't deny the calling, she couldn't quite deny pathetic Morty Vance.

He was such a dumb-ass loser creep.

Just what she deserved.

His pale blue eyes all but absorbed her. "You know, breakfast is the most important meal of the day."

She'd never thought in terms of meals because her life had never been routine. She slept when she could. Ate when she remembered. Fought when called upon. Destroyed as instructed.

And when time allowed, she drew and narrated her graphic novels.

The comics had gained instant popularity with the underground community. Gaby kept them out of the hands of reputable publishers. They were too gory, too bloody.

And too damn real.

The last thing she needed was someone putting two and two together, and equaling her involvement.

Saying nothing, Gaby allowed Morty to lead her into his kitchen. At the chipped Formica table, she turned a chair around and straddled it. Watching Morty dish up eggs and sizzling sausage, she took another long draw of the coffee. God, the food smelled good.

Like a kitchen should.

Wishing she remembered how to smile, Gaby studied Mort's stringy brown hair, the amateur tattoo on his scrawny white shoulder, the paunch that protruded over the waistband of his pants. At twenty-six, a few years older than her, Morty should have been out dating and having the time of his life.

Instead, he lived in his stupid comics, believing in superheroes and the theory that good could triumph over evil.

No one ever triumphed over evil because evil never ended. It was inestimable, coming and going with no predictability, a relentless, driving influence with forces too intimidating to conceive or even consider.

Disgusted with herself, Gaby set the mug aside and crossed her arms over the chair back. "How come you don't date, Mort?"

With his aura shifting and undulating, he glanced up and away. His unshaven chin, patchy in the way of a sixteen-year-old, quivered. "No time. Besides, most girls are bitches."

Or stupid. Or naïve. Just like most men.

"So?" Gaby tracked Mort's progress across the floor while he set the table and brought out condiments. Not one for tact, she said, "You could clean up. Get rid of the baggy clothes and nasty hair and—"

"Dig in." He dropped into his own seat and scooped up a large bite of egg. "I threw in some special seasonings. See what you think."

At his expectant look, Gaby turned in her chair, ate several bites, and shrugged. "It's edible."

She'd almost finished the meal when Mort visibly worked up his nerve. "You never date, either."

"No." She spent all her time surviving.

Hesitation throbbed in the air before he asked, "Why?"

"It'd be pointless for me to date."

His expression lifted. "Really? Why?"

Swallowing down the last bite, Gaby shoved back the plate. "I'm . . . asexual. Uninterested and uninteresting and I sure as hell don't have time for stupid questions today." Or any other day. She pushed her chair away from the table and stood.

"Where are you rushing off to?"

Because he'd never before asked, Gaby stalled. Good God, had turning twenty-one made some miraculous change in her demeanor, somehow led him to believe he could grill her?

Encouraging more than a quick meal could be disastrous—for him. He wouldn't understand. Hell, he wouldn't even believe her. Best to set him straight right off, though she hated to hurt him. He'd had enough hurt in his miserable little life.

Taking one big step, Gaby towered over Mort, holding him in her unflinching gaze until he shifted in discomfort and a touch of fear, pressed back in his chair as if it might absorb him. "Mind your own business, Mort."

Embarrassment and worry flushed his face. Awkwardly, cautiously, he eased his chair from the table and rose to his feet. "I don't mean to pry."

The colors encircling him faded to soft pink and lilac, indicating his compassion . . . for her?

Fuck that.

Gaby turned and strode away. She didn't need the likes of Mort Vance. She was Gabrielle Cody, God's tool on earth, the hammer that smashed savage monsters without regret, without—

Mort rushed after her. "Gabrielle, I'm sorry. Please. Please, don't go mad."

God, he was so fucking wretched. So alone and weird, and . . . sad. Some lost kernel of sympathy wormed its way into Gaby's cold, blackened heart. At the apartment door, she turned. "I told you from jump that I don't like questions."

His hands twisted together. "I just . . . sometimes I worry about you."

Oh hell no. Her feral growl had him backing up a step. "Tell me that's a joke."

He swallowed. "I don't want to see you hurt."

Then he should damn well keep his eyes closed around her because even now the pain boiled inside her, leaving her flesh raw, her insides tortured.

"Fine." She leaned toward him and color leached from his face. "Then quit grilling me, because your nosiness is a real pain in my ass."

He jerked back as if slapped, and Gaby went out without another word. Just as she stepped outside, she heard his door close with a near-silent click.

Had she hurt his feelings?

For a single moment, a niggling of guilt squirmed through her. But she had serious work to do with no time for distractions. Forcing Mort from her mind, she went down the three painted concrete steps to the street.

The moment her feet made contact with the blacktop, heat shimmered up her body to cling to her skin without penetrating. Temperatures, both sweltering and frosty, affected her differently than they did normal people. When she had a job to do, she remained impervious.

Cold didn't make her shiver.

Heat didn't deplete her strength.

Her entire being focused on what had to be done, with no room left to consider mundane attributes like the weather.

Already sinking into the zone, Gaby slipped on reflective sunglasses and scanned the area, seeking out the trigger. She wouldn't need her car today. How she knew that, she couldn't explain. She just knew it'd be better not to have it. The old white and rust Ford Falcon wasn't that reliable anyway, whereas her feet had seldom let her down.

Pain pulsed through her veins, driving her forward. As a child, she'd fought the bone-grinding agony, thinking it physical. She used to curl up in her bed and sob, trying to comprehend the inexplicable. She'd been too young to understand the magnetism of what she had to do to make the hurt go away.

When doctors could find nothing wrong with her, the wards had grown disgusted. They showed her no sympathy, and even punished her for refusing to leave the bed. They doubled her chores, hoping to reprimand her out of her hypochondria. She'd grown strong, physically and mentally. She'd isolated herself from others.

But the pain had continued to plague her.

As a teen, she'd met Father Mullond, and from the start he took acute interest in her, as if through her appearance alone, he could see the difference in her. There'd been no one else in her miserable life, only foster homes and dispassionate strangers, so to her, Father became her family: brother, parent, uncle, confidant—he filled every role.

He cared about her.

And he understood her.

Oh sure, some might call what he'd done unethical. The church definitely wouldn't have approved. But like her, Father had accepted that certain things were out of God's hands. He would smile and say that God had singled her out, recognizing her as a paladin. He made it sound almost . . . special.

He made *her* sound special, instead of freakish.

Through guidance and care, he'd taught her to cope. To this day, Gaby could still hear his voice coming to her in the darkest moments of her life. "Smile, Gabrielle. He has named you a paragon of chivalry. A heroic champion. It's a gift that comes with great responsibility. You and you alone have the ability to protect the innocent."

Not all innocents, Gaby thought, reminded of those she didn't save. She did what she could, but it was never enough. A hundred paladins wouldn't be enough. But at least she'd had Father on her side.

To reinforce that her ability was right and good, he'd taken the confessions of sinners too evil to inhabit the earth. Together they'd waged a war, and in the process Gaby had learned how to sharpen her skill, to understand the summons, to follow an urge to the rightful conclusion.

She wouldn't die. God wouldn't let her, even during the lowest points of her life when she'd pleaded for death.

The same couldn't be said for Father.

Long before she'd been ready to face the world on her own, he'd been taken from her. Not by the evil so many feared, but a disease just as heinous: cancer.

Never again would she open herself to that depth of emotional devastation. Fighting a league of demons alone was much, much easier than losing a beloved friend.

Drawn into herself, concentrating fiercely on the mental trail, Gaby had traveled nearly two blocks when a wolf whistle split the air, startling her out of the disturbing memories.

Without noticing, she'd come alongside the local bar overflowing with idiots who never went home, or didn't have homes to go to. Given the slums she lived in, lewd comments and sexual harassment were as common as the decayed-brick scenery.

A muddy brown aura hung in the air, indicating that evil lurked here, preying on the despondent, the emotionally weak. Pausing by a lamppost, Gaby surveyed the area with a dispassionate eye. Leering men pushed away from the doorway to encircle her.

One by one, Gaby looked at the drunks—and dismissed the taint of their influence. Most of their destruction would be wreaked inwardly, on their own persons.

Stupid bastards.

She would have walked away. Unfortunately, for them, they didn't allow her to do that.

Well hell. It needed only this.

Chapter 2

Gaby braced herself.

"Don't go jumpin' out of your skin, baby girl," said one man as he closed the distance to her. "I jus' wanna get to know ya."

From right behind her, another said, "Damn, you're a tall drink. Ain't never seen a bitch so tall."

"Who gives a fuck if she's a giant? She smells clean." A misshapen nose sniffed the air around her.

Childish name-calling could neither distract nor insult her. She had too much to do.

Gaby started to step around the men. One brazenly blocked her way. "You might be tall, but you ain't got much in the way of tits, now do you?"

A lot of knee-slapping and roaring good humor followed that gibe.

Gaby said, "Drop dead," and shoved past him. But she'd taken only two steps when she got worried. She glanced at the vast sky and whispered, "Just kidding, okay?" She didn't really want some sad sap dead on her account—not that God listened to her all that often. But just in case . . .

A hand circled her upper arm, drawing her to a stop.

Shit. She did *not* have time for this.

"Uppity bitch," the drunk complained. "Why're you in such a hurry?"

The other losers snickered, egging him on.

Gaby didn't want to hurt anyone—not yet anyway. In her current mood, her control would be iffy at best. If she let go, she might kill the miserable fool by mistake. No loss to humanity, but her conscience could only take so much baggage.

In motions slow and precise, she pivoted to face him. Even slouched with drink, he stood tall enough to meet her eye to eye. Jesus, he smelled like ass and looked like death.

She slipped off her sunglasses to give him the full brunt of her discontent.

A spasm of surprise slackened his mouth, and the damp fingers clutching her arm flinched, then tightened with obvious dread.

Yeah, when in the zone, she had that effect on people. She didn't know why—maybe she appeared more menacing, or her determination became tactile. Whatever, most people in their right minds got out of her way.

This guy didn't, which only proved that too much drink had addled his common sense. More out of shock than deliberate intent, he hung on to her.

The stench of sweat, combined with the oily, alcohol residue of his skin and breath, sent a lurch through Gaby's stomach. She had to force herself to continue looking at him, to open her mind to him.

An atmosphere of depression and desolation heaved

around him. Disturbed, yes, but not demonic. Definitely not the one who had gotten her out of bed.

When she didn't react, he shored up his nerve and reached for her rear, filling his hand with one cheek. At least he hadn't touched the small of her back and discovered her knife. Gaby considered that far more serious than a little grab-ass.

Laughing like hyenas, his friends shouted encouragement and suggestions.

Emboldened, he squeezed and cuddled her, saying, "A tight ass, too." His mean smile showed discolored teeth. "But I don't mind much."

She didn't move away as he'd probably expected her to. She didn't cower, or tremble. Her rage built in tandem to his nervousness. Sweat beaded on his upper lip and tracked a slow path down his temples; his hand stilled. Even the slowest of minds felt the power within her when she had the call.

Gaby was already in motion when he let go and started to back up, too late to avoid her attack. She smashed her bony knee into his jewels. Face contorting on a soundless wail, he collapsed forward, and she struck his nose with the heel of her palm, finishing him off.

His friends scattered as he sank backward, wheezed once for breath, and keeled over. His head clunked hard on the concrete walkway. Lucky for him, he had enough alcohol in his system that he didn't get back up. If he had, she'd have done more damage to him.

Dangerously on edge, Gaby lifted her penetrating gaze to the onlookers. No longer could she see them clearly, only the haze of their nervousness, the blistering of their fear.

Knowing she'd wasted too much time, Gaby sucked in a slow, calming breath, turned to leave—and ran face first into a hard chest. Acting on instincts, she struck out, left hand, right elbow, fast and hard. Swifter movements blocked each blow before large hands curved over her upper arms, alarming her.

But these hands weren't damp or cruel. They definitely weren't weak.

Holding her secure, keeping her upright, they burned through the fog of her purpose.

An atavistic montage of alarms scuttled throughout Gaby's system, not unlike what she experienced when receiving her call of duty. Only . . .

Only the acute pain *lessened*.

And that couldn't be good. She needed the pain to keep her focused, to keep her instincts sparking.

Wary over what she might see, Gaby took the time to gain her breath, to clear her head. Once she had her rage tempered, she looked up by small degrees, taking in a trim waist belted by black leather, buttons of a pressed white dress shirt, the loosened, burgundy-printed tie, a tanned throat, a strong chin.

Filled with trepidation, she raised her gaze to a face— and fell into calculating chocolate eyes that contrasted sharply with fair hair and a frown that bespoke concern rather than anger.

Jesus, he stood taller by a good three inches.

Beneath the nice suit, broad shoulders gave testament to incredible power. And he smelled of goodness, an unfamiliar, drugging scent.

Whorls of soft yellow, pink, and orange framed him with the same serenity as a sunset. The colors showed optimism, strength, purpose, and compassion. She didn't dare acknowledge the way her knees weakened and her stomach bottomed out.

Tugging her closer, keeping her on her tiptoes, he asked, "Are you all right?"

That deep, resonating, and somehow alarming voice caused Gaby to shrink back. But he didn't let her go far.

This man would be much more trouble than the drunks, mostly because he affected her in some odd, freakish way. Rage she understood. Fear, deliberation, disgust. All the garden-variety emotions.

What she felt now, with him, was something faster, almost raw, definitely urgent and disorderly.

Infused with an inclination she didn't understand, Gaby reacted instinctively, again jerking her knee up with precise aim.

He shifted, and rather than meet her target, she thumped against a muscled thigh. He winced, but didn't release her. "Calm down," he told her, as if she hadn't just come close to unmanning him.

Wow. Amazing control.

Amazing reflexes.

And an incredible poker face.

He'd moved so fast, she hadn't had a chance to counter it—something that had *never* happened to her before. The success of her talent depended on her skill. She had to be better than everyone else, faster and stronger and more intuitive . . . or innocent people would be consumed by savagery.

Or maybe . . . he was innocent, so she couldn't hurt him.

That thought left her confounded, and she shied away from it. No one was totally innocent. No one.

Curious, Gaby stared at him. Even with her attack, his gaze didn't falter, his voice didn't change. Other than the slight winging of one dark brow, he showed no reaction at all.

Eyes shining with awareness, he asked, "Is there some reason you're assaulting me?"

She had to get away.

Now.

The longer she stayed near him, the more disconcerted she got, and she *never* got disconcerted. She couldn't allow old-fashioned jitters to jeopardize what must be done. Enough time had passed to threaten the probability of the outcome.

Letting evil escape was not an option.

If she didn't get her ass in gear, some poor soul would suffer. She'd fail in her duty, and the awful pain would linger and burn until it almost drove her mad.

His knees bent, bringing his face level with hers. "Hey, anyone at home in there?"

Gaby narrowed her eyes, annoyed at his teasing. She'd never known a man to act so weird. She didn't like it. She sure as hell didn't understand it.

Forgoing a verbal reply, she stared down at first his left hand, then his right, both firmly latched on to her arms just above her elbows.

He released her and took a step back.

Without wasting another second, Gaby started around him.

This time he only caught her arm to regain her attention. Full of incredulity and dangerous antagonism, her fist cocked back, Gaby whirled to confront him. He dropped his hand. Again.

"I'm a cop." Reaching into his pocket, he pulled out a black wallet and flipped open a badge. "Detective Cross." He offered an encouraging smile. "Luther Cross."

The air squeezed out of her lungs so fast that dark spots danced in front of her eyes. She detested cops. They never understood. They couldn't.

By virtue of their chosen careers, they were diametrically opposed to her and to what God forced her to do.

After a quick glimpse at the badge, which looked real enough, she met his gaze with insult. "Good for you." Again, she turned—and again he caught her arm.

Snarling, Gaby jerked free. "Back off, shithead, all right?"

In the universal sign of surrender, he raised his hands. "I just want to make sure you're okay."

Right. So that must be altruism emanating from him in scorching waves, making her head swim and her belly flinch? Even if her mission hadn't heightened her sense of smell, she would have seen through the lie.

Suspicion filled his dark eyes.

Curiosity.

And something else, something she didn't dare ponder.

"Great. I'm fine." This time when she stalked away, he kept pace with her. *Oh Christ.* She could *feel* him there, big and hot and powerful—and somehow amused, though he showed no expression. She had to shake him off. No way in hell could she take care of business with him tagging along.

Cops weren't keen on seeing people slaughtered.

What to do?

Torn by duty and caution, and the new, alien edginess, Gaby halted with an unmistakable show of exasperation. *"What?"*

Those dark eyes grew more intense as he scrutinized her. Somehow, he managed to appear bigger. Taller. And mean.

Being physically ripped apart couldn't hurt this much.

He struck a concerned frown. "You're still shaken. Look at your hands."

Gaby glanced down and bit off a lurid curse at her white-knuckled fists. She closed her eyes, carefully opened her hands, stretched out her fingers, loosened them until she appeared relaxed.

"Better?" he whispered.

Fuck off. No, she'd better not say that. Pain shredded her nerves. His appeal nearly destroyed her. Together, the dual influences could do her in.

She gritted her teeth. "Just dandy."

He took a step closer. "Where're you headed?"

The pain amplified, signaling an urgency to the moment. His presence had at first blunted the pain, but now her time had run out. She all but panted to keep control. "And that's your business because . . . ?"

Something within him sharpened; she felt it like tiny pinpricks from a million needles. He kept his expression enigmatic, but the strength of his purpose enveloped her. "You assaulted a man."

Resisting the wild urge to run, Gaby rested her weight on one hip and crossed her arms over her chest. "Self-defense."

"Yeah?"

"He grabbed me."

Detective Cross agreed with a slow nod. "I saw. You acted like Satan himself had you."

Her chin shot up. For a minute there, she hadn't been sure.

A quirky smile lifted the corners of his mouth. "Bogeymen aren't real, but unfortunately jerks are."

Both she and God knew that he couldn't be more wrong. Bogeymen, demons, vile incarnations and perversions of the sickest kind . . . they walked the earth in greater might than all the jerks combined.

But she had neither the time nor the inclination to school him on reality. She'd amused him enough.

"So where'd you learn to move like that? Most women would have slapped his face and started crying. You knocked him out." He snapped his fingers. "Just like that. You've had special training?"

If you could call God a trainer.

But Gaby couldn't tell him that. The pain in her belly ruptured, boiling up her throat and into her lungs and heart. *She had to go.*

Arms curled around her middle, her back teeth sawing together, she sought coherent words. "Are you arresting me or what?"

His head tilted back and something flickered in his expression, as if he'd just noticed her discomfort. The seconds ticked by, driving her urgency, sharpening the mauling agony.

Very softly, with a tip of his head, he said, "Not."

She let out a broken breath. And this time when she strode away on stiff legs that made her gait awkward, he didn't follow.

But damn it, Gaby felt his gaze and couldn't resist the urge to look over her shoulder.

She wished she hadn't.

He stood there, staring after her, somehow dark and bright at the same time. He looked . . . speculative, and the last thing she needed was some damn nosy cop wondering about her.

Thank God, he hadn't asked for her ID or even her name. If she became known in the area, she'd have to move on.

Again.

Blaming him for the excess of her pain, Gaby glared, and he began walking backward, moving away from her while keeping her in his sights. Gaby watched, waiting for him to round the corner, to go about his business, whatever that business might be.

He didn't. When he reached the drunk still sprawled on

the walkway, he stood over him a moment, then knelt down and helped him sit up. Gaby's eyes widened. Damn it, the scuffle in front of the bar was *her* business, and she wanted Detective Luther Cross's nose out of it.

The drunk's friends staggered forward, and with horrified realization, Gaby watched as the detective began to grill them all. *Shiiiit.*

She didn't trust that cop, not even a little. She considered intervening, but . . .

With Detective Cross no longer a threat, the real menace throbbed throughout the air like a thundering heartbeat, consuming her. Had she missed her chance? Was she too late after all?

Would she have to carry the pain for days instead of a couple of hours?

No.

She couldn't bear that. She wouldn't bear it. Somehow, she'd make it on time.

No cop had ever succeeded in halting her activities. She'd be damned if she'd let one get in her way now.

Teeth clenched, Gaby replaced her glasses over her eyes and broke into a hobbled run. At first, the agony nearly crippled her, but exerting herself physically helped give the pain guidance into her legs and lungs. Her stride became more fluid, faster. Through a deeper precognition, she followed her way to the trigger much as a dog trailed a scent.

Without tiring, without bumping into people or hazarding traffic, Gaby ran the length of the narrow street.

She saw no one, felt nothing.

Noise surrounded her, but beyond the slapping of her flip-flops and her own coarse, grating breath, she didn't hear a thing.

Less than a mile into her run, Gaby's urgency for speed

waned, as did the pulse of life. Devoid of traffic, conversation, and children at play, an eerie stillness pervaded the area. No drunks fouled the air with insults. Birds didn't sing. The air stilled.

Gaby glanced around. Startling silence roared in her brain; she drew a strained, heavy breath.

Sweat glued her hair to her forehead and sealed her shirt to her flesh. In the furthest recesses of her mind, Gaby still felt the burning of her muscles and the tripping beat of her heart, but she remained unaffected by physical dominion.

In front of her, looming dark and still, an abandoned factory lured her. Determination and duty carried Gaby up the slight incline, over broken glass, sharp twigs, and crumbling concrete. Dead, moldered bugs crunched beneath her feet.

At the oily remains of an old discarded engine, Gaby paused. She was close. With each step she took toward the bulky, blackened brick face of the factory, the more her vision blurred. Eventually, she knew she'd see only vague outlines haloed by constantly shifting colors, tints, and hues to guide her actions and infuse her with necessary information.

Her feet moved by rote, taking her to a burned-out lot that butted into decaying woods concealed at the back of the building.

The core of the misery nestled here.

Bile burned in Gaby's chest, her pace lagged—and then it seized her in its awful, unrelenting vise. For too many heartbeats, the choking impact squeezed her gangling body. A futile cry gurgled in her throat before she regained herself, accepting the pain and deciphering its instruction.

Reflective heat undulated from the asphalt, seeping through Gaby's rubber flip-flops, sealing her within the pain so that it was a part of her, and her a part of it.

Forcing her heavy, plodding limbs to move, Gaby circled around the minacious face of the structure. Black as sightless eyes, broken windows stared at her. Her breath came in silent wisps, inadequate to feed her starving lungs.

The horror of what she knew she'd find shrieked in her brain.

She didn't want to do this.

But, oh God . . . she knew she had no choice.

She never did.

Chapter 3

A chaotic inferno of rich colors—bloody red, darkest brown, and writhing black—danced frenetically before her. The turbulence of the twisting hues indicated pain and fear, but not just pain and fear from the hapless victim. Such an explosion of color could only emanate from more than one person.

Where? *Where?*

Standing near a putrid Dumpster ripe with the stench of rot, feeding maggots, and refuse, she saw the sobbing child. Narrow arms stretched out, trying to fend off a nightmare of hideous features.

With the plethora of enraged colors indicating many things, Gaby tried to clear her vision, to better see through the auras to the physical features of the attacker. But still she saw . . . things she didn't quite comprehend or believe.

Sure, monsters existed. She knew it because she'd sent plenty of them to hell. But to the world, they looked like everyone else. They looked normal. Only with her divine talent did she see an exterior that matched their rotted souls.

But this time, she saw more.

She saw teratoid deformities. Gruesome. Inhuman. Sickening . . .

Revulsion raced up her spine as she stared in slack-jawed distaste at the target. Yes, she'd been summoned to this . . . this . . . whatever it might be.

Tall, but obviously old with a hunching posture that nearly bent the emaciated body in half. Bowed legs seemed inadequate to support the frame, and gnarled hands sported short, fattened fingers that gave the appearance of mittens.

Gaby swallowed convulsively. Aged, wrinkled skin bunched and puckered on the cheek and forehead, making room for a violation of odd fleshy protrusions. Except for the quivering, gelatinous blobs of vein-riddled, dimpled flesh that clung to the side of its head, the form appeared human.

A wail of sheer terror snapped up Gaby's attention. She looked beyond the creature and focused on the little boy.

Did he see the figure the same as she did? Did he realize that which tried to defile him wasn't human? Did that poor little boy comprehend the demon in the guise of a barely human form?

Visually as well as mentally, Gaby was accustomed to perceiving the truth. But this little boy wouldn't be.

How could he bear the sight of the awful dastard?

Kids and animals generated much pity. They were so sweet and pure, they couldn't comprehend the brutal depravity often heaped upon them.

Sounds passed Gaby's ears: needy, gulping whimpers mixed with unintelligible pleas, and finally helpless mewling. In her present state, the words were indecipherable, but she understood the appeal.

The kid, who couldn't have been more than eight or nine, begged for help and a justice that only she could give. He was hurt and horrified, but evil hadn't gotten what it wanted.

Not yet.

It only toyed with the boy, frightening him, setting him up, weakening him with raw terror. She still had time.

Thank you, God.

Pain meant less than nothing to her when faced with saving a child. She would not let him down. She would not let herself down.

Bigger and stronger with purpose, Gaby slid her knife free of the sheath. Razor-edged steel on weathered leather emerged with a lethal hiss, bolstering her, empowering her. Steps metered and sure, she approached the scene, placing herself center stage, gaining sudden attention.

With a shock of displeasure, evil's face knotted and gnarled. The clumps of live flesh, covered in a glossy sheen, jiggled and flushed with ripening fury. The weight of the grotesque appendages kept the semihuman form off-kilter, listing to the side, adding to the loathsome image.

It released its grip on the trembling boy.

The child looked at Gaby, and even through the haze, she saw the awful anguish that would haunt him for all of his years.

He'd met the bogeyman, and he would never forget.

Gaby inhaled a painful, shuddering breath—and accepted the truth: she was on time, and yet, sadly . . . she wasn't.

"Go." She didn't hear her own voice; she never could, not when duty dominated her every sense. Most normal humans would have wanted to console the child, to reassure him.

That wasn't her job.

She didn't know shit about consolation.

But destruction . . . oh yeah. That she knew.

All her senses stayed tuned to the wicked face of corruption. As if the apparition felt confusion at her interference, or maybe over its own inclinations, bright violet and dark indigo churned together. The monster hesitated before taking a step toward her.

Oh yeah, Gaby thought, *come to me*.

And the colors mutated.

Bursts of blood red erupted, broken only by black holes boring through the crimson. This demon suffered excruciating pain and physical imbalance.

Gaby didn't soften an inch.

Because of her present insight, Gaby knew that the soul of this enmity had devoured many children. To her mind, it deserved to suffer. Without her intervention, it might have gone on to ruin other innocents. But now, finally, it had erred.

It came within Gaby's reach.

God wanted it gone, and she'd damn well see to it—gladly.

The boy back-stepped on weak, clumsy legs, faltering, shuddering, removing himself from her peripheral vision. Gaby allowed herself to be drawn into the evil, to understand it and experience it.

The better to destroy it.

"Go," she screamed one last time, and the boy turned in a stumbling rush, sobbing hard, fleeing as fast as he could. The vulgar, monstrous head turned to watch as its prey got away.

"No," Gaby taunted with certainty, "you won't ever touch him." Though fever burned through her, evaporating the sweat on her skin, her fingers were icy-tight on the bone handle of the lethal blade. "You're mine, you malformed bastard. All mine."

Quite often, demons were too stupid to be afraid. This trigger proved no different. Wailing its fury at her interference, deceived by her slim stature and the blank stare of her hollow eyes, the aged apparition crashed toward her.

Like great globs of brain tissue exposed to the elements, the excess flesh swung around the face. Pale eyes watery with age or tears displayed a bone-deep hatred. Parted on a fierce cry, wrinkled lips exposed toothless gums.

One bony limb lifted, creating an arc of blistering red and smoldering gray, intent on striking her.

Perfect.

In a straight, well-aimed strike, Gaby slashed with her knife, using the momentum of the attack to aid her. The finely honed edge penetrated the chest wall with ease. Gaby stuck her knife long and deep through loose, buttery flesh, until it deflected off a brittle rib.

The demon staggered, bent—and Gaby severed the windpipe, turning the shriek of pain and surprise into a repugnant gurgle.

She could have stopped there.

She *should* have stopped; it would have been less messy.

But when in the zone, Gaby lacked control. And when it came to the abuse of children, she considered mere death a feeble cop-out. For as long as the creature gasped for air, for as long as it could feel the slashing of her wrath, Gaby would administer her own fitting punishment.

Teeth bared in the grisly semblance of a smile, she hacked again, sinking deep into a blackened heart that accepted her blade like a stick through a marshmallow, soft and squishy.

Easy.

Satisfying.

Determined to give as much as she could, Gaby twisted

the blade and wrenched it back out, doing as much damage on her exit as she'd done on the thrust.

Uncaring of the writhing, incoherent pleas and the chubby, dwarfed hands that batted at her in futile defense, Gaby gouged into wet, twisted guts, into those awful, bulbous growths on the head.

The body stilled, all movement ceasing, and still she used both hands, her breath coming in grunts as she sawed through organs and muscle.

Even in the afterlife, this malevolence would never again menace a child. When the coppery taste of blood polluted her mouth, Gaby finally stopped. She smelled the tang of the blood, felt the sting of it in her eyes.

The blood and gore was . . . everywhere. Bits and pieces of flesh, skin, and bone splattered and spilled on the ground, on the remains of the body . . . and on her.

Gasping, Gaby took a hasty, appalled step backward. She gagged, spat, and swiped an arm across her eyes and mouth.

Silenced by the violence of her own acts, she waited for the ease that followed a kill. Nothing moved but her rapidly pumping heartbeat and the bellowing of her chest as she sucked in stale, hot air. Anxious for the return of sanity, she closed her eyes.

But the relief didn't come.

Alarm clung to her; pain prodded and pulled.

What the hell was happening?

Abruptly, she whiffed it in the air, the rancid scent of immorality. Accepting the prickling of fresh alarm, Gaby tried to prepare her depleted body.

Somewhere near to her, a presence lurked. The colors flowing in and around the area shifted with ominous overtones, all shades faded and greasy in deceptive connation, moving with the speed of a turbulent river, too fast for her to decipher. She sensed another's gleeful satisfaction and dawning perception, a perception that perhaps matched her own.

Blinding pain ripped a groan from her soul that she couldn't silence.

The knife, now slick with blood, almost slipped from her numbed fingers. She clung to it, bracing her feet apart to stay upright, to stay alert.

Whatever stalked her, she had to defend herself.

No one else would.

Thankfully, no sooner did Gaby have the thought than the alarm began receding, sliding away until only her thrumming grief remained.

She searched the area, searched her own senses, but could detect nothing. Slowly, through a lessening of misery that told her all was now well, Gaby came back to herself.

Whatever had plagued her, whatever had *watched* her, was now gone.

Nausea rolled over her. Her vision cleared and the brilliance faded, dissolving into the air until only the drab, washed-out colors of patchy grass, scorched trees, and hazy sky remained. They were a dull contrast to the rich hues of auras.

They were the real world. If only she never again had to leave it.

A breeze tickled over her, reviving her.

Gaby didn't want to look. She hated looking, but facing the destruction had become an inexorable tangibility for her, a penance she forced herself to pay, no matter the cost.

Eyes burning, body taut with trepidation, she lifted her lashes.

Her knees buckled and she dropped down hard.

The man whose head barely remained attached to his neck, lying in a dark pool of his own body secretions, in no way resembled the demon she'd just destroyed.

Deformed yes, although now, thanks to her, most of the deformities were gone, hacked off, no longer a part of his body. He looked . . .

He looked like someone's grandpa. Someone's *murdered*, mutilated grandpa.

All but decapitated.

Hand shaking, Gaby reached out to smooth his gray, disheveled hair, clumpy with blood, gore, and the remnants of chunky flesh and displaced muscle. She nudged his skull over, putting it more in line with his shoulders. Grizzled eyebrows framed soulless eyes, frozen with the horror she had delivered so skillfully.

She guessed his age somewhere in the mid-seventies.

His destroyed body was so gaunt as to be cadaverous. Had his deformities affected him mentally, turning him into a monster, robbing his body of strength, his mind of conscience?

No. She remembered her certainty of his past misdeeds. Perhaps the body had caught up to the soul. Life would be so much easier if all monsters looked like monsters.

But she knew that would never be.

Gaby looked at his hands, now red with his own blood. His fingers were short and blunt. There were no nails. Just discoid tips.

By accident, or had some disease eaten away at him?

An invisible fist squeezed at Gaby's heart and she wanted to howl, to deny that she, Gabrielle Cody, had butchered him in so many places that meat hung from his body, and only bones held him together.

He would never hurt anyone again.

No one, except her.

Regardless of what she knew him to be, despite the fact that she'd saved a child, probably many children, she would never be able to forget him.

She never forgot any of them.

They became part of her, in some ways adding to her strength, in other ways tearing her down until she felt like nothing at all.

As she did now.

Only moments ago, rage had guided her; now a pervasive weakness sent quivers rippling up and down her spine. She gagged, still tasting the blood, identifying the scent as it baked on the hot asphalt beneath the blistering sun. A fly buzzed close, landing on the man's exposed intestines.

Gaby heaved—and lost control. Hot loamy spew regurgitated out her nose and mouth.

Ah, shit.

Swallowing convulsively, she fought back the last of the bile until the spasms receded. She hated puking, and not just because it left evidence behind. Hands braced on the rusted metal of the Dumpster, she drew deep, slow breaths, calming her mind with thoughts of other things, quieter times, until her belly quit trying to crawl up her throat and out of her nose.

When she could breathe again, she straightened and curled her hands around her aching middle.

Fucking eggs Morty had forced on her didn't want to stay down. She might never eat eggs again.

Knowing she couldn't linger, she dragged a bandanna from her back pocket and, keeping her back turned toward the body, scrubbed the blood from her face and hands, up to her elbows. There wasn't a damn thing she could do about her ruined shirt. At least it was dark—a deliberate choice because it made it harder to detect the blood on her walk home.

And thinking of her walk . . . she had to get to it, shaking limbs or no, nausea or no.

She couldn't rest.

Couldn't indulge pity for herself or her victim.

Couldn't change her life, or the curse that haunted her.

Couldn't deny who and what she was: God's minion. For better or worse.

No one else would see that man as a demon. No one else would know that she'd done humanity a favor. They'd see his disfigured body and label *her* as the monster.

If he knew the truth, Detective Cross would try to arrest her, locking her away so that evil had free rein. She didn't want to fight with Cross. She didn't want to have to hurt him.

Blind fools, all of them.

Closing her eyes, she said a quick prayer, crossed herself, and thanked God for guiding her, for putting her there in enough time to keep that child safe.

She asked forgiveness for her weaknesses and her guilt, and she asked for the courage to continue doing what she must, just as Father Mullond had instructed her to do.

With that complete, Gaby dragged both sides of her big knife over the dead man's sleeve to clean it. She replaced it in her sheath and made sure her T-shirt covered it.

Mentally calculating her location, she decided to head for the nearest gas station. She needed water in a bad way—both to drink and to wash.

Putting her shoulders back made her feel stronger. She started out of the lot—and heard footsteps approaching. Her heart shot into her throat and, without even thinking about it, she sought cover behind the brick building.

Darting one quick, cautious glance around the corner, she spotted Detective Luther Cross methodically picking his way up the incline toward the factory.

Son of a bitch.

Had he followed her? But how? *Why?*

To minimize her chances of getting lost, she wanted to return the same way she'd come. But Cross effectively removed that option. By the second, he drew nearer. She looked over her shoulder, seeing the carnage of the demon's body in all its gruesome display. She saw the Dumpster filled with rot, and beside it, her own vomit.

A telling scene.

It wouldn't take a genius to put it all together. If she got herself arrested, who would do her work?

Think, Gaby. Do something.

Her frantic, searching gaze fell on the path the boy had taken when he'd left her. Though she hadn't been able to focus on him at the time, her subconscious now supplied her with the image of him stumbling into a cluster of trees that overgrew the property.

Gaby didn't waste another second. She ran. And this time, running hurt like hell. Without the summons to guide her, to make her movements sinuous and economic, she stumbled in her flip-flops. Twigs and stones nicked her toes. Her lungs labored and her sluggish limbs refused to help. Once safely buried in a thicker cover of trees, she paused to look back.

Through the leaves and limbs, she could barely see Detective Luther Cross standing over the body and cursing a blue streak while scanning the area. Gaby watched him with narrow eyes and burning annoyance.

Why did he have to interfere?

And why did an almost ethereal white veil drift gently around him?

The detective was a good man, but not good enough to divine her purpose. Not good enough to be trusted by God. He'd arrest, condemn, and lock her away without a moment's hesitation.

Just once, Gaby wished someone would trust in her the way Father Mullond had.

Cross pulled out his cell phone and punched in a call,

barking into the phone while walking a wide circle around
the area, careful not to disturb the evidence.

Making no sound, Gaby slunk away, farther and farther
into the woods. God must have been guiding her, because
no twigs snapped. No leaves crunched. When she was far
enough from Cross that he couldn't hear her, she began
running again, as fast and hard as she could push her
drained body.

Within minutes, the whole area would be swarming
with cops. She didn't intend to be anywhere around when
they got there.

❦

As Gaby skulked deeper and deeper into the dank woods,
itchy sweat, earthly grit, and the stench of fear coated her
skin. She stumbled along until her lungs burned and her
thighs felt leaden. She didn't dare stop. Cops could be
tenacious, and she knew they'd be looking everywhere for
their supposed murderer.

Frustration clouded her eyes, but she'd long ago given
up on crying. Anyway, cursing made her feel better than
crying did, and she gave in to the urge to voice her discontent.

After several lurid, coarse words, her foot caught on a
broken piece of concrete. With a grunt of surprise, she
pitched forward and landed on all fours.

A mere inch from her nose, a stone slab crawling with
wild ivy and multilegged insects rose up from the earth.

She'd almost cracked her head open.

So close to the unforgiving stone, Gaby couldn't quite
read the stamped letters. They blurred into unrecognizable
gibberish until she cautiously levered herself away. Dead
branches from a thorny bush cut into her palms and knees.
A broken twig gouged her upper arm.

She barely noticed.

The marker sat crookedly upright on the weedy ground, an eerie specter of past life. Filled with a deviant trepidation, Gaby stripped away the knotted, entwined vines and read aloud, "Mulhauser County Isolation Hospital."

A hospital?

In the middle of the woods?

But a quick look around assured her that the area hadn't always been wooded. The abandoned building was the victim of neglect. "Erected AD 1850 by the Board of Chosen Freeholders of Mulhauser County."

Not since Father died had she been anywhere near a hospital. Her heart stuttered in familiar rage.

The cold stone boldly displayed the names of a director, supervisor, medical advisor, architect, and assistant. Eyes narrowed, Gaby whispered aloud, "Cancer Research Center."

Sound and sight receded. Seconds stretched into a full minute. Memories overtook her mind, playing in rapid, clicking succession with the jarring clarity of a movie reel.

Father Mullond growing ill.

Losing weight.

Losing strength.

Losing his sanity.

Medicines and medical treatment had only robbed him of his dignity and multiplied his suffering. She remembered all the clerics praying, to no avail.

She remembered her useless tears, which hadn't changed a thing.

Most of all, she recalled the tragic, yet merciful end that had taken too long to arrive. By the time God claimed him, Father had become a wasted, shriveled being, hollow in body and mind, in no way resembling the powerful man he'd once been.

With a shock, Gaby sucked in a gasping breath and fought

off a recurrence of the nausea. She wouldn't think about those awful days, and weeks, and months. She wouldn't think about the year when her world had crashed down around her, when the only friend she'd ever known had been tortured by nature—by the very God she worked so hard to appease.

She wouldn't think about being alone in a life plagued by evil forces that only she could see.

"Screw this." Using the marker for leverage, Gaby pulled herself to her feet. Bloody fingerprints remained on the stone as she peered around, at last seeing through the woods to the forsaken hospital lurking within.

Staring at the building, she sneered, "So it looks big and imposing? It's also dead and empty and . . . nothing at all."

Covered in abundant plant life, cut off from human traffic, few people would remember this place or even see it. Life would buzz around it, never once making notice of the atrocious structure.

"If things get critical," Gaby whispered, "this just might be the perfect place to hide."

Chapter 4

Curiosity kept Gaby studying the area. Toward the back of the largest building, which she assumed to be the main part of the hospital, smaller buildings sat like forsaken headstones. Picking her way past poison ivy, needle-sharp thorns, and hungry insects, Gaby moved to see all the property.

Icy, murky auras shadowed the perimeter of the grounds, moving around her in unsettled displacement, possibly depicting paranormal activity. Unhappy spirits? Vengeful wraiths?

Evil?

Through practice, Gaby had learned to see all the layers of an aura, to disentangle the meanings and nuances. Proper diet, fresh air, exercise, and sunlight strengthened an aura, just as neglect, alcohol, drugs, stress, and lack of rest weakened them.

These auras looked massive, filling the surrounding sky, the very air that fed her lungs. It was as if many small auras had combined into one, because despite the size, they lacked real power or purpose.

Beneath the menace lurked great suffering, crippling pain.

And more.

Contact with others could enable an exchanging of energy, or in some cases, the draining of it. Certain people, places, even memories, could suck the very life out of a being. Whenever Gaby felt herself tiring too quickly, as she did now, she removed herself from the source. But this time, she couldn't.

She edged closer, drawn to a courtyard overlooking the abandoned hospital. The property was so bulky that it even had its own power station.

A mosquito buzzed past Gaby's ear, landed, and bit her neck, drawing a bead of blood. She swatted it away, engrossed at the sight of yet another structure.

Enormous trees and waist-high weeds cloaked a ramshackle house off to the side, perhaps the home of someone who once ran the hospital. Between it and the hospital, a swamp that had once served as a pond festered with mosquitoes and thick moss. A disturbed breeze carried an awful stench off the pond to the air around it.

Wrinkling her nose, Gaby looked back at the house. The roof of the covered porch sank low, threatening to collapse. Paint peeled from every surface. Shingles and shudders had gone missing. Toxic vibes emanated from every unbroken window.

Remnants of a past life, or warning of a current resident? Gaby didn't know. At that moment, she didn't really care.

A deserted playground, hazardous with broken equipment that had once held swings, a jungle gym, a teeter-totter, indicated there had been a children's ward, too. Now only crows flapped around, pecking at crawling insects and cawing to one another in high-pitched screeches that cut the stillness with alarming ferocity.

Gaby started to move closer to the pond, and from nowhere a cold wind went up her spine, making her flesh prickle and the hairs on her nape stand on end. She jerked around, her knife already in her hand as she prepared for battle, ready to face another nightmare.

Only the eerie, soundless lull of the woods greeted her.

Cautious and unconvinced, Gaby turned back to the isolation hospital. Multipaned windows were broken, boarded up, or black with age, cobwebs, and filth. No one looked out at her—at least, no one with eyes that she could see.

And still Gaby had the disquieting sense of being watched, of being mentally dissected. It unnerved her and, knife still drawn, started her on her way in a rush.

"Fucking paranoia," she cursed to herself, but it could have nothing to do with the eerie hospital and everything to do with the meddlesome detective hot on her trail, so she thrashed her way out of the clinging underbrush.

Burs caught in her jeans. Muck stuck to her flip-flops and oozed up between her toes. Her panic was a strange counterpoint for a person who fought and defeated the vilest evils, and yet she left the ominous woods as fast as possible.

One smaller building she passed, separated from the isolation hospital, had brick walls riddled with graffiti claiming it to be someone's "place." A sign even pointed to the BEER ROOM, making Gaby wonder if it had once been home to a fraternity of some sort.

Did college kids lurk inside, chuckling at the way she fled? Did she care?

No.

She'd always been a freak to society. Nothing new in that.

As she circled the grounds and finally found her way to a clearing, she tucked the knife away in her sheath at the small of her back.

Oddly enough, she found that the main complex of the Cancer Research Center was visible from the road. The broad face of the building easily hid the smaller hospitals behind it, but anyone driving by would see it.

Did they not sense the evil? Were they all so obtuse, so self-absorbed, that they paid no attention at all to such a blatant, rancorous threat?

To get her bearings, Gaby looked around and saw unkempt, suspicious businesses, dark alleyways, bums, homeless transients, and prostitutes.

The unfamiliar slums reeked of depression and poverty, but it didn't frighten her. In a way, it explained how the hospital remained so obscure. Once upon a time, the area might have been lucrative and in need of a hospital. In days gone by, the old houses, tall and built close together, might have been the homes of doctors.

Now they accommodated several families, and from what she could tell, a few of them served as crack houses.

Relieved that no one would recognize her here, Gaby set off again.

Every bone and muscle in her body ached. Exhaustion pulled at her. She felt like she could curl up in a corner and sleep—but the luxury of rest was something she couldn't afford, not until she'd reached the safety of her apartment.

Wherever that might be.

As she walked along, she looked down each alleyway, always guarding against threats. After a time, she spotted three men in an alley between an ambiguous novelty store and a vacant building. They clustered around a can fire, cooking something and, given their postures, stoned out of their gills.

Surrounded by cardboard boxes and shopping carts laden with other people's discards, it appeared that they lived in the narrow lane.

Perfect.

Most sane people would have avoided darkened seclusion that harbored sinister, desperate men; Gaby thanked God for it.

When she'd gotten within six feet, one man pulled out a knife. That amused her. He shook so badly, and his eyes were so unfocused, he wouldn't be able to hit the wall, much less a person with her skills. "What're you cooking?" she asked, hoping to ease the tension.

"There ain't enough fer ya. Go away."

It looked like squirrel to her, probably roadkill. Her still-jumpy stomach pitched in revolt. Such pitiable people. Desolation clung to them, but not malice.

It'd be best for her to get to the point. "I need a shirt."

"Ya got a shirt. Now git."

"I need a different shirt." She dug in her pocket. "Here's five bucks. I'm not picky."

Two of the three men conferred. The third was too high to even acknowledge or notice her. He stared off at nothing in particular, swaying gently from his cross-legged position near the wall. Gaby briefly studied him. Eyes sunken, complexion sallow and damp, body gaunt, he wouldn't last out the week. His addiction was so ripe that disease riddled his body. Poor schmuck.

The man with the knife lumbered awkwardly to his feet. Holding the blade out straight, as a novice might, he staggered, steadied himself, and said, "I'll take the money, then you'll git."

"Not without a shirt." Gaby held his gaze. She felt the power blossom in her and knew he wouldn't cut her—even if he really wanted to, which she doubted.

As she stared at him, he blanched and backed up a step.

Gaby followed. "I don't want to hurt you, but I can." She kept her tone even, calm, and filled with dead sobriety. "If you don't play fair, I'll show you the kind of pain you've never experienced."

Beneath grim and bristly whiskers, the man's face went white and his jaw slackened. She could see the wild pulse thrumming in his throat, the sweat gathering at his temples. The hand holding the knife drooped at his side.

"We ain't got much," he whispered.

"That's why I'm willing to pay, rather than just take what I need—which I could do." She strode past him to the grocery cart, rummaged through the discarded items until she found a man's navy blue T-shirt with a tear on the shoulder, paint stains on the hem. "This'll do."

Facing the man, who'd made no move to hurt her when her back was turned, she nodded her gratitude and tucked the five in his front shirt pocket.

"Sorry to do this, but . . ." She shrugged, stripped off her ruined shirt, and tossed it in their fire. Black smoke billowed out, and then the shirt caught and flames consumed it, singeing the poor critter they intended as a feast for dinner.

She wore no bra, saw no reason to with her mostly flat chest, and so the two coherent men got an eyeful. They stared, not with lust but with utter surprise. They were so far gone that they'd never remember seeing her, much less be able to detail the exchange.

Being sure to keep her mouth tightly closed as the material passed her face, Gaby pulled the shirt on over her head.

Though it felt clean, God only knew where the shirt had been and what filth might cling to it.

She started to take her leave then, but instead she hesitated. Cursing herself for showing any softness, she reached out and removed the man's knife from his limp hand. It was so dull as to be useless.

"You hold it like this," she explained, turning the knife so that the blade faced his body, the handle his opponent. "That way, your forearm conceals it. And when you lift your arm to stab, you have your entire body weight behind the blade. And you know, it makes it easier to slash across the face or throat."

She exhibited that by guiding his arm through the motions.

As if the touch of a woman, even a woman of her dubious attributes, threw him off-kilter, he held himself stiff as a board. Gaby released him and took a step back, but she took his knife with her. Examining it, she said, "You should really sharpen this if you expect it to be a threat or protection."

He shook his head. "I jus' wanna be left 'lone."

Gaby flipped the knife in her hand and presented it back to him with the handle first. "Fine. Don't say I didn't warn you, though."

She'd taken two steps when he said, "Uh . . . thanks."

She looked over her shoulder, a brow raised.

"Fer the money."

But not the lesson on defense? He had his priorities screwed up, but it wasn't her problem.

With a nod, Gaby took herself off. She had a long walk ahead and no time to chitchat. It was back to business.

After crossing the street, she entered a gas station that smelled of oil and had seen better days. Off to one side was an old, broken air pump, and toward the other, a sign that read RESTROOM.

Using her foot to open the filthy door, Gaby went inside. Given the unrecognizable splatters on the walls and floors, she had to wonder if hookers used this particular john to fulfill assignations. Flies crowded the room, along with a few spiders.

Careful not to touch anything, Gaby inched her way to the scum-encrusted sink, barely connected to the wall by exposed pipes. So many chips and cracks marred the porcelain that using it would be hazardous.

Gaby wrinkled her nose in revulsion and knew she couldn't let it matter. Using a sliver of hair- and dirt-encrusted soap, she washed away all signs of the mutilated man's blood.

Though it was disgusting, she even splashed her face and rinsed out her mouth. The water tasted as metallic as the blood, but her head knew the difference and she felt better.

Next, standing on one foot at a time, she removed her flip-flops and cleaned all traces of mud from between her toes, then cleaned off the shoes, too.

She pulled out her knife and washed it, taking her time, being methodical.

When she finally left the restroom, thick gray clouds had rolled in to hide the sun.

Not a storm, she silently prayed.

Anything but that.

Luckily, she made it to her building without a single raindrop falling. She was so exhausted that she wanted only to lock herself in her room and pass out on the bed. She did not want to visit with Morty—but with him sitting on the front steps, more or less waiting for her, she couldn't avoid him.

He jumped to his feet at her approach, and Gaby noticed his red-rimmed eyes, his blotchy cheeks.

She drew up short. "No fucking way have you been crying."

Indignant, he shook his head and swiped a forearm past his nose. "No. Course not."

But she knew he lied. She always knew those sorts of things, even when she'd rather not. Gritting her teeth, she took the most expedient way out of the confrontation.

"Look, I'm sorry, okay? I've been tired lately. Not up to snuff. I don't mean to be a bitch. I just . . . am."

His expression softened. He rubbed the back of his neck. "Yeah, I know. It's okay."

Nonplussed, Gaby glared at him. He *knew*? So he didn't intend to deny her bitchiness?

"Great," she said, all but grinding out the word. "Then if that's settled . . ."

He shifted, effectively blocking her entrance into the building. Gaby lifted a brow.

He dared?

Clearing his throat, Mort said, "That's, um, not why I was waiting for you."

"No?"

He hemmed and hawed around, shuffling his feet.

"Jesus, Mort, spit it out, will ya? In case you can't tell, I'm beat. I need to get some rest and—"

"A cop stopped by here, looking for you. A really big cop. Detective Luther Cross, I think was his name. He said he'd come back tonight. I just . . . I thought you should know."

Eyes narrowed, mistrust prickling, Gaby moved forward with slow, precise purpose. "What did you tell him, Mort?"

When Morty flushed, she caught him by his shirtfront and dragged him close.

"Mort?"

"Nothing. That is . . . not much." He groaned as if in pain. "I told him you were a good person, Gaby. I told him you'd never have a run-in with the police. He wouldn't tell me why he wanted to see you, but he asked all kinds of questions, like what you do for a living, where your family lives. Stuff like that."

How dare he? "Nosy bastard."

"Yeah, well . . . He wanted to know where you were, and Gaby, I'm sorry, but I had no idea what to say."

Which was exactly why she never told him shit—so he couldn't give anything way. "So you said nothing, right?"

He shook his head. "He kept staring at me and I'm not a good liar. I had to say *something*, so I figured it'd be better to just admit that you keep to yourself, and that I don't know that much about you."

She nodded.

"He asked me how long you'd been my tenant, and when I told him, I don't think he believed me." Nervousness flushed Mort's cheeks. "He kept asking me if we ever talk, if we have any casual conversations . . . all kinds of stuff like that."

"Screw him." Gaby released Mort, even smoothed down his wrinkled shirt. "Who cares what he believes?"

"Uh . . . I thought you might."

Weary to the bone, she shook her head. "I need to shower. And sleep. If the cop shows back up, tell him to go away."

That instruction left Mort wide-eyed with incredulity. "But he's a cop! What if he insists . . ."

"He can't insist without a warrant, so unless he has one, don't bother me."

Hands twisted together, Mort asked, "And if he does?"

Gaby sighed. "You know where to find me."

"He, uh, he seemed like a nice guy."

"Yeah, right." Big and good-looking, and so full of himself. And he had that gentle, superior aura floating around him. Gaby snorted. "He's a regular superhero."

"You say that like you don't believe in heroes."

Mort sounded so wounded that Gaby blinked at him. "What? And you do?"

"Well . . . yeah."

"You've been reading too many graphic novels." He'd been reading too much of *her* work. "Granted, there's a few fools left out there who hope to save the world. But they're wasting their time."

Morty went soft. "Gaby, don't say that."

"It's a lost cause, Mort. Trust me." She had the emotional scars to prove it. "The world is not a comic book, and Superman isn't going to fly in and save a damned thing."

"Gaby?" Confusion filled his tone and marred his expression.

She felt like she'd kicked a puppy. What did it matter if Mort had his illusions? For most people, that's what got them through the day.

"Forget I said anything." Pushing past Mort and into the building, she trudged up the steps. Once inside her room, she secured the doors, removed the leather sheath strapped around her waist, and, still wearing the nasty shirt and soiled jeans, stepped into the shower.

What better way to scrub the grungy clothes clean?

As the soap and warm water helped wash away the remnants of the woods, Gaby's thought scuttled around at Mach speed.

What had she felt at the isolation hospital—horrific memories, or current misery? A threat?

And that damn Mort, looking to her for reassurance, and for so much more. She shied away from that thought, and focused on Detective Luther Cross instead.

Feeling marginally revitalized, she pictured the cop as she'd last seen him, watching her walk away, and then talking to those bums by the saloon. So he knew where she lived? And he thought he had reason to talk to her?

That probably should have bothered her more than it did, but so much turmoil twisted through her exhausted mind, grasping one particular worry seemed impossible.

Maybe he wouldn't come back at all. And maybe, someday, she'd be a normal woman.

She wouldn't place a bet on either possibility.

For six straight hours, Gaby gave herself over to sleep. Before lying down, she'd taken every precaution she could to ensure her own safety. She'd never slept through an intrusion, no matter how exhausted she might be. But chance was a commodity she couldn't afford.

She woke disoriented and dehydrated, and immediately wanted to write.

That's how it always happened for her. Writing wasn't a hobby or a true occupation. It was a passion. A necessity to her body and organs and soul—like breathing.

Like killing demons.

Using vivid descriptions in her novels helped her exorcise them from her mind. The details of her missions for God went into the stories, there for the entire world to see if only people would wake up and acknowledge the truth.

Gaby guzzled water until her head cleared, then dressed in another clean top and jeans. Her wardrobe consisted of dark tunics or T-shirts, well-worn denim, and simple flip-flops. In winter, she alternated with oversized hooded sweatshirts and black sneakers.

The lack of variable attire was a deliberate choice on

her part. If anyone ever claimed to see her in the area of a murder and tried to identify her by what she wore that night, it'd prove nothing. She always wore the same. Their memory could be of a Tuesday or Friday, the deli or the gas station.

Wind whistled outside her windows, a clue about weather to come, but for once Gaby barely heard it. She unfolded the metal stool and seated herself at her desk. From a nearby bin, she retrieved her latest manuscript, her inks, markers, straight-line tools, and fresh paper.

In no time, she'd immersed herself in the novel, sketching with a frenzy and writing out the truth as she knew it. Her peripheral vision constricted as she placed the day's details into still frames and rich dialogue that would complete her latest work.

Writing and illustrating graphic novels gave her the satisfaction of showcasing talents that didn't involve real death and destruction. She had a way with words, with the depiction of details that critics said brought readers into the moment.

Her drawings were vivid and explicit, showing the pain, the conflict, and the inner struggle of right and wrong.

No one gave her direct credit for her storytelling abilities because she remained anonymous. But she had the pleasure of seeing Morty's face light up when he got the newest loose-leaf manuscript. He'd spend the day devouring her work, and then he'd gush to her about the story, all but swooning in his excitement.

He didn't know Gaby was the creator, and he had no concept how his appreciation pleased her.

Devout fans flocked to his comic store in search of the next episode. Hordes of Goth kids checked in regularly, hoping to find a release date, putting their orders on hold.

Preppies sneaked in and left with the novel in a plain paper bag. College kids shouted out their victory when they got their copies.

All in all, her stories were well loved.

Most graphic novels included credits not only for the writer, but also for a penciler who sketched the artwork, an inker who inked the sketches, and a colorist who added the color. Gaby did it all herself, pouring her bitter heart and tortured soul onto the page and into the illustrations.

Depending on her mood and her most recent destruction, most of her stories ranged anywhere from fifty pages to more than three hundred. This one would be long. After the day's events, which she felt compelled to include, it'd probably run three-fifty.

Writers usually dealt with an editor and traditional publisher. Not Gaby. When she finished a graphic novel, she mailed the manuscript to Morty under a fictitious name. He sent whatever payment amount she named to a P.O. box outside their city.

The rest was up to him, and thanks to Mort, she had an enthusiastic underground publisher who didn't mind the X-rated, violent quality of her life.

Mort had been approached by bigger publishers, but as per her instructions, he kept to the lesser-known, underground circulation. The fewer people who got curious about Gaby, the better her odds of not being exposed.

She didn't want her natural and very cathartic outlet ruined by misguided fame. She saw the world through images, through the most basic truths, and with single-minded ferocity she put that on paper, sometimes working through the night.

Like an inside joke, or maybe a whimsical prayer, she wrote her character as an avenging angel rather than an iconic freak. Even with blood under her nails and brain matter splattered into her hair, Gaby's illustrated character remained a bright vision.

Like the rest of the normal world, Gaby romanticized the ugliness; she romanticized herself, and it made it easier for her to stomach her duties.

But as always, even in this, she remained alone.

Chapter 5

Hours later, after darkness had fallen, Gaby scripted an ornate THE END onto the page. Only one lamp, aimed at her desktop, lit the room. Shadows crawled and shifted around her, over the floor and up the wall. Wind pushed against the loose windowpanes.

Leaning back on her stool, Gaby studied the images of Detective Luther Cross. Somehow, they had encroached into her story.

Disgusted with herself, she closed her eyes and released a humid, pent-up breath. She hadn't planned to write in Cross. It had just sort of happened. In her memories, in the phenomenon of her anguished life, he was there, now a part of it all.

She'd drawn him larger than life, big and hulking with a firm but gentle hand, and kind but perceptive eyes. He looked like a pure angel, ready to stand beside her . . .

Jesus.

She had to stay away from him. She hated to contemplate new change, but maybe it was time to move on. She needed to be well out of Cross's realm.

Too antsy to stay still, and dying for something to eat, Gaby stacked the pages all together and secured them in a large padded envelope. She'd mail them first thing in the morning, as long as no other summons came.

Sliding her feet into her flip-flops, she checked the clock, saw it was nearing ten, and headed out. Even from the stairs, she could see a light shining from beneath Morty's door. She didn't want a repeat of their earlier awkwardness, so she crept past, using an inborn stealth that came in handy even when she didn't need to kill someone.

Oppressive air washed over her skin as she stepped out into the sultry night. Keeping her head down, Gaby ignored her surroundings and made her way to a joint that served what she liked to think of as real food. No preformed burgers or frozen salads. Chuck's Grill dished up chili or soup, subs or sandwiches, or a hearty breakfast—made fresh each day. At Chuck's she didn't have to worry about eating a random cockroach or catching a nasty disease from the filth.

This time of night, only his outside window remained open for service. Gaby stepped up and tapped on the glass. The youthful worker glanced up, nodded to acknowledge her, and indicated he'd be right with her.

In no hurry, Gaby tucked her hands into her pockets and lounged back on the stone face of the restaurant. Colored strobe lights from a nearby bar blinked and hiccupped, sending random, diffused light around the area. Vehicles passed, their tires hissing on the steamy pavement. An unsettled, angry breeze continued to stir the night air.

To Gaby's right, a couple of sleazy hookers touted their wares with halfhearted enthusiasm. To her left, a group of knuckleheaded kids with absurdly colored hair and more piercings than she could count tried to act tough. She doubted they fooled anyone but themselves.

On the opposite side of the street, a blue car eased up to the curb and a gangly young man, so dark that he blended in with the night, emerged from a shadowed doorway to make a drug deal. The whores called out to the driver, trying to entice him over to them. The dealer shook a mean fist toward them, making a valid threat in the coarsest terms. The punkers cracked up, laughing too loud and too long.

This was her life, each thing familiar and mundane and easy to ignore. She blended in here.

"What can I getcha?"

Gaby turned. The waiter looked nice enough, if a little worn down. "BLT, heavy on the B. A few pickle spears and chips on the side. And a Coke."

"Got it. Be about five minutes."

"Thanks."

He had no sooner shut the window than a deep belch of thunder rumbled through the night sky. Gaby shivered with dread. Maybe it was a remnant from the way her mother died that made her dread storms so much.

Whatever the cause, she detested them, not that she ever expected to admit it to anyone.

Since no one else even bothered to look up at the black, starless sky, she couldn't very well cancel her order and scurry home in a frightened rush. Besides, she was depleted and needed food. She had to—

Her reasoning failed when lightning slashed through the atmosphere, raising the fine hairs on her nape. Through sheer reaction, Gaby flattened herself to the wall. When the accompanying thunder crashed, louder this time, her heart tried to punch out of her chest.

"That'll be eight forty-eight," the worker said, and Gaby nearly jumped out of her skin.

Her face might've been blue from holding her breath when she turned to him, because he tilted his head and asked, "You okay?"

Even though prayers seldom gave the answers she wanted, they tripped through her mind. "Yeah." She took one breath, forced the scowl off her face. "I'm dandy." She pushed a ten through the window. "Keep the change."

"Hey, thanks." He handed over a white bag and a Coke. "Looks like rain, huh?"

With her thoughts on avoiding that rain, she didn't bother to answer him. She couldn't get out of there quick enough. Driven by hunger, Gaby unwrapped the sandwich and took a huge bite. Holding the bag of chips under one arm, she popped the tab on the Coke. It wasn't fun, but she intended to scarf her food as she made haste right back the way she'd come.

With her concentration on the impending storm, she almost missed the burn of intense scrutiny. But once she felt it, it sank into her bones, assuring her that someone had her in his sights.

Slowing her pace, Gaby mentally sought out the direction of her stalker.

A car pulled alongside her. Gaby glanced at the driver, but dismissed him. He wasn't a threat. Shoving another big bite in her mouth, she surreptitiously took note of her surroundings, studying everything and everyone to her left and right in quick but thorough glimpses.

She saw only stark buildings, dark shadows, familiar denizens, and empty alleys.

"Hey darlin'," the driver called out hopefully. "Where ya headed?"

"Away from you, jerk. Get lost."

"Bitch." The car sped off, leaving the scent of burned rubber behind.

An amused laugh sounded behind her.

Stopping dead in her tracks, Gaby went rigid. It might have been any number of people who'd laughed. The streets this time of night crawled with perverted souls who found humor in the most morbid things.

But somehow, she *knew* that laugh.

Detective Luther Cross sidled up beside her and eyed her food. "This gives new meaning to carryout."

Slowly, filled with a mystifying dread, Gaby turned her head and looked at him.

It annoyed her to realize that she hadn't done him justice in her novel. He was even bigger than she remembered.

He'd changed into jeans and a printed T-shirt that read SECRET SERVICE, and in smaller print beneath that, YOUR BOYFRIEND NEVER NEEDS TO KNOW. The soft cotton hugged his biceps and chest, making her heart beat a little too fast in an atypical way, sort of like anxiety but not as unpleasant.

The wind had played with his blond hair, leaving it disheveled. His slow smile teased, but his dark eyes saw everything.

And something inside Gaby churned in the most erratic, unnerving way.

Too bold for his own good, he chucked her chin. "Cat got your tongue?"

Sucking in air too fast, Gaby inhaled a piece of food and started choking. To her mortification, chewed bits of bacon and toast sprayed out of her mouth to land on his shirt.

Calm personified, Cross relieved her of the food bag and Coke, setting it all on the sidewalk so he could tap her between her shoulder blades. "Easy now. Small breaths."

Wheezing, Gaby snarled, *"Fuck off."*

"Do you kiss your mother with that mouth?"

Pain clenched around her heart. She got hold of herself, curled her lip, and whispered, "My mother died birthing me, asshole. Thanks for the memory."

And she stormed off, completely forgetting her food, praying he wouldn't follow.

As usual, her prayers went unanswered.

Or the answer was no. Whatever.

She had nearly reached the vacant playground near her apartment when Cross caught up with her. He kept pace at her side, carrying *her* food.

He peered down at her, looked away. Sighed. "I'm sorry."

Gaby had nothing more to say to him.

Three long strides later, he added, "I didn't know."

Bastard. "You don't *need* to know." She lengthened her stride, all but running.

He easily matched his gait to hers. "But I'd like to."

No, and no again! "My life is none of your damn business," she exploded. "Now get lost." She started away, thinking it was no wonder she'd felt stalked. How long had Cross been observing her, and why the hell did he bother?

He stayed right with her. Humor sounded in his tone when he said, "I'm not as easy to scare off as that driver." Bordering on cheerful, he strode along with her as if invited. "Besides, I do know some things about you already."

Gaby's heart tripped, then thumped so loud in her ears it nearly drowned out the rattling thunder. Leaves and litter scuttled across the roadway, carried by the approaching storm. She kept going, one foot after the other.

But he was there, and she knew it down to the marrow of her bones. Doing her damnedest to ignore her unreasonable weather-related fears, she muttered, "You don't know shit."

"I know you have a foul mouth."

"Wow, you are astute, aren't you?" *God, Gaby. Just shut up. Don't reply to him. Don't give him reason to keep replying to you.*

You don't want to have to kill him.

She clamped her lips together.

"I know that you live in a dump. That you have the oddest landlord I've ever met and that you have a penchant to talk with your fists."

She tamped down the urge to tell him a few things—with her fists.

"I know you don't frighten easily, either."

No, she didn't. Despite what she'd just told herself, she heard herself say, "Huh. You learn those awesome profiling skills in fancy detective school?"

The sarcasm didn't faze him. A hand appeared in front of her, offering her the sandwich. "Take it. I know you're hungry."

True enough. Because it was her food and she'd paid for it, Gaby snatched it from him and bit in. Talking with her mouth full, she said, "Know this: I don't like pushy cops who grill my landlord and stalk me."

"Stalk you? Acquit me of that much, at least. I was just cruising the area, and you showed up."

"Right." She'd felt him watching her. Or . . . did she *still* feel someone watching her? Maybe. But damn it, his presence messed with her perception, and she couldn't be sure of jack shit.

"I have an idea."

With her gaze straight ahead and a one-finger salute, she told him what he could do with his ideas.

He paid her suggestion no mind at all. "Let's sit on the bench over there at the playground while you finish eating, and I can ask you a few questions."

She stopped so abruptly, he passed her by and had to

turn back around. When she leveled her outraged stare at him, he sighed, then moved to lean back against the chain-link fence, her can of Coke in one hand, the white bag in the other. Standing six feet from her, he looked expectant, as if he assumed that she would agree, when she had no intention of doing any such thing.

Gaby opened her mouth to blast him—and evil sank its claws into her.

She had no further doubts that someone watched her, someone vile and cruel.

Not Cross, no way.

This was that same teeming malevolence she'd experienced earlier by the hospital. As substantial, thick, and dark as a mudslide, it clogged the air around her.

Tensing, Gaby perceived rather than heard the chuckle as someone or something scrutinized her reaction, toying with her, testing her.

The power of it was unbelievable.

Until his strong hands wrapped around her upper arms, she almost forgot about Cross.

"What's wrong?" he demanded.

This didn't make sense. She stalked evil, not the other way around. When summoned, she had all the control. But . . . *not this time*. She felt like a puppet on very short strings.

Unacceptable.

Utilizing all her concentration, Gaby focused herself.

Cross took her face in his hands, speaking urgently to her. What the hell was he trying to do? She didn't have time to be coddled.

She pushed him away, and to her surprise, he allowed the distance. He even stepped back to give her room. "What is it?" he asked again.

"Something's wrong."

"Okay." Taking her at her word, he turned a full circle, searching the area. He held his body in the deceptively relaxed pose of someone who knew how to kick serious ass.

Gaby blinked at that. Later, she'd muse over his quick and easy acceptance, which was something she'd only ever gotten from Father. For now, she needed to get a handle on things.

Moderating her strained breathing, keeping her thoughts calm and free, Gaby took her time scanning the area. She detected the commonplace turbulence of humans out on this muggy, electric night—but not the red-hot evil she sought . . .

Until she again faced Cross.

It lurked *behind* him, in the playground.

Gotcha.

Stepping around the detective, Gaby strode determinedly toward the evil. She put her hands on the fence, ready to vault over it—and she sensed it taking flight, evading her, running from her.

Body braced to leap the fence, Gaby paused. Like a candle, once snuffed, only a wisp of smoke remained as a reminder of the flame. She wanted to follow, to hunt the malignant corruption and chase it to ground, but damn it, Cross stood there, watching her, waiting.

If she went, he'd follow. She knew that.

Damn him. Because she couldn't risk him or her secrets, she *couldn't* proceed, and that pissed her off so much that she cast him a quelling glare.

"Fascinating," he said, without a speck of humor. "Now tell me what the hell is going on."

Like hell. "Nothing."

"Baloney."

Baloney? Would he say "golly-gee" next? What a putz. A big, powerful putz, but still . . .

Affecting her most antagonistic expression, Gaby growled, "You calling me a liar, cop?" and figured that ought to get him out of her face.

Not the least bit intimidated, he said, "Absolutely. The way you looked—"

A furious bolt of lightning fractured the night sky, cutting him off. Electricity snapped through the air just as a cackling clap of thunder sent a violent tremble over the ground beneath her.

In the next instant, the skies opened up to dump a deluge of icy rain. Cursing, the detective bolted for the safety of an overhang.

Gaby couldn't move.

Irrational, deep-rooted fear kept her grounded to the spot, her limbs useless, her mind a frozen quagmire. From far away came a voice. She wanted to focus on it, but she couldn't.

How long she stayed like that, Gaby didn't know. A couple of times during her life, she'd been caught in storms. It was never pleasant, but other than her lacerated pride, she always survived.

Surely, she'd survive this time, too.

An eternity later, the panic waned beneath an onslaught of fragrant warmth and obscure security.

She was . . . tight.

Safe.

And for that reason more than any other, Gaby refused to relax, to succumb to temptation.

She couldn't be that weak, couldn't let down her guard. Not for a single second.

So lethargic that it took major concentration, Gaby got her eyes opened and, with some confusion, studied the warm skin in front of her. A throat. A man's throat.

Oh shit. "Cross?"

"The storm spooked you." His hand cupped the back of her head. "Why?"

If only she'd had her faculties about her, she'd have thought of a great rejoinder, a witty reply. But nothing felt familiar right now. She couldn't match wits with him, not like this, and so, in a toneless whisper, she said, "I'm told my mother died from a lightning strike. It brought on her labor, killed her moments later, and I was born an orphan."

At her admission, a great stillness fell around them. She felt something she hadn't felt often—sympathy. From Cross.

The bastard.

His big hands began coasting up and down her back, urging her closer. She had no memory of ever being touched so tenderly . . .

A nose nuzzled against her temple. "I'm sorry."

Gaby stiffened.

He said, "Shhh. It's all right, now."

No, it was not all right. Far from it. But what to do?

"Your food's ruined. Washed away. I forgot all about it when you went into shock on me."

He thought she'd gone into shock? Well, good. That explanation worked better than anything she could have come up with.

Peering around, Gaby saw that they stood in the recessed doorframe of a nine-to-five business. The storm had chased everyone inside, leaving her alone with Cross on the flooding street. Illumination from other establishments shone in the windows, but didn't quite reach them.

In a quiet, lulling rhythm, the rain continued.

"I don't remember coming here," Gaby said with accusation. Had he dragged her?

"You were pretty much out of it." He pushed back to see her face, and as if he'd read her thoughts, he added, "You don't weigh much."

He kept looking at her mouth, disconcerting her. Did she have bacon left in her teeth? Anger roiled. "You *carried* me?"

One big shoulder lifted in a halfhearted admission. "Yeah, so? You needed help, so I helped you. Is that so odd?"

It was fucking absurd.

While Gaby contemplated ways to kill him, he brushed wet hair away from her face, then cupped her cheek—and scared the hell out of her.

Apparently, big beautiful cops ran neck and neck with thunderstorms, as far as how they affected her yellow streak.

"Get. Off."

"Don't panic on me again," he soothed.

"I'm not panicking!" But she was. In a very big way. "It's just . . ."

He waited, his gaze warm and filled with curiosity.

She shook her head. Soaked through to her skin, her hair sopping wet and dripping down her neck, she still felt more comfortable than she could ever remember. It was an alien thing for her. Not even with Father had she experienced anything like this, because he always plotted on how to make use of her talent, how to do God's work.

Father was kind, but single-minded in his pursuit of justice, not in the least demonstrative with his affections. She couldn't recall him ever touching her affectionately.

Expression bordering on tender, Cross said, "It's all right, Gaby."

Her alarm—and rage—escalated. In a lethal whisper, she asked, "You know my name?"

"Your landlord told me."

Of course, he had. Poor, dumb Mort. He didn't have the mental equipment to deal with someone like the detective. "You had no business grilling him."

"I didn't."

She snorted.

Cross looked at her mouth again, his expression so intent that she rolled in her lips and glared at him.

His gaze lifted to hers, and she could have sworn his eyes were smiling. "Come on, let's get you home."

She yanked her arm away from his grasp. "Let's don't."

When he took a stance, determined to have his way, she said, "It's right there," and pointed one block up and across the street. "I can damn well walk on my own."

"But I'm going to see you get there, so no, don't start going all scary on me again. I've already made up my mind."

Did he have to keep throwing her curveballs? "Scary? What the hell does that mean?"

"We'll talk on the way." He reached for her arm, caught her venomous look, and held up his hands instead. "Sorry."

At least he learned.

He gestured for her to precede him, and because she didn't really want to murder him, Gaby gave in.

They walked a few feet, stepping around puddles, ignoring the sprinkling rain that softened the night. Crickets sang out; the occasional owl hooted.

"Did you know your face contorts?"

Gaby stumbled over her own feet. *"What?"*

"Your face. At certain times, it sort of . . . morphs."

The very idea of it made her palms sweat. She was different from the creeps she removed from the earth. She had nothing in common with them. "You're wrong." He had to be.

The evil ones morphed; she did not.

He glanced down at her and shook his head. "No, not like that. That's just annoyance. And when the storm hit, you looked paralyzed, but not frightening. I'm talking about before that. When you said something was wrong.

Your face was different. Somehow . . . I don't know. Unreal. Sharper."

Oh God, no. No way.

Never had Gaby heard such an idiotic accusation—but then, no one had ever been with her while she dealt with evil.

Sickness seeped through her guts. Did she turn as ugly and menacing as the targets she defeated?

"How?" Eyes burning, throat tight, she stared at Cross. "What did I look like?"

"I can't exactly explain it." He steered her around a dripping overhang. "It was strange."

The sickness squeezed up around her heart. "Strange?"

He shook that off. "More powerful. A little vague, as if you'd slipped your control. Not worldly." He chewed his upper lip, stared straight ahead, shrugged. "Sexier."

Her feet stopped moving, halting Gaby beneath a streetlight.

Sexier?

Not horrific. No. But . . .

Her brain felt like a great void, no words coming to her, her thoughts tumbling.

Was he myopic?

Some sort of sick jokester?

He couldn't be that desperate. No normal man could be, and definitely not an attractive, powerful man like Luther Cross.

It wasn't true and she knew it. She stood tall and gangly, without curves but with stringy muscles. Her face was as average as it could get, her attitude antagonistic on good days, threatening on the rest.

Cross played her; that was the only thing to make sense. And God help her, she let him get to her.

She had to escape him. Right now. "I'm just across the street."

Detective Cross moved to stand over her, shadowing the light, so potent that she nearly choked on the air surrounding him. "I figured you must have an illness of some sort, but what? I've never heard of anything that alters your features that way. Is it some kind of seizure?"

She took a step back. "Leave me alone."

Apologetic, he said, "I can't do that."

Rage replaced other disturbing emotions. "You will."

"I've lived by my instincts, and every time I'm near you, warning bells go off."

She denied that possibility with a shake of her head. "Don't be idiotic."

"It's more than that, though." He put a hand to his chin, eyeing her up and down. "I feel drawn to you, Gaby. That's odd, isn't it?"

"Fucking insane."

His lips quirked. "Such a nasty mouth. I've never known a woman who talked like you."

He'd never known a woman like her, period.

"I can't decide if I like it or not."

"You don't. Trust me."

"You're probably right." Before she could accept that, he added, "But I'm intrigued."

She narrowed her eyes. "Then you should really seek some help. Tonight. Right now." She started to go around him.

"I mean, why would a woman like you—"

That halted her again, sending new ire to fuel her attitude. "Like me?"

"Smart. Capable. Strong. Why are you living in this hellhole? What do you do for a living? And why do you look so afraid of me, even when I'm not crowding you?"

Fury consumed her. "Don't delude yourself, detective. You *don't* scare me." But his perception of her did.

"I will have answers, Gaby."

She wished he'd quit calling her by name. "Here's an answer for you: go fuck yourself." With that parting shot, she gave him her back.

"You don't want to leave yet."

She meant to keep walking, she really did. Glancing back, she sneered, "Wanna bet?"

He reached behind himself and produced her knife. "This is illegal, you know."

Chapter 6

As Gaby eyed her knife in Cross's hand, her breath left her in a whoosh. No way. Disbelieving, she searched the small of her back and found the sheath . . . empty.

Rage brought out the worst in her.

Her teeth gnashed together.

Her muscles tightened.

Splashing muddy rainwater in a high arc, she again stormed across the space between them. *"How the hell did you get that?"*

Unfazed by her temper, Luther lifted one shoulder in a negligent shrug. "When you were out of it, I picked you up and felt it there. To keep from stabbing either of us, I took it."

She thrust out her hand. "Give. It. Back."

Ignoring her outstretched arm, he examined the blade with the edge of his thumb—and watched as a bead of blood welled up. "This thing could be dangerous."

"Well duh, Sherlock. What would be the point of carrying it otherwise?"

His gaze locked with hers. "Why *are* you carrying it?"

The lie tripped easily off her tongue. "Look around you. Would you wander this neighborhood unarmed?"

He went back to examining her blade. "This is a mighty big knife for such a little girl."

Asshole. Gaby's chin shot up. "You took advantage of me."

His slow smile made her uneasy. "No, but I could have."

She should take the knife from him and be gone from the area before Cross knew what to think. It'd mean hurting him, though. A lot.

And she hesitated to do that.

He turned speculative. "I should confiscate this—"

"I wouldn't try it, if I were you." Proficient in the use of most weapons, she didn't need her knife, but she wanted it. Silent and deadly, clean and neat when she wanted it to be, it was a part of her.

Breaking necks and gouging out eyes, among other deadly means, was much messier.

As if she hadn't spoken, Luther said, "But I'm not going to."

And reminiscent of her earlier gesture with the man in the alley, he flipped the knife around and offered it to her, handle first.

Choosing silence, rather than some lame reply, Gaby took it, slid it into the sheath, and walked away.

He followed.

She kept going, across the street, the sidewalk, up a step, then another to the apartment door. "Good-bye Detective."

"Call me Luther." Without making a sound, he'd moved so close she felt his breath on her shoulder.

"Drop dead, Luther."

His warm fingers curled over her upper arm, guiding her around so that she faced him. "You're not wearing a bra."

And just what the hell did that have to do with anything? "So? I never do. Why should I?"

Holding her gaze locked in his, he slid his hand down her arm, to her elbow. "Because of this?" And he pressed a hand over her chest.

Brown eyes darkening, he caressed her, made a small sound of pleasure, and dropped his hand.

Gaby was too stunned to move. A riot of combustible sensations jerried inside her. *Why would he do such a thing?*

And why had she allowed it by standing there, silent, numb, stupefied?

By God, *she wouldn't allow it*.

In delayed reaction, with no clue to her intentions, she punched him in the jaw.

Hard.

He wasn't expecting the blow. He didn't prepare for it, didn't try to dodge her fist. She connected solidly, and his head snapped to the side.

Eyes narrowed, teeth bared, he said, "Son of a—"

Gaby took another shot, this one coming low and swinging up, aimed at his midsection. But she'd given him a warning with that first strike, and he easily sidestepped her, caught her elbow, and jerked her off balance.

He'd forgotten they were on steps, and she went down them.

He cursed as he tried to catch her arm so she wouldn't fall.

She didn't. She leaped down the steps, immediately turned, and squared off with him again. He blocked her kick to his ribs, her elbow to his head.

"Christ, Gaby, I don't want to fight you."

"Too bad," she growled, and landed a knee to his thigh.

His leg crumpled, but on his way down, he caught her ankle and tripped her.

Neither of them stayed down.

"I don't fight women," he warned.

"Then plan on staying in bed tomorrow."

"Is that a threat—or an invitation?" He blocked another blow, frustrating her.

No one blocked her strikes.

"You can jam your invitation." Stupid bastard. Her next kick caught him in the biceps, making him curse. *Good. Let him be distracted.* She swung for his face—and he caught her fist one inch from making contact with his straight, very handsome nose.

She would have broken it. She still wanted to.

"I'm sorry I fondled you."

Fondled her. How ridiculous that sounded. "Not yet," she warned, "but you will be." Her left almost connected before he caught it, too.

Gaby jerked free and then retreated a step to prepare for her next move.

He eyed her expression, flattened his mouth, and said, "If you pull that knife on me, you'll be the sorry one."

"Ha!" She eyed him up and down. "I don't need my knife for the likes of you." She didn't want to kill him. She just wanted him to bleed some.

Moving fast, he ducked under a punch that would've blacked his eye, and came up behind her. She managed an elbow to his midsection before he pinned her arms to her sides and squeezed the breath right out of her.

He kept his face tucked in by her shoulder, so she couldn't head-butt him, and he hefted her right off her feet, so she couldn't stomp his toes.

Not that she'd have done much damage in her flip-flops, anyway.

She went limp, giving him her dead weight. But he didn't let go, didn't give her any leverage.

"I shouldn't have touched you," he said, breathing hard and fast. "That was wrong and you have my sincere apology."

"Bastard," she gasped out around the restriction of his hold. Sparks lit in front of her eyes as she went lightheaded from lack of oxygen.

Cautiously, Cross gave her a bit more room. With his face so close beside hers, his breath teased her neck, his wet hair touched cold against her skin.

"I've never in my life done anything like that. I don't blame you for being pissed, and I swear to you, it won't happen again." He paused, cursed under his breath, and added, "Unless I have your permission."

That made her jerk and howl, determined to get free and bludgeon him into the ground.

His arms tightened like a vise. "But I need to talk to you now, Gaby, and you *will* act civilized."

His superior attitude bit big-time, but what could she do about it? At the moment, nothing. She couldn't get free of him without causing him a serious injury, possibly even killing him, and that she wouldn't do.

She killed enough bad people.

She didn't want to kill a good one.

He waited, and much as it nettled Gaby, she gave a small nod.

Being smart, the second he opened his arms, he separated himself from her. In less of a hurry, Gaby turned to face him. He'd gotten his way, but there were things he should know.

Her gaze locked with his. "If I'd wanted you hurt, you would be hurting."

He acknowledged that with a nod of his own, rubbed the

back of his neck, and paced two feet away. "Where were you earlier today?"

Gaby tracked his every movement. "What's it to you?"

He flashed a fearsome, annoyed frown. "A man was murdered."

She stared back, her expression carefully blank. Had he somehow connected her to it? Impossible. He'd seen the body, the damage she'd done. Yet he hadn't hesitated to cozy up to her, to confront her and . . . *fondle* her.

Just thinking that word left her feeling oily. She didn't like it.

Surely, if Cross believed her capable of such a grotesque deed, he wouldn't have taken her on.

Far from discouraging him, her lack of response made him edgier. He slashed a hand through the air. "Scratch that. He wasn't just murdered, he was destroyed."

A question burned in her mind, and Gaby couldn't help asking, "Who was he?"

"Hell if I know."

A sliver of moon crept out from behind the clouds, forming a bluish glow around Cross. Mesmerized, Gaby studied him. A gutter dripped. Beneath the streets, water rushed through sewer lines.

Judging by his auras, Detective Cross was pure.

She couldn't forget that—no matter how badly he annoyed her. "What do you mean, you don't know?"

"He was elderly, a denture wearer, so there's no way to get dental records. No one has reported him missing, but he should be easily recognizable." Something hardened in his features. He rubbed his brow. "Cancerous tumors grew all over his body."

Cancer.

The word brought back such horrific nightmares. Gaby knew cancer intimately, had dealt with it, suffered for it, hated it. But those strange growths . . . she'd never seen anything like that.

"He was pretty cut up, but from what we can tell, the tumors were exposed, most of them on his head. Sort of heavy and fleshy." He glanced up, caught her direct gaze in his, and his mouth tightened. "That doesn't make you flinch?"

She'd killed a demon. She knew it, even if he didn't. Whatever had ailed the elder, it didn't matter in the final scheme of things.

Cross looked her over, but not with admiration. "You are a tough little nut, aren't you?"

Gaby refused to react to the gibe.

"He'd also been mutilated."

Mutilated, dismembered, almost beheaded. "You mean during the murder?" She'd done what needed doing. She wouldn't fall apart over it now.

"Not exactly, but whoever killed him did a job of it. No, I meant that someone had hacked off the ends of his fingers. I think on purpose."

Hacked off? The odd stubbiness of his hands flashed briefly in Gaby's mind. So that hadn't just been part of the apparition. "Why?"

"We can't know for sure, but my guess is so there wouldn't be any fingerprints."

Realization dawned. Without dental records or fingerprints, no one could identify him—whoever he might be. "Dear God."

Cross laughed without humor. "I doubt God had much to do with any of this."

Gaby knew that he couldn't be more wrong. God had sent her to kill the demon; that made Him very involved.

Remembering the way evil had pursued her earlier before the rain, thinking of the black omen she'd encountered in the woods, Gaby decided she needed time to ponder things.

"This is all . . . disturbing," she lied. "If you're done annoying me, I'd like to go in now." She started to do just that, and Cross stopped her.

"I asked you where you were today."

"Out walking. Far as I know, that's not a crime."

"No, it's not. But you had a blade on you, and while I don't think you have the strength to commit that grisly murder—"

"Why not?"

He looked at her in disbelief. "You can't weigh more than a hundred pounds." His gaze went to her upper arms. "You don't have enough meat on your frame to cut through bread, much less bones. No, whoever diced that old guy up had to be a big son of a bitch."

"Yeah?" Luckily, Cross was as clueless as everyone else. "So what do you want with me?"

His mouth opened, and then he shook his head and closed it again. "That's a loaded question, Gaby."

Not again. "Quit wasting my time."

He shifted position. "I don't think you did the damage, but that doesn't mean you can't be working with someone else."

Her smile taunted him. "I work alone."

"Got any witnesses?"

Her snort was deliberately rude. "Just those goons you already spoke to."

Luther crossed his arms and surveyed her. "Ah. The guy you flattened, and his cronies."

"We already agreed he had it coming."

"Maybe." He came closer to the steps, staring up at her with blatant suspicion. "They didn't know much."

"About me or anything else, I know. Dunces, all of them." She kept her stance calm, bored, and insulting. "But I don't make a habit of chatting up the locals, so they're the best I've got."

"Meaning you have no way to confirm your whereabouts."

Now she needed confirmation? "I asked you this once today, Detective, but it seems I need to ask again. You planning to arrest me?"

"No." He looked plenty annoyed that he couldn't. "At least, not yet."

"Then I'm done talking." Gaby jerked the front door open and walked face first into a dead, mangled creature hanging from the overhead hall light.

Drying, sticky guts swung back and forth, almost slapping her in the face. The awful smell of it assaulted her nose.

For one of the few times in her life, surprise brought a shout of horror from her throat.

In one agile leap, Cross shot up the steps, only to draw back when he saw the ghastly thing dangling there. "Shit."

"Smells like," Gaby agreed. She stared at the unrecognizable creature that had surely been dead for at least a week.

Mort's door hit the wall and he ran into the hallway. "Gaby! Are you—" He, too, nearly collided with the animal remains hanging from the foyer light. In terror and revulsion, he stumbled back, lost his balance, and fell on his ass. Eyes bulging with fright, face gone pasty white, he whispered, "Oh my God."

Mort wore only his yellowed underwear. His eyes were puffier than before, his nose red and watery. *Fuck, fuck, fuck.*

Forgetting the disgusting animal remains, Gaby demanded, "Are you still crying?"

Mort stared at the dead critter, mute. He looked ready to barf. Or faint. Or both. He put a hand over his mouth and gagged.

Pathetic. "Suck it up, Mort. It's only roadkill." Using her knife, Gaby cut it down and, holding it by the rope used to hang it, tossed it out the door and into the corner where the buildings met. Blocking Mort's sight of the door with her body, she said, "Just someone's sick idea of a joke, that's all."

Cross growled behind her. He stared at the rotted animal corpse, then slowly brought his gaze up to zero in on Mort.

"Or maybe," he suggested, "it's a threat."

Gaby didn't like the sound of that. "Don't deliberately scare him, Detective."

Cross looked from Gaby to Mort and back again. "Why the hell is he crying?"

Mort objected to that. "I'm not!"

She shrugged. "He's not."

Unconvinced, Cross continued to look between them. "You two have a fight?"

Gaby just glared at him, but Mort—looking more morose and *guilty* than any man should—swallowed hard and shook his head. "No."

Eyes narrowing, Cross whispered, "A lovers' spat, then?"

Gaby considered slugging him again. "You're warped."

The detective just shrugged. "After three years together, you two claim to barely know each other." One brow arched up. "But now I'm getting a different impression."

"Good night, Detective." And to Mort, "Get rid of that carcass, will you? It'll stink up the place."

Distaste wrinkled Mort's nose; he gagged pathetically and nodded. "All right, Gaby."

Making sure Gaby would hear him, Cross said, "I'll help, Mort. Then you and I can talk some more."

"Talk? About what?"

"About you and Gaby having a dispute."

Meddling prick. Gaby stomped up the rest of the stairs, went into her room, and slammed the door.

But she couldn't sleep, and trying to hear the detective over the outside noise of traffic and human chatter was a waste of time. With nothing much else to do, she sprawled out in the bed and let her thoughts drift away.

Evil had stalked her, taunted her, and then escaped her.

Unthinkable.

Definitely unacceptable.

Tomorrow she'd start the hunt. One way or another, she'd figure things out. Evil didn't stand a chance.

It never did.

Shoving aside the stack of reports and his empty coffee mug, Luther sat back in his leather chair. Even two days after tangling with Gaby, a twinge in his ribs had him rubbing the spot—and smiling in memory.

Maybe Gaby was right. Maybe he was warped. Why else would a lingering ache, caused by her dead-on kick, amuse him?

"Something funny?"

He looked up at Ann Kennedy, a veteran detective and longtime friend. "Not really."

She propped her perky ass on the corner of his desk. "You're rubbing your ribs. Get in a scuffle?"

Luther dropped his hand. "Not really, no." But he believed Gaby when she said she could have hurt him if she'd wanted to. Which meant . . . she hadn't wanted to.

"Being evasive?" Her gaze turned speculative. "C'mon, Luther. Spill it. You know I'm not going away until you do."

"It's nothing. Really." Swiveling to face her, he asked, "You ever heard of a disease that sort of . . . morphs a person's expression?"

Both brows lifted. "Morph?"

"Yeah." He straightened in his chair. "You know." He moved his hands around his face. "Makes you look different."

"In a weird way?"

"Not so much." It was all too freaky and strange, but never at any point had Gaby looked weird. Maybe otherworldly. But still a woman. "Just . . . not the same."

Ann laughed. "Well, that'd be different." She tipped her head. "So who'd you see morph?"

Earnest, even eager, to figure Gaby out, he still wanted to protect her—why, he couldn't say. She'd already proven she could protect herself. "Just a lead I'm following."

Ann looked ready to launch into more questions when Gary Webb dropped mail on his desk and said, "Maybe it's like in *Servant*."

Both Ann and Luther peered up at him.

"Oh, come on. Are you two so old you can't keep up with pop culture? Rhetorical question. You're both ancient."

Luther laughed. He supposed to a guy barely out of his teens, thirty-something did seem old. "I don't mind a young'un like you giving me shit, but Ann here, she can be deadly. You should show more caution."

"Indeed," Ann said.

Unconcerned, Gary launched into speech. "*Servant* is an underground graphic novel. Really cool, too."

"A comic book?" Ann asked with disdain. "You're still reading those?"

"God save us." Gary dropped the mail pouch and scowled at her. "It's not a mere comic book. Graphic novels are books with illustrations, and *Servant* is a *great* story with awesome drawings. Trust me. It's some super-creepy shit." He nodded at Luther. "Including bad guys who morph."

Luther met Ann's commiserating gaze. "Yeah, well, somehow I think we're talking about two different things. But thanks anyway."

Irked at their ignorance, Gary retrieved his mail and stalked away to finish his intern duties.

"Crazy kids these days." Ann swung one foot. "You're a detective, Luther. If you want to know what sort of disease someone has, just ask."

He had—and got a foul-mouthed reply instead of an answer. "Most people would be irked at that kind of nosiness."

"Maybe. So ask someone who knows the person." Ann lifted herself off his desk. "But whatever it is, it sounds horrid, and unlike anything I've ever heard of."

Watching Ann leave, Luther admired her curves in a detached yet automatic way. He'd known her a long time, but he wasn't an idiot so he kept work and his social life separate.

Except that he'd slipped up with Gaby.

He still couldn't believe he'd copped a feel. And of what? The woman barely had any curves to speak of, and what she did have she kept protected beneath of a lot of poisonous thorns.

Yet he hadn't been able to help himself. It was a part of his personality he'd never encountered before. He always kept his head, always controlled himself.

Fuck.

After running a hand through his hair, Luther looked at the not-quite-finished reports and made a fast decision. He'd come back to them later.

He pulled out a clean sheet of paper and a pen and made himself a list.

Background check on Mort. He'd start with a face-to-face and see what he could find out just through chatting.

Investigate morphing. God, that word sucked, but he

couldn't think of one better, not to describe the way Gaby had altered right in front of his eyes.

Check into her mother's death. One of the few times he felt Gaby had been straight-up honest was when she mentioned her mother.

Luther started to fold the list, and on impulse scrawled, *Cancer in background.* The mutilated man had a strange sort of cancer. Yet when he'd told Gaby, she'd kept such a stony expression that he couldn't read her at all. Perhaps cancer had touched her life in some way. Maybe it even had something to do with the odd way she changed appearance.

Tucking the note into his pants pocket, Luther left his desk.

He'd start finding answers now by first visiting with Mort. And maybe when he finished that, he'd visit with Gaby again, too. The woman had secrets that might, or might not, be related to the grisly murder of an old man consumed with cancer.

Until he found out, Luther knew he wouldn't be able to get her out of his mind.

Gaby pushed her lank hair away from her face and realized it now hung an inch or so below her shoulders. Time to cut it off again. She got out her shears, big and sharp enough to be lethal, and in one fist gathered the hair together at the back of her neck. Doing it this way wouldn't make an even cut, but who gave a flip?

She didn't.

She eased the blades around the hank of hair and was just about to hack it off in one big chunk when a strange sensation crawled over her. She went rigid, jerked back, and the point of the scissors gouged her in the top of the shoulder. A single drop of crimson blood trailed over her pale skin and down to her collarbone.

The evil was back.

Dropping the scissors into the sink, Gaby strode to the window and looked out. At late afternoon, the sun held high in the sky, casting tree shadows around the surrounding area. Kids of all ages scuttled around the playground, shrieking, jumping, creating a boisterous sonance of laughter and ephemeral happiness.

Gaby tuned them out to listen for other sounds, baser sounds. Besides the kids, nothing stirred, not even a breeze, and yet, she felt it. Hot.

Sticky.

Calculating.

Close to the innocent children. But uninterested in them.

By rote, Gaby reached behind her and fingered her knife, safe in its sheath beneath her baggy T-shirt. She inhaled slow and deep, once, again, a third time. Her senses sharpened, but not by God's will.

No, this was mere human instinct, pathetic in comparison, but all she had at her disposal.

So the evil didn't plan anything. Yet. It only watched her. But why?

And what difference did that make? One way or another, she had to destroy it. She felt it studying her, so she knew it was close. She sensed it lurked just beyond the playground, so it had dared to come within reach. It wanted to hide, but that wouldn't do.

Gaby would go to it, force a confrontation, and then demolish it.

Turning away from the window, she strode to the side of her bed and slipped her feet into her flip-flops. Key in her pocket, she went out the door and rushed in silent haste down the steps.

Thankfully, Mort didn't appear. She didn't want any interruptions that might give the evil an opportunity to escape.

Keeping half her attention on avoiding Mort, Gaby shoved open the entry door—and almost collided with Luther Cross.

They didn't make actual contact, so he had no reason to grasp her arms. But he did anyway.

"Well, well. Going out for another stroll, Gaby?"

Sensations exploded. Thoughts of Luther had plagued her all through the long, lonely nights, until she concluded that she'd have to get rid of him.

Permanently.

Other than the possession of her knife, he had no solid reason to suspect her of anything.

That meant, as aberrant as it might be, his interest came from a different source.

Strange bastard. Didn't he know that put him on a level with goofy Mort? Surely, he couldn't want that.

Cold with deliberate and somewhat feigned disdain, Gaby looked down at his hands on her arms. "Let go."

He stupidly ignored that. "You're cut." Using his hold, he tilted her to the side and examined the bead of blood on her pale skin. "What happened?"

"I'm fine. Now let go."

"Cut yourself shaving?"

His attempt at humor only incensed her further. "I said. Let. Go."

Dark lashes lowered over narrowed eyes. "You're in one hell of a hurry, you look pissed, and you have blood on your neck. I think I have good cause to ask a few—"

This time Gaby gave him no warning, and for some odd reason, he wasn't as prepared as he'd been during their first scuffle. Her bony knee slugged hard against the inside of his thigh. She hit high up, close to his groin, hard enough to cause him to cringe not only with pain, but with inborn defense of his jewels.

When he lurched forward trying to cover himself, Gaby brought her elbow up and in, and then shot it back into his jaw in a clean strike. His head snapped back, his arms flailed, and his foot landed just beyond the top step. He tumbled backward in an awkward heap.

Gaby jumped down around him, sprinted across the street, and scaled the chain-link fence around the playground—all before Luther had picked himself up off the steps. After one quick glance back, Gaby kept her attention focused forward. Somehow she knew he wouldn't follow her, but even if he did, once she'd wound her way in and out of alleys, he'd have a hell of a time finding her again.

The children at play paid her no attention at all. It would have been disgustingly easy for her to harm any of them— if she'd had that intent. Still at a fast pace, she went over the fence again, this time toward the back, then beyond the empty school.

When her lungs burned and sweat smothered her skin, Gaby drew to a pause. She'd allowed herself to run freely, trusting a sixth sense developed through pain and purpose, to guide her in pursuit of the archfiend haunting her.

When she perused her surroundings, she found herself in front of a hospital, facing the entrance for the emergency room.

Abhorrence overtook her. Her detestation of all things medical squeezed her throat in a viselike grip, making deep breaths problematic. Chills chased away the sweat. Revulsion churned in her belly.

She remembered being here—not at this specific hospital, but to her wounded psyche they were all the same. Misery hung heavy in the air. Fear, desolation, and anxiety wafted in and around the human cattle. As many security guards as medical personnel mingled through the masses.

Through constantly breached doors, Gaby detected the voices, elevated in both pain and anger. A hacking, wheezing body bumped her as it passed, making slow, stooped progress into the unit. Ambulances came and went; people of all sorts talked, ate chips or cookies, and swilled caffeinated adrenaline.

It should have been chaos, but to Gaby's jaundiced eye, it appeared more like frigid, choreographed efficiency.

She stood there, taking it all in, letting it stir her memories until it became a part of her.

And hurt her. Again.

Gathering her wits, she studied the ambulance drivers talking as they replaced a gurney, then the nurse in her tidy white uniform, sharing amicable conversation with a woman in a suit. Her impulses tightened. Her stomach knotted in dread. She curled her hands into fists.

Then she went in to find the fiend who'd led her here.

Chapter 7

Angry black clouds filled his vision. When he got his hands on her, he'd throttle her. Twice.

Luther tried for a calming breath, but calm remained well out of reach. Gaby had done him in, and it hadn't even taken much effort on her part.

Where the hell was she going in such a hurry? And how had she gotten cut?

"Son of a bitch."

Cursing didn't make him feel any better, and in fact, it only served to bring Morty Vance scuttling out of his cubbyhole.

The scrawny landlord gaped down at Luther in disbelief. "Detective Cross. What are you doing on my stoop?"

Luther sat up and dusted off his hands. His leg hurt. His head pounded. Trying not to growl, he said, "Taking survey."

Mort looked around the dark, deserted streets and along

the dirty sidewalk in confusion. The baking sun amplified the rancid scents of God-knew-what. Discontent buzzed in the air. "Survey of what?"

"My bones. I wouldn't swear to it, but I think they're all in one piece still." Had Gaby missed his crotch on purpose, or did she have faulty aim? Somehow he doubted the gangling barbarian ever missed unless she meant to.

Luther worked his jaw, tamped down on his blistering temper, and got off his ass. "Gaby leveled me."

Mort's mouth drooped open, then snapped shut. "She did what?"

Nodding toward the uneven doorframe where Mort hovered in trepidation, he said, "She came barreling out of the building, damn near ran into me, then laid me low. All without so much as a how-do-you-do."

"But . . ." As if seeking explanations, or looking for Gaby, Mort rubbernecked around. Finding nothing but the same old dirty surroundings, he shifted his bony shoulders. "Well, I'd say that doesn't sound like Gaby, but I guess it does. She's not much for small talk."

"You don't say." A dirt stain marred the front of his gray slacks. "She was bleeding." He looked at Mort. "From the throat."

His curled hand pressed to his mouth. "Much?"

"What?"

"Was she bleeding much?"

Luther wanted to punch a hole in something. "You're not surprised that she was bleeding? You just want to know how much? Does that mean you're the one who hurt her?"

"No!"

Crossing his arms, Luther waited. Silence had a way of making small-minded people spew their innermost thoughts. He doubted it'd work with Gaby. No, she'd just stride away. But Mort . . .

"I would never hurt her. I swear, I wouldn't. She's a friend."

"Then who did?" He looked beyond Mort to the shadowy entrance. He could see the peeling paint on the battered walls, the chipped wooden floor. "Is there someone else in your building?"

"No way." Mort shook his head in surety. "Gaby never has anyone over."

"Never?" That was a pretty long time. But it didn't surprise him.

"Not since I've known her. Not even once."

"Hmmm." Pondering that, Luther said aloud, "I suppose she could have done it to herself. Hopefully an accident. It didn't look too serious—"

"Thank God."

Luther drew back, perplexed at Mort's reaction. Had he been in an agony of suspense, not knowing how badly hurt Gaby was when she fled the building? But why assume such a thing anyway? "Why all the relief, Mort? You've seen her hurt worse, have you?"

Showing some belated spine, Mort straightened. "No. And why are you bothering Gaby? What did she ever do to you?"

Luther did an abrupt and unplanned about-face. "I'm not bothering her. Actually, I came to see you."

"Me?" Astonishment and worry muted his pleasure. "But . . . why?"

"You've lived in this area for a long time, right?"

Excitement made his voice stronger. "About a decade now. My mom used to own the building and I lived with her." He realized how that sounded and cleared his throat. "I took care of her, made sure she had what she needed . . ."

"Yeah, I get it. That's real noble of you." Putting an arm around Mort's shoulders, Luther led him inside and toward his apartment. With a slow groan of rusty hinges, the entry door crept shut behind them. "Where's your mom now?"

"She passed away about five years ago."

"Two years before Gaby moved in?"

Nodding, Mort stepped to the side and allowed Luther to enter his apartment. Everything looked the same as it had two days ago: cluttered, meager, and impoverished. "I'm sorry about your mother."

"Thanks." Mort ran his hands up and down denim-covered thighs. "Why d'you care how long I've been here?"

"There's been some trouble in the area and I figured you had to know people, right? I thought maybe you could lend me a hand."

"You want my help?"

"Sure, why not? The police can always use a little outside assistance. Given your proximity to things, you're a good candidate to help now." Luther stared right at him while telling the lie. "I can trust you, right?"

"Yeah, I mean, sure. I'm glad to help however I can." Shifting in nervous ebullience, he stirred the air, sending the odor of unwashed skin to Luther's nose. "You want something to drink, maybe?"

After a discreet cough, Luther nodded. "If you make it strong, coffee would be good."

Mort's thin face lifted. "Cool. Let's go in the kitchen."

Rushing ahead, he emptied dirty clothes off a chair and piled them in the corner, then began clearing the tabletop of comic books and unpaid bills. Luther sat down and, trying to be subtle, asked, "You said Gaby keeps to herself, but you don't get much company here either, do you?"

"Nah, but it's okay. When I have the store open, I stay plenty busy."

Luther pictured the ramshackle store that abutted the two-family structure. Enough filth marred the windows to impede a view beyond the bent, stained, and faded signs crookedly hung. Handwritten messages pronounced the sale of comic books and other fan magazines. "You own the connecting building, too?"

"Yeah. I inherited both this place and the comic book store from my mom. But I didn't feel like opening the store today."

"Under the weather?" When Mort glanced at him in edgy suspicion, Luther said, "I noticed you had some allergy problems or something with your eyes. It hits a lot of people this time of year."

"Yeah." He turned away to fix the coffee. "So you wanted to ask me some stuff about the area?"

Absently, Luther picked up one of the comics on the top of the pile. He thumbed the edges, making the pages flip. "You heard there was a murder?"

"There always is." After he finished the coffee preparations, Mort turned to face Luther. "It's sad, but around here, we're used to it."

Very true. "Lots of hookers getting killed, the occasional robbery gone wrong."

Mort nodded.

"This one was different, Mort. A man was mutilated."

Mort said nothing, but his Adam's apple bobbed in his scrawny throat.

"He was so hacked up, body bits were everywhere."

"Hacked up, huh?" He rubbed the back of his neck. "I heard some stuff . . . people around here talk. I guess it was pretty bad?"

"He was nearly decapitated. Almost every bone broken. Ribs sawed through. His guts spilled out." Luther watched Mort. "Pretty macabre stuff."

Both hands covered Mort's mouth. "That's . . ."

"Disturbing. I know. And then you had that mutilated

critter hung in your foyer." Luther tossed the comic aside and picked up another. "I wonder how someone got in there to do that, without you hearing or seeing anything."

"I was in bed a lot that day, and Gaby wasn't here."

"Where was she?"

"I already told you I don't know." He paced away. "I don't know how I didn't hear it."

Probably because he'd been crying too hard, the poor schmuck.

Fear overtook Mort's expression. "You think the two things are related?"

"In this neighborhood, who can say?" Luther lifted his shoulders. "I do know that Gaby shouldn't be out alone at night—like she was a few nights ago." He waited a second or two. "She *was* alone, wasn't she, Mort?"

"I don't know." He almost wailed that. "Gaby doesn't tell me anything. I wasn't lying about that. She's real private."

"She's been here three years. You must know something about her."

The second the coffee machine quieted, Mort took out the carafe and filled two mugs. As a type of warning, he said, "I know she keeps to herself and doesn't like questions."

"How does she support herself?" When Mort again glared at him in suspicion, Luther tapped the comic book against the tabletop. "I'm just asking because I'm worried about her. It doesn't seem she works during the day, but if she has a night job somewhere, she could be at risk. Until we catch the lunatic who committed the murder, no woman should be out alone at night."

Mort grunted. "Yeah, well, you try telling Gaby that." He held out a mug of coffee, and Luther started to toss the comic away.

That's when he noticed the cover.

Servant slashed across the front in a scratchy font above

the depiction of a tall woman, her hair blowing back in the wind, her eyes narrowed in what appeared to be pain and resolution.

He accepted the coffee in one hand and lifted the graphic novel with the other. "You read this?"

"Are you kidding? It's the best. I've collected them all. They're my most popular item. They—"

To Luther's surprise, Mort suddenly clammed up. "What?"

He shook his head. "Nothing. I just . . . I realized how you might look at it, me reading graphic novels."

The lie showed all over poor Mort's face. For some reason, he didn't want to talk about the story. With more to ponder, Luther again skimmed the cover.

Something about that cover depiction drew him. The claws of curiosity dug in, and Luther couldn't let it go. "Mind if I borrow this?"

"Why?"

"I've heard good things about it."

Suspicion showed again. "Yeah? From who?"

Thanks to Gary, he didn't have to lie. "There's a college kid who hangs out at the station, getting in some credit time. He cleans up, runs errands, hands out the mail . . . that sort of thing. He mentioned the novel to me just this morning. Raved about it, actually."

Staring down at the floor, Mort muttered, "He's probably getting anxious for the next installment. I know I am."

"So can I borrow it?"

Drawn back to himself, Mort looked at Luther. "Uh, sure. But . . . you'll bring it back, right? I mean, they become collector's items. I wouldn't want anything to happen to it."

"I'll keep it safe. Soon as I'm done, I'll return it to you."

"Thanks. Take your time. I've already read it, but a new

one should be out soon, so I was just rereading it until then."

It occurred to Luther that he could accomplish a lot by becoming Morty's friend. "When do you expect Gaby back?"

"I don't. That is, she comes and goes on her own. Most of the time I don't even hear her. I swear, she's like a ghost."

Did Gaby sneak out, or was stealth a natural part of her personality? "Sounds like you have plenty of time to visit."

"Sure."

Luther glanced at his watch. "Let's order a pizza. My treat. It'll give us a chance to get better acquainted, and you can tell me more about the people around here."

Specifically, he could tell him more about Gaby.

Blending into a hospital couldn't have been easier. Watching the woman covertly proved simpler still. Curiosity was sharp, but then, to a scientific mind that never rested, this new phenomenon held almost as much interest as the cancer growth.

Thinking of the cancer growth wrought both satisfaction and annoyance.

Too many medical critics want to proclaim that the procedures violate a cardinal rule of surgery by leaving dead tissue in the body. Of course that can—and usually does—lead to sepsis. But on a dying body, what difference did a massive infection make? Why can't the skeptics grasp the underlying significance in what we can learn, what advancements can be made in the field of cancer research?

Idiots.

But not this one, not the spiritual girl. She saw too much, and understood everything. She had a similar intelligence, sharp and unwavering, and a way of dealing with things that proved almost as satisfying as a major medical break-through.

Stepping into a patient's room gave all the cover needed. The girl went on past, her long ragged jeans dragging the hospital floor, her lank hair in her face, her eyes almost unseeing. She'd turned her thoughts inward, and for the moment, forgotten her purpose.

Interesting.

So not only lightning distracted her, but an inflated empathy for the ailing took her off course, too? Good to know.

And even easier to use.

But first, like the cancer subjects, this would be tested. After all, brilliant minds insisted on analyzing all that they could. Then, with the results in hand, the knowledge gained could be put to good use.

For an extended length of time, Gaby wandered unnoticed through the hospital. Silent as a wraith and just as devoid of her surroundings, she went up elevators, down halls, in and out of waiting rooms. At times her senses prickled, but overall, the despondency of strangers overwhelmed her. She heard soft sobbing, loud wailing, and witnessed restless, worried pacing.

If she'd had a heart, it would have broken into tiny little pieces.

But what she'd once claimed as a heart had been shredded years ago.

Eventually, as she again became familiar with the suffering, everything blunted enough for her to concentrate on her unease. By then, she could detect no evil, and in fact felt the power of angels lurking about. Auras, eight feet square, showed strength of purpose. The exact opposite of the draining auras near the abandoned isolation hospital, these hues fed her, strengthening her, giving her clarity.

Whomever she'd followed had gotten away.

Time for her to leave, too. Next time, Gaby assured herself, she'd do better.

To get her bearings in the sepulchral hall, she looked around and realized she'd wandered into the cancer ward. Several yards away, a nurses' station stirred with lights, machines, sounds, and kindly looking women.

No. Not here. Making haste, Gaby turned to leave before she got noticed.

Mere seconds before she reached the elevator, she detected the soft cooing of a woman. It was a familiar sound, one of insanity and surrender.

One without hope.

Her eyes closed. Father had made those indecipherable sounds, too, when the cancer had reached his brain and modern medicine numbed his pain. They sounded placid enough, but Gaby knew the truth. They meant nothing, no more than the body issuing them.

Unable to help herself, she slowly turned and looked into the room.

A shrunken female form, barely clinging to life, rested flat on her back in the bed. Beside her, a plump nurse gently eased a damp cloth over her arms. The cancer victim made another pleasurable sound, and the nurse smiled.

"It's all right, Dorie. I'm here. Your family has been to visit, but they needed to go home. You know you're very loved, my dear. Very, very loved. They all care so much. And I care. I'll be here until morning, and then Eloise will take my place. You know how you like it when she brushes your hair."

Hot tears welled in Gaby's eyes, choking her, blurring her vision of the deceptive scene. Someone touched her arm, and she flinched away, coming back to the here and now in a crashing disturbance.

"Hey, it's okay," the man said. He wore a cleric's collar and a sympathetic smile. All around him, a swelling purple aura swam and shifted, indicating a noble and spiritual soul. "Is Dorie a relative of yours?"

Gaby straightened as much as she could. To her horror, she could feel her nose running, but she had nothing to wipe it.

The man handed her a hankie. "It's so difficult, I know."

Gaby snatched the hankie and wiped her eyes first, then blew hard. Uncaring of decorum, her voice broken with pain, she said, "It's fucking inhumane."

The man peered in at Dorie and nodded. "It's not something we can easily understand. But we all do what we can."

"There's nothing that can be done!" Gaby didn't mean to raise her voice, but memories of Father growing weaker by the day still infested her mind. Over and over, she visualized the awful treatments that made him suffer more than the worst torture. She remembered his agony, his prayers, and then his blankness. She remembered . . . everything.

"Sometimes, no," the cleric agreed. "But the tenderness does help soothe the pain."

"You can't know that." But Gaby prayed that somehow he could.

In answer, he patted her and his compassionate smile came again. "I thank God often for the angels here on earth, the ones with the patience and caring to take on so much suffering day in and day out."

Damn it, her eyes flooded again and the hankie received another loud honk. Choking out the words, Gaby said, "I can't be in here. I have to go."

He squeezed her shoulder. "Of course, child. Go, collect yourself."

But Gaby knew the nurses would stay.

The cleric would stay.

They weren't cowardly like her.

Angels on earth, he'd called them. It must be true, because even as she rushed to escape, she felt the cottony softness in the air, and around the black spots of imbalance and the gray shadows of sickness and lugubriousness, she saw the cocoon of sympathetic green and calm blue hues. They came from the caregivers.

They came from angels.

Two nurses rode the elevator with Gaby, speaking low to one another, giving her privacy in their averted gazes.

One said, "I wish Dr. Chiles could always be on call. I really don't like dealing with Dr. Marton."

"No one does," the other nurse replied. "Talk about clinical."

"And lack of feelings . . ."

The nurses grew silent, leading Gaby to wonder about Dr. Marton. Was he like the doctor Father had, detached to the point of leaving a body shivering cold? Gaby had hated talking to the doctor, listening to his evasive non-answers and lack of respect toward a man who was no longer a man, but a shell with a disease.

The elevator doors opened and Gaby launched out, almost running, so anxious to breathe in fresh air that she thought she might hurl. In the very back of her mind, she thought she sensed a laugh, but the distress of her body kept her from reading it clearly.

She burst through the emergency room doors and, doing all she could not to fall to her knees, sucked in the humid summer air.

She could have returned to her apartment at that point, but she didn't want to.

Ignoring the strange crowd loitering outside the hospital,

hoping to buy prescription drugs or trade sex for favors, Gaby headed for the street. She had a few miles to go before she'd reach the apartment. But she intended to go beyond that.

She intended to seek out the woods where she'd located the abandoned isolation hospital.

For some reason, she felt drawn there.

Chapter 8

A sweltering, setting sun cast the dreary neighborhood in a muggy haze. The reflection off the blacktop patches on broken concrete roads could blind a person and added to the smothering heat, but Gaby didn't move from her position at the front of her apartment building. Sweat dampened her scalp and pasted her hair to her forehead, temples, and neck. Even though she'd cut it, her hair still felt too thick and smothering.

Sunglasses in place, flip-flops kicked to the side, she sprawled boneless on the scabrous steps and surveyed every inch of the surrounding area. For the past four nights, she'd tried to go back to the isolation hospital. Each time, she had to alter her plans, knowing someone followed her.

Detective Cross?

Morty?

Or someone, *something*, else?

Sleep became elusive, as did peace of mind. Her thoughts

twittered with too many possibilities, too many questions. For once, she begged for a calling from God, a summons to attack, a divine guide to the evil that plagued her.

No summons came.

She wanted to curse God, but it wasn't easy. Commination against Him stuck in her throat. Her faith was such that if He didn't send her after the demon, she knew there had to be a reason.

It just sucked that the reasons were never in her understanding.

As Gaby pondered her quandary, a shadow climbed the stairs and crept over her.

Already sensing whom she'd see, she glanced up, and there stood Luther Cross. Too tired and strung out to care, she diverted her gaze away again.

Dressed in another button-front shirt and tidy slacks, he sank down to sit beside her. "You are one hard woman to track down, Gaby Cody."

Her first and last name. What else did he know of her? "Drop dead." Mentally, she retracted that order, just in case He was listening—which she doubted. God couldn't be bothered with such pettiness. She just didn't want to take any chances. Her soul had blackened enough already.

"I'd rather not, thank you. And I'd rather not arrest you, but I will if you make me."

"Yeah?" Stiffened arms braced behind her, Gaby tipped her head back so that the sun caressed her throat. "For what?"

"Assaulting an officer?"

In her tautened position, the laugh sounded more like choking. "An officer who molested me?"

He chuckled—and Gaby felt his gaze on her chest. "Touché. Not that anyone would believe you."

Too drained to measure her words, Gaby straightened

and asked, "Why not? Because I don't have anything to grope, or because you have a pure aura? We both know you still did it."

For half a minute, Luther remained utterly silent. Gaby listened to the rumble of engines and the quieter thrum of tires on pavement as cars went past. She heard the muted congestion of voices across the street, a few doors down, at the end of dark alleys. She heard doors opening, a dog barking, and off in the distance, the lone but not unfamiliar wail of a siren.

"Okay." Luther propped his forearms on his knees. His eyes narrowed and his brow pinched. "Let's skip the strange comment for just a second to clear up something else."

"If you insist."

"Yes, we both know I did it, no way for me to dispute it. But we both also know that's not why you ran from me."

"When did I run?"

"A few days ago. With blood on your neck." His jaw flexed. "After you tried to unman me."

Her smile quirked. "Listen up, cop. If I'd tried, you'd be a choirboy. Believe it."

Luther accepted that without expression. "So why'd you run?"

Sighing, Gaby knew she couldn't lie. She had run, he'd seen her, so denying it would do no good. But her reasons would remain her own. Curious, she asked, "Why do you think?"

Without missing a single beat, Luther stated, "You know something about the murder and you don't want to tell me."

Well hell. Gaby took off her sunglasses and scrubbed at her eyes. She had to throw him off that scent somehow. "Yeah, you've got me dead to rights, officer. I know all about it."

"Don't be a smart-ass, Gaby. If you saw something that night, it's your duty to tell me."

"My duty." How ludicrous that sounded.

Luther firmed even more. "If you're afraid of retaliation, I can protect you."

That brought about a genuine laugh—of amusement and bitterness. "If you want to think so, who am I to say otherwise?"

His irritation hit her in waves. "What exactly does all that sarcasm mean?"

Time to run away. Again.

But before she'd even gotten her ass off the step, Luther blocked her. "I won't let anything happen to you, Gaby. I swear."

Temper snapping, she rounded on him. "Good God, man, don't be a complete imbecile. You can't protect me. *I'm* the one who—"

She cut herself short on that awesome disclosure. Breathing hard, she stared at Luther and saw his fascination, his interest. *Oh God.*

Rot out her tongue. Make her mute. Let her faint. *Something.*

But the only thing that happened was Luther's puzzled frown. "You're the one who . . . ? What? Murdered that old man? Mutilated his body?" His voice deepened to a feral growl. "Lopped off his damn head?"

Shaken, depleted, Gaby pulled herself to her feet. She stared across the street as she asked, "Where'd you get that idea?"

Slowly, Luther stood, too. "I didn't. Have that idea, I mean. I was being facetious."

"Oh. Good." She needed to go inside. No. One glance at the dreary entrance and she knew there was nothing in there but her restless thoughts. She started across the street instead, going where, she didn't know yet.

Just away from Luther Cross.

"Let me tell you something right now, Gaby. You're a nanosecond away from being arrested."

Gaby waved that away. "Leave me alone. You're nuts."

"I will arrest you."

"No you won't."

Growling again, he warned, *"Don't try me."*

Gaby stopped, but didn't turn to face him. "What do you want, Luther?"

She counted five heartbeats before he replied.

"Having you say my name is a start. But I have questions, and I want answers."

Over her shoulder, Gaby took his measure. "What kind of questions?"

"The kind best handled in conversation instead of at the station with you in handcuffs."

Another tired sigh almost took away her knees. She moved two steps closer to him. "You were telling the truth? No one would believe me if I told them what you did?"

He stepped closer, too. "I don't know, but is it worth the effort when you look so beat?"

It didn't take her long to decide to give in. "Come on. I'll buy us Cokes and we can sit by the playground."

"The same playground you used to lose me last time." But he fell into step beside her.

Neither of them spoke. When she reached Chuck's, she went to the window and gave their order. "Anything else?" she asked Luther.

"I'm good."

Yeah, he was. The colorful sunset enhanced a large orange halo encircling him. Optimism, strength. He had both in spades. He'd make a good teacher, a capable leader of others.

Gaby dug two bills from her pocket and paid for the drinks. The cans must've sat in ice because they dripped frosty chips, and when she popped the tab, a fog escaped.

After a deep drink, Luther put a fist to his mouth to muffle a belch and said, "Good. Thank you."

Gaby rolled the cold can over her forehead and, knowing he'd follow, went up the street to an empty bench. With each step she examined the playground. Metal equipment wore shades of rust. A cracked wooden swing offered splinters to an unknowing hiney. But the few children still at play didn't care. Shirtless, most of them shoeless, they mellowed as evening approached, carefree, unaware, and happy.

Just as they should be.

Gaby's stride kicked up brittle leaves. The sun sank further into the horizon until lengthening shadows encompassed everything. Most of the kids would head home now. Others, more neglected, would linger or wander off to different, less puerile amusements.

Gaby stopped by the chain-link fence. As lampposts flickered on, mothers called their offspring home, their voices carrying on the stagnant air.

The youthful crowd thinned—and an older crowd crawled out.

The nightlife started, and with it came a force of hookers, dope dealers, drunks, and thugs. Gaby started to sit.

"Careful."

Luther used the toe of his shoe to nudge away a dead, dried-up mouse curled around the bench leg. She felt much like that critter—used up and frangible.

Cradling her canned drink in a loose hold, Gaby plopped down. "So. You on duty?"

"I got off an hour ago."

"And came to see me." She pushed her sunglasses to the top of her head and indulged a slow drink. "You do realize how pathetic that makes you, right?"

"You think so?"

"Definitely." The thought occurred to her, and spilled off her tongue. "Don't you have a wife tucked away somewhere, or at least a significant other you could hassle instead of me?"

"Sorry, I don't have either." He didn't smile, but he didn't frown. "What about you?"

"No wife."

That got a chuckle out of him. "Good. Husband, significant other? Now or . . . ever?"

"No."

An odd inquisitiveness gleamed in his dark eyes. "How old are you, Gaby?"

"Just turned twenty-one."

"Just?"

"I met you on my birthday, Cross. Now what kind of queer gift is that, do you think?"

"I didn't know." That seemed to bother him.

"Even if you had, so what? It doesn't mean anything." Except that she'd survived another year, and that, perhaps, was something worth celebrating.

"I thought you were older."

"Do I have wrinkles?"

"No, but you have older eyes. Eyes that have seen some ugly things."

Gaby groaned at the absurdity—and truth—in that. "Let's cut the melodramatic crap, okay? Between that and the heat, I'll puke."

His halfhearted smile came and went. "All right. Then I'll start with my first question. You said your mother died birthing you. So who raised you?"

Tracing her fingertips through the sweat on her can gave Gaby something to look at other than him. "The state."

"Always?"

"Yep. I had a few foster homes, but they didn't last long." She pressed her thumb inward, denting the can. "I was too weird for normal people to put up with." She glanced his way. "I freaked people out. They didn't want me around their real kids. *They* didn't want to be around me."

"Maybe as a kid you misinterpreted things."

"No. They spelled it out." Hell, she could still hear the conversations in her head, blunt, to the point, but not deliberately cruel. It was too hot to shrug, so she simply said, "I didn't blame them. I was weird enough that even I realized it."

Luther watched a bird light on the sidewalk in front of them, snatch up a bug, and then take flight again. "I think you're unique, Gaby, but I wouldn't call you weird."

"That's 'cause you're weird, too." She looked him over. "Why else would you have groped me?"

Exasperated, Luther plunked his can down on the sidewalk and turned on the bench to face her. "All right, since in typical female fashion, it keeps coming back to that—"

"Typical female fashion? *Me?* Now you're delusional."

"I groped you because there's some sexual chemistry going on between us."

Gaby worked up a believable gag. "There, you see? I told you. Heat. Bullshit. It's a combo guaranteed to turn my stomach."

"You do it to me even when you're gagging." He held up his hands. "But I'm practicing a 'don't touch' policy. At least until I figure out what you're hiding."

As straight-faced as could be, she said, "I'm not hiding anything."

"And I'm a saint."

"Sexual chemistry." The words felt funny on her lips, sounded imbecilic, but still, they stirred her mental acquisitiveness. "Explain that."

"Explain what?"

"This . . . sexual chemistry stuff. What is it?"

"You're pulling my leg."

"I can kick your leg if you want. But I'm not pulling on it."

He scoffed, but not with conviction. "You're telling me that you don't know what sexual chemistry is?"

She didn't like the implication that she was stupid. "Fine. Forget it. It's not like I really give a shit anyway."

He caught her arm, and quickly released her. "Don't go off in a huff. I didn't mean to insult you. It's just . . . It's hard to believe a twenty-one-year-old woman could be so . . ."

"Stupid?"

"Innocent."

Gaby blinked at him as she absorbed his accusation, and on the third blink, her eyes narrowed with rage. "There's nothing innocent about me."

"Have you ever had sex?"

She didn't really mean to, but she punched him. Right on the chin. And because she hadn't realized her intent, he'd had no way of anticipating it. If he'd had a glass jaw, he'd have been out for the count. As it was, his head snapped to the side, and in the same movement, he surged off the bench in a rage.

"Goddamn it, woman. Stop attacking me!"

Impervious to his upset, Gaby didn't stand. She didn't even flinch. She looked at him, at his heaving, his flared nostrils and red face, and the strangest thing happened.

She snickered.

Luther looked ready to shoot sparks out of his head. And that amused her even more.

She patted the bench beside her. "Sit down, Detective. I promise I won't hit you again. At least, not without provocation."

He appeared more inclined to choke her, but when she patted the seat again, he dropped down. Jaw jutting forward, he warned, "I mean it, Gaby. Keep your fists to yourself or we're going to end up at the station."

"Yeah, yeah. I got it." Still amused with him, she slanted him a look. "No, I've never fucked anyone. Truth is, I've never been kissed, either. Other than your big paws, no guy has touched me. So maybe that explains why you bring out my anger. I just don't get you."

That all hit Luther in an odd way. He went mute. And something, some strange emotion filled with perturbation and energy, emanated from him.

He leaned into her space. "Never?"

"Nope."

"Not even a peck?" Skepticism kept his eyes narrowed and his gaze precise. "Maybe on the cheek?"

"Nope."

Thoughtful, he sat back, took a drink of his Coke, and after a few nods of understanding—for himself, not her— he zeroed in on her again.

Very intent, he launched into explanation. "Everyone has . . . nuances—a way of walking or talking, *emoting*, that draws other people or repels them. Every so often, you run into the right people—or maybe in your case, just the right person—who reacts to what you have. Whatever it is. Scent. Attitude. Expression."

He had to be kidding.

"In your case, I think it's all three. Your attitude definitely does it for me."

"Does it for you?"

"Stirs me. Turns me on." Expression bordering on helpless, he shook his head. "At times, I swear, you wreck me. I can't explain it. But I like it."

"Pervert."

He laughed. "Yeah, maybe."

"All that makes you sound like a damn masochist."

"Doesn't it though?"

"Everything you said sounds like a bunch of hooey to me."

"Yeah, well, it sort of did to me, too. I guess it's not something that's easy to explain or decipher."

"My scent?" Without looking away from him, Gaby turned her head and sniffed at her own shoulder. She detected soap, a little sweat, and that sun-warmed aroma that came from being outdoors for an extended time. "I don't smell bad, but I'm not exactly a flower, either."

"Really?" Utilizing great caution, moving very slowly, Luther leaned forward. "Let me see."

Gaby's heart did a funny little flip.

By infinitesimal degrees, Luther closed the distance between them until his nose touched her ear.

She heard the rise of his breathing, deeper, richer. He made a small sound that she took as earthy pleasure—and then he jerked away, and said nothing. He swilled the rest of his Coke.

"Well?"

Luther shook his head. He ran both hands through his hair, tugged a little, looked away into the distance. "Yeah." He cleared his throat. "Not too bad, I guess."

She didn't understand him at all.

"And people think I'm flaky." When he said nothing more, Gaby looked across the street at two whores strolling along in amicable conversation. "What about them?"

As if glad of a distraction, Luther focused on the two women in comparable stages of calculated undress. "They're hookers. What about them?"

"You telling me it's their smell that draws the customers and earns them a living? Because I have to tell you, I've walked past a few of them and they sometimes stink to high heaven."

He choked on a laugh. "No, it's not their smell. Sometimes sex is just sex, with nothing else involved." He paused to ponder his own words. "Actually, I'd say that's usually all it is. With a business transaction, that'd be the case."

She eyed him. "I take it you have experience?"

Appalled, he pulled back. "Not with hookers, no, thank God."

He'd grilled her, so Gaby had no qualms about reciprocating. "With other women who aren't hookers?"

Querulous disapproval stiffened his shoulders and tightened his expression. "This is an extremely peculiar conversation."

"You started it."

His sigh held a note of frustration. "Fair enough. Yes, I have experience. For Christ's sake, Gaby, I'm thirty-two. It'd be more than odd for me to be a virgin."

She supposed that made *her* more than odd.

He must've realized the same. "I didn't mean . . . Look . . . Surely you've learned enough about sex from television and music to know how most men operate."

"I'd say you were unlike most men." She could be a master of understatement. "But it's a moot point anyway. I've never owned a TV and I've never been a fan of music."

He did another double take. "You've never owned a television?"

"No. When I lived in foster homes, they had them, but I

wasn't exactly invited to curl up with the others at family time." And it was safer to keep to herself.

Luther sat very still, just looking at her, enrapt. His hand lifted and he touched her hair. In a benign voice laced with tenderness, he whispered, "You keep cutting little pieces out of me, Gaby, and you don't even need that machete you carry to do it."

An alien sensation unfurled in her belly. It left her unsettled, even a little shaken. She slapped his hand away. "Keep your mitts to yourself, cop."

Rather than take offense, he smiled. "I gather the subject of sex is over."

"You got another subject?" Night air settled over her, cooling her overheated skin. In the playground behind them, the crickets came out to sing in tandem with other insects. The night should have been peaceful, but Gaby knew too much to ever be fooled. "Because if not, I should get going."

"Where?"

She had no idea. "Away from you." That'd be the first priority.

"Fine." He let out an aggrieved breath and, all business, settled back into the bench. "What do you know about cancer?"

The question hit Gaby like a cruel blow, deadening her wits.

"Well, well," Luther murmured, "there's an honest reaction for a change. I take it you've known someone with cancer?"

For lack of a better response, she said, "What's it to you?"

"The man who was murdered—"

"Yeah, you told me." She didn't want or need to hear the lurid details again. "He had cancer."

"He more than had it. He was eaten up with it."

Gaby eyed him. "Listen, Detective. I'll admit the whole

sex talk thing was interesting. Maybe even a little educational. But now you're just boring me." She did not want to talk about cancer.

"Boring or not, I expect an answer."

She could see that he did. Even a good guy like Luther Cross couldn't be dissuaded from his course, especially not when he thought he had just cause for an interrogation. What that cause might be, Gaby couldn't guess.

Deciding it'd be best for her to give him what he wanted so she could then seek solace away from him, she nodded. "Sure. I know cancer."

Brows coming together, Luther frowned at her. "You say that like it's a living thing, an acquaintance you've made."

"And you think it isn't? Trust me, cancer is very alive— alive enough to massacre without mercy."

Laying his arm along the back of the bench, Luther studied her for several terse moments before drawing some conclusion. "Convince me that it's alive."

"Do your own damn research."

"I'd rather get your perceptions. Or can't you back up that statement with explanations?"

Gaby snorted at the challenge, but she wouldn't back down. She finished off her Coke, crushed the can in one fist, and tossed it a few feet away to an overflowing trash receptacle.

"Good shot."

"Thanks." She sprawled out further. "The docs have fancier names for it, but when you break it all down, cancer is nothing more than rebel cells. Real ass-kickers with the ability to populate out of control."

"Metastasize."

She shrugged. "Call it what you want. I call it a siege, a long-term, decimating invasion that lasts until death."

"Sounds right to me," Luther agreed.

In acknowledgment of the detestable topic, Gaby's voice went low and cold. "Normal cells have a life span. The old die off to make room for the new. But cancer isn't normal. It gets stronger, jacking up into great ranks, invading and wreaking havoc. Cancer's a son of a bitch, robbing from normal tissue until body parts, and eventually the body, dies from deprivation."

Luther kept a close watch on her as she spoke.

"Occasionally cancer shows mercy and snuffs away life before people realize what's happened. It spares them the excruciating, violent process." Her muscles tightened. "But most times it lacks any humanity at all, slowly and methodically eating away at sanity and strength."

Luther stroked her hair, the side of her throat. She flinched away, but of course that didn't stop him.

Memories had her breathing hard and fast even as they dropped her voice to near nonexistence. "Cancer rots organs and bores holes in the brain until disillusionment takes over. Where a good soul used to be, cancer leaves behind a shell."

In the far reaches of her consciousness, she felt Luther's caring touch. "You've put an awful lot of study into this, Gaby Cody."

"No," she whispered back. "I haven't studied it." She fixed her gaze on him instead of the abominable images from the past. "I lived it."

Apprehension cleared his face of all other expressions. "You've had cancer?"

Misleading him hadn't been her intent. "Worse." It would have been so much easier if she'd been the one wasting away. And more appropriate. "He was a very good man who I cared about."

"A friend?"

"Sort of." They hadn't been friendly in the typical way. They didn't share chitchat or have dinner out. Father had been a mentor, guiding and counseling her, often serving as her conscience, her parental influence, and her only confessor.

Strangers strolled by, rambunctious with too much drink. A woman's stagnant perfume hung in the air, and a man laughed too loudly at nothing at all.

"He was a very good person." Gaby waited until the strangers had passed. "Cancer killed him."

"I'm sorry."

"Why? You didn't even know him."

Again, Luther teased his fingers through her hair. "I get the feeling there haven't been many people you've cared about. Losing someone is always hard, but doubly so if you don't have anyone else."

Like a scalding cauldron, emotions tried to bubble up and over. But therein lay weakness and lack of caution. *Careful, Gaby,* she warned herself. *Don't let a simple dose of concern turn you all mushy and talkative.*

To free her hair from Luther's fingers, she slouched sideways into her seat and turned her face away. "Anyway," she said, "cancer's not contagious, but it sure as hell affects everyone who comes into contact with it. I was just one of millions who got to know it on an intimate level."

The silence that fell between them helped amplify the night sounds. Somewhere down the street, a fight broke out. A bottle broke. Loud music competed with rank cursing. Running footsteps retreated.

Into the stillness came the rustle of Luther moving closer. "You cut your hair, didn't you?"

At a loss how to deal with him, Gaby chose mockery. "Now see how observant you are? Nothing gets by you."

"It's a lot shorter and not all that even. Anyone could figure out that you cut it yourself."

"Few enough people even look at me, Detective, and no

one else would pay any attention to my stupid hair." *She* barely paid any attention to it.

"Why did you cut it?"

"Would you want long hair hanging down your neck and getting in your face with the temps we've had?"

His gaze slipped over her, warm and tactile. A second later, his thumb followed the same path. "That blood I saw on you . . . you have a mark here now." His thumb brushed the spot. "It wasn't there before. Is that from the cut that made you bleed?"

"Jut a nick from my hair-cutting efforts."

"You hair wasn't cut then."

He really was attentive to details. "I'd damn near slit my throat. I decided I should wait till morning." And other things had taken precedence.

"So instead of a trim, you chose to thump on me?"

Sitting still for so long didn't suit Gaby, not like this.

Not with a man.

Out in the open.

Pulling her legs up to sit Indian style, she struggled to get comfortable. "You got in my way that day. That's all."

"A deadly bad mistake, apparently."

His humor proved nearly as addictive as his kindness. "Anything else, detective?"

"Yeah, one more thing. But I doubt you'll want to cooperate, so I want your promise up front that you won't resort to violence."

"I make no promises." Gaby stared at him, waiting.

"Such a tough nut."

He didn't show any real concern for bodily injury, but he did hesitate, giving Gaby an unspoken warning that she wouldn't like his new subject matter.

"You told me your mother died birthing you. That lightning struck her."

"God Almighty." Before he could even think about stopping her, Gaby surged from the bench. "Are all cops as freakin' hard-hearted and intrusive as you?"

Uncaring whether he liked it or not, she began striding away.

But she couldn't stop the flow of words spurred on by ire. "Isn't *anything* sacred to you?"

"Gaby, wait."

"Fuck you, cop."

"I said wait, damn it."

"Why?" Walking backward allowed her to sneer at his face as she withdrew. "You want to dig up any other unpleasantness for me? Wanna talk about my years in foster homes, or how the other kids all hated me and called me a freak?"

"No." He looked annoyed with her.

"Why the hell don't you just poke me with a stick, you coldhearted bastard? What gives you the right to dig into my life anyway?" Because he was getting closer, she turned back around and lengthened her stride. "It's no wonder this town is in such sad shape, when the cops waste time—"

A hand on her arm snatched her around. Luther had caught up quicker than she'd realized. She collided hard against his big, solid body.

Chapter 9

"Why won't that cop just *go away*?"

The frustrated voice carried on the wind, but no one was around in the darkness to overhear. The cop and the very strange woman were several yards away, on the other side of the fenced playground, well out of range.

Almost impossible to see.

Even with the streetlamps shining down and a fat moon overhead, the night remained pitch black around every corner, behind every building and down every alley.

The hour grew late. The watchdogs grew tired.

This would be the perfect time to accomplish a great deal. There were things to be done, things with the failed test subjects.

And things with that girl.

But not while a law official lurked nearby, causing complications. If the police got suspicious and started snooping around, they could ruin everything accomplished through careful research, great risk, and enormous sacrifice.

Hopefully the girl would send the cop on his way, and soon. Burning the candle at both ends had a draining effect on even the most brilliant minds. Each day held so many responsibilities: working at the hospital, studying and tending the test subjects, getting rid of failed experiments, and following the girl.

Something had to be forfeited.

The girl, obviously, would have to go. Yet she was so fascinating . . .

"Maybe, just maybe," the doctor spoke aloud, "I need to get rid of the police officer first." Yes, that plan made sense. With the detective gone, everything would go smoother.

And that would leave the path wide open to get to the girl.

But how to do it?

Distracting the woman would be a problem, but thinking of the weaselly landlord . . . "Maybe it won't be an insurmountable issue at all." Everything needed was in quick supply, stored a short distance away—or right at hand.

Smiling, the doctor tugged on the length of rope, and got a groan in return. "Yes, I know. Not much longer now. I've just thought of a brilliant way to make use of you one last time. Your death will not be in vain. You will have another opportunity to atone for past sins."

An odd noise echoed out around the area; it was the doctor's laughter of eagerness and delight. But given the other night sounds, no one would pay any heed.

There were benefits to hanging in the slums.

The rope grew taut, then slack again with submission.

No one cared what happened or to whom it happened, and that made medical experimentation so much easier.

Before she could deck him, Luther said, "I'm sorry, Gaby." And he meant it.

But damn it, she tripped him up at every turn. What should have been simple became too complicated to unravel, especially when Gaby lost the belligerent aggression of a pit bull, and instead mirrored a small wounded female.

Once again a pit bull, she shoved him back. "Keep your hands to yourself, will you already?"

"Yes." But he knew he wouldn't. For whatever reason, he couldn't. "Will you let me explain?"

"Do I have a choice?"

He wanted to tell her that she did, but it'd be an outright lie. Much as he might sometimes dislike it, he was a detective, and that meant certain things had to be disclosed. "I'm trying to understand you, Gaby. Yes, out of personal interest, but also because, as a cop, I've lived by my gut instincts much of my life. And alarm bells clamor whenever I'm near you. Something isn't right."

Her lip curled. "I told you. I'm a freak."

It wasn't easy to draw a calming breath, to keep from berating her over such self-inflicted castigation. "I asked about the death of your mother because I think it might explain a few things."

"Like my *life*?"

She was so hurt, so angry and antagonistic—and untouchable. The walls around Gaby weren't just sturdy; they were all but impenetrable.

As Luther was a male chauvinist of the first order, her barriers only made him more determined to get beyond them.

"Your life, and how that life might play into my perceptions now. You see, I researched lightning strikes and—"

Throwing up her arms, Gaby complained, "Oh God, you've got to be kidding me."

And oddly enough, it didn't seem a mere expletive so much as a rebuke. At who? "Lightning can affect all organ systems, sometimes in long-term or even lifelong ways."

In a huff, she examined a fingernail. "Fascinating."

Luther locked his back teeth. "It can cause all kinds of problems."

"Yeah, uh-huh."

"Nerve disturbances. Movement disorders. Dementia. Decreased—or increased—reflexes."

Her gaze swung up to his and she pursed her mouth, maybe to keep from laughing. "I get it. You think the way my mother died somehow explains what you saw when I laid out the bums by the bar?"

"How you move, yes. But also how antagonistic you often are, and why you looked . . . different when I first met you. The way your facial expressions, even your appearance, altered." Because he couldn't stop himself, Luther eased closer to her. "It seemed such a phenomenon, I figured there had to be a medical explanation, but I had no clue what it might be."

At the mention of her transforming countenance, Gaby froze up. "You've got a damn screw loose." Pointing a finger at him, she said, "Leave me alone. I mean it." And she turned to head back to her place.

"I can't do that, Gaby." Once again, he found himself following close behind her.

"Try." Shoulders tense and tread stomping, she kept on going.

Damned stubborn twit. "You're just digging yourself into a deeper hole."

"Go fuck yourself."

His patience wore thin. "Is foul language your answer for every damn thing?"

Vibrating with fury, she halted, then jerked around to square off with him. "No, asshole. I like to talk with my fists. I was making an exception for you because you're such a pretty boy. But since you refuse to back off . . ." She widened her stance and poised herself for combat.

Blood thrummed in Luther's veins. "Here we go again." He braced for her attack.

He anticipated grappling with her again. She wouldn't hold back, so by God, neither would he.

Then a bloodcurdling scream blasted from her building.

Their locked gazes afforded Luther a firsthand view of Gaby's singular reaction. She went still and calm, but alive with a flood of energy unlike anything he'd ever seen.

So fluid she nearly became a blur, she spun around and charged for the apartment building.

"Gaby, damn it, wait!" Who knew what she might run into? Luther's longer legs didn't help much in catching up to her, not with her unholy speed.

He drew out his gun and got up the front steps two paces behind her, just in time to see her open Mort's door and, without an ounce of caution, storm inside.

She had that razor-edged blade in her hand, and a look of anticipation that turned his blood cold.

"Mort!" Her voice rang out. "Mort, where the hell are you?"

Luther did a quick surveillance around the small apartment and saw nothing amiss.

He tried to get in front of Gaby, but after she scoured the rooms, she headed back to the foyer.

"Mort!" she bellowed again.

And they both heard the whimpers.

Gaby shoved Luther aside and went to the bottom of the

stairwell. Almost at the top near to Gaby's rooms, Mort hunkered down.

On nearly every step beneath him, thick, sticky blood pooled and dripped.

"Shit." Gripping the handrail with one hand, Gaby levered herself up the stairs three at a time, avoiding the spill of blood as much as she could. At first, she went right past Mort and checked her door. When she found it still secured, she stowed her knife and came back to Morty. "Talk to me, Mort. Let me know you're okay."

White with shock, he stared at her and began to babble. "I was seeing if you were in. I wanted to tell you about the newest *Servant* manuscript I got, and how mind-blowing it is. But you didn't answer and then I thought I heard you come in, so I turned to call down to you, but . . . You weren't there. No one was there. It was just . . . all that blood."

"None of it is your blood?" Gaby knotted a hand in his spiky hair and worked his face this way and that, checking him for injuries.

Watching her, Luther sighed. She had a shitty bedside manner. And poor Mort looked ready to expire from her attendance.

"Come on, Florence Nightingale." He returned his gun to the concealed holster at his back. "I'll help you get him down from there, and then I'll call it in." Being as cautious as Gaby had been, Luther went up three steps and stretched out an arm.

"Butt out, cop." Ignoring his proffered hand, Gaby pulled Mort's limp arm over her bony shoulders, put her arm around his waist, and stood. "We don't need your kind of help."

Like acid through his veins, the rejection burned. Luther didn't move, didn't retract his offer or his arm. "You will take my hand right now, Gaby, or so help me you won't like the consequences."

Morty stirred from his horror-induced trance. Lips trembling, he whispered, "Thanks, Luther." And he reached out.

"Fine." Gaby let him go with a slight shove. "But try not to track it all over the place, will you. It's going to be a bitch to clean up."

Rather than pamper Mort, Luther did the expedient thing and slung him over his shoulder, bounded down the remaining steps, and put him back on his feet. "You all right?"

Morty shuddered. "Just grossed out. I mean . . ." He spared one fitful, fleeting peek at the bloody stairwell. "There's so much of it, and there are *chunks* of things in it, too. And I can . . ." He gagged. "Smell it."

Frowning, Luther looked again at the blood.

Gaby crouched down on one of the steps and she, too, took a better study. "He's right. Looks like hunks of flesh and skin and stuff. Maybe some bone." She made a face. "And hair."

"This is too much." Luther pulled out his radio. "Try not to disturb things too much until the forensics guys can get here."

"No."

He stabbed a glare at Gaby. She leaned over the rail and slid down on her belly to keep her feet out of the blood. When she reached the bottom, Luther automatically helped her down around the broken wood finial at the front post.

Again, she brushed him off. "Put the radio away, Columbo. There's nothing here worth bothering the specialists."

She amazed him at every turn. "You don't think a gallon of blood warrants inspection?"

"Why? It's just another damned prank. Likely from a

slaughtered pig. If you want to do some investigating, start at the butcher's around the block. You can find it by the raunchy stench."

Luther looked at the blood again. "You think that's from an animal?"

Her light blue eyes rolled up in annoyance. "No, it's from the president's wife."

Luther didn't appreciate her sarcasm.

"What? You thought it was human?"

"I don't know."

She shook her head, as positive as a person could be. But how? "It's not."

"No?"

"It's an animal. And unless you know something about cult worshipping and sacrifices taking place in the area, which wouldn't surprise me, it'd almost have to come from a place with lots of spare blood."

She held out her hands, encouraging him, and Luther dutifully replied, "The butcher."

"Exactly. If there was another murder, you'd already know about it, right? If anyone was slaughtering house pets, you'd probably know about that, too." She gave him a superior look. "Or am I wrong?"

If he replied to her at all, Luther knew he'd lose the fragile thread on his temper. He directed his questions at Mort. "Have you pissed off anyone lately?"

"I don't think so." Folding his arms around himself, Morty turned his back on the gore. "People come into the comic book store to sell stuff or buy stuff, and sometimes I don't need what they have, or don't have what they want. It makes people pissy, but I don't think I've made any real enemies because of it."

Gaby lounged back on the wall. "I bet I know what it is."

Both men looked at her.

"You." She held Luther in her pointed gaze. "Look around the neighborhood, Detective. This isn't Sesame Street. Around here, cops are the bad guys, especially the kind who wear suits instead of uniforms. And yet old Mort has played nicey-nice with you, chatting you up, inviting you in. That can't be good for his social standing." Her lip curled. "Do us both a favor and go solve some real crimes, will you?"

Shit. She could be right about that. He disregarded her last dose of disparagement and said, "So you think someone managed to throw in a bucket of pig's blood without Mort noticing?"

Gaby slanted her attention at Mort, who wore a blank, befuddled expression, then back to Luther. "Hardly seems possible, huh?"

Her wisecracking added to his tension. Luther rubbed the back of his neck, undecided. "Maybe. But I still need to have this checked out—"

"So you can get even more people hating Mort? Sure, why not. He's got that coming."

Morty started to panic. "Now wait a minute. I don't want more stuff like this to happen." He grabbed at Luther's sleeve. "C'mon, Luther. Do you really have to make a fuss about it? What if I promise to keep the entry doors locked from now on? Only Gaby and I will have keys. Will that be okay?"

Something in Gaby's expression convinced Luther. Though she tried to conceal it, and from most, she succeeded, he still saw that she didn't want the cops there.

In fact, she was outright rigid about it.

Somehow, Luther knew that if he pushed her, she'd disappear. He couldn't chance that. Not until he got everything neatly resolved.

"Yeah, all right, Mort. That'll be fine."

Gaby left her slouched position on the wall. "What are you asking *him* for? You own the damn building." As she walked between them, she gave Morty's chest an arrogant shove. "If you want the front doors locked, then lock them."

"Where are you going?" Luther demanded.

"To the storage closet to see if Mort has any cleaning supplies. Someone's got to get this mess cleaned up, and I'm afraid if he does it, he'll pass out."

Morty nodded. "She's probably right." Then in an attempt to be stronger, he said, "But I'll help, Gaby."

Turning his wrist, Luther looked at his watch. What the hell. "I'll help, but I can't stay too long. I do plan to go by this butcher's you mentioned, just to look around. I'll say a few choice words to anyone there, and hopefully that'll put an end to it."

"Yeah sure." Gaby returned. With one hand she dragged along an industrial-sized mop and bucket, and in the other she held a large plastic garbage bag and a bundle of old rags. "Knock yourself out."

It took more than an hour to get the worst of the mess cleaned up. Luther looked around, and decided it was time for him to go.

Gaby, still behaving like a prune, walked off to dump the bag of blood-soaked rags in the basement near the washer and dryer.

Mort changed the mop water for the fifth time and prepared to go over the stairs again. He'd promised to have a new lock put on the doors first thing tomorrow morning.

That made Luther feel marginally better, but he still didn't like it. Something was up.

He felt it.

❧

Just as Gaby had said, he caught a whiff of the meat market long before he reached it. The unique smell of a fresh kill hung in the air like sweat in a closed locker room.

It wasn't far from her apartment, just a few blocks over. Rather than announce himself, he parked at the curb half a block away and started in that direction. But before he'd reached the butcher shop, he heard a soft, mewling noise.

Luther glanced around but saw no one. Still, he felt the attention directed at him, and knew he was being watched. Gaby? Maybe she wanted to make sure he checked out the butcher, as she'd suggested.

But he didn't think so.

She was far too pissed at him right now to be dogging his heels for any reason. Hell, if he didn't keep going to her, ignoring her rapid-fire insults, he'd probably never get to see her again.

He knew without doubt, she'd never come to him.

Eyes narrowed and temper soured, Luther scanned the area, peering at the closed businesses, the dark doorways, the overflowing garbage cans.

One empty building, boarded up and darker than sin, caught and held his attention. Drawn to it, Luther approached the front but found it locked up tight. He tried a side door.

No one answered his knocks.

He heard another low-pitched whine and moved closer to investigate.

Jaws snapping, a muscular dog lunged out from the shadows. Blood hung from the animal's mouth and mottled the fur around its face.

Luther stumbled back and cracked his spine on a metal railing by the side door. *"Damn it."* His feet slipped in something wet and he barely caught his balance.

Fur on end, muzzle undulating, the dog continued to menace him. It circled, licked its chops, and inched forward.

Unwilling to shoot the animal, Luther stomped a foot and said with his own mean snarl, *"Git. Go on, go. Get lost."* He slapped his hands together, all but attacking.

The beast turned and ran.

Heart still thumping, Luther caught his breath, rubbed the bruise on his back, and then turned a semicircle to get his bearings. The partially blocked alley led to a back entrance and, on alert, he moved in that direction.

He heard another, barely audible whine.

The dog was gone, so where . . . He looked, but saw nothing.

No one.

After releasing the leather latch on his holster so he could get to his gun quickly, he said, "Who's there?"

No one answered.

Drawn deeper into the alley, beyond where the illumination of streetlights could reach, he withdrew a penlight and scanned the area. There on the ground, a large black stain caught his attention. Moving closer to investigate, he stepped around discarded crates and cartons and a few sealed-up bins that didn't warrant investigation.

A fat rat scuttled by, barely missing his right shoe.

Glistening with evening dew, a web stretched from brick to brick. The black stain looked like oil.

Or blood.

Luther bent to touch it, but stopped before making contact. A foul stench reached him, rank enough to make his stomach flinch. With one hand he covered his mouth and nose, and with the other, he shone the penlight.

The black stain trailed away toward a large metal garbage container, and beside that, what looked like . . . guts, bones, intestines.

Forgetting the smell, Luther shot to his feet and dropped

his hand. The narrow beam of light bounced around as he moved closer and closer.

So many possibilities worked through his brain that it took him a moment to recognize the remains as discards from the butcher next door.

Damn dog. So that's what he'd wanted to protect, why his mouth had been bloody?

There was nothing here. No one.

Luther had no reason to be so suspicious. He let out a breath and headed back for the street.

Maybe if his thoughts hadn't veered to Gaby, remembering how she slung that heavy mop, her obstinate attitude and her take-charge manner, things might have gone differently.

He might have had a chance.

But he did have Gaby on his mind, and because of that, he heard the odd wet, scraping, dragging noise a moment too late. He turned and barely had time to catch sight of the nightmarish apparition pitching toward him. The odor intensified.

The body, missing an eye, dragging one useless leg, drenched in a gel-like substance, moaned a complaint, an entreaty, and fell toward him.

Shocked and sickened, Luther lurched to the side, hit the brick wall, and scuttled back into the alley to avoid the grasping arms. "Fuck."

It reached for him again, slavering from a gaping maw that might have been a mouth, and he stumbled away, unwilling to be touched. "Hang on," he said to the malodorous creature. "Just . . . hang on."

He jerked his radio free to call for help—and something solid hit against his temple. Pain ruptured, bowing his back, blocking his vision. "Oh shit."

As he slipped down, down, down, he realized his error and cursed his own stupidity. He had one single moment of cognizance, one second to know he'd failed not only himself, but Gaby, too.

And then cold blackness snuffed out all thought.

❧

Gaby pulled the chain hanging from the low ceiling in the basement. The bare light fixture clicked, but no light came on.

A prickling of unease raised the short hairs on her neck.

She dropped the bag of blood-soaked rags and, using the dim light from the stairs, looked around. Casting thick shadows, the mismatched washer and dryer were to her right, connected to a laundry tub. Piled high with discarded clothes that Morty never wore anymore, a rickety table sat to her left.

A subtle shift in the air assaulted her, and Gaby looked above the table at the small slider window.

Wide open.

Things came together in a snap. How the perpetrator had gotten in with the bucket of blood, and earlier, the dead carcass. Had the person left? Or had he been around when Gaby sent Luther to the butcher?

What if . . . ?

The pain seized her suddenly, clutching Gaby in a suffocating lock.

It was so severe that it dropped her against the moldy wall with a groan of agony. *"Oh no."* Not here, not now, with Mort only a few feet away. No, it had never happened this way before.

It *couldn't* happen now.

But she had no means to stop it. What usually crept up on her with adequate warning now struck with blinding trauma. Weakness pervaded and she slid down the wall until her tush connected with the dingy, dank concrete floor.

"Gaby?" Mort called down the stairs.

Go away, she screamed silently, but she knew he wouldn't, and she couldn't find the breath to tell him to.

He slunk down the steps in nervous trepidation. "Gaby, you still down here?" When he spotted her, he froze on the bottom step. Voice shaking, he asked, "Hey. What are you doing?"

When she couldn't reply, he hurried to her side. "Gaby, are you all right?"

"Yeah." The word emerged as a gasp of agony. Summoning lost reserves, she squeezed her eyes shut and slowly straightened, crawling her way up the wall until she had her feet under her. Her stomach burned and her muscles knotted. "I have to go."

"What?" Mort fluttered around her as she tested the strength in her legs. "Gaby, *no*, you're hurt, or, or something. Let me call an ambulance. Let me . . ."

At his sudden silence, Gaby got her eyes open. The pain was so strong she could barely see, but she sensed Mort's fear. Fuck. "Go upstairs, Mort."

An audible swallow broke the silence. "What's wrong with you?" he whispered.

She couldn't speak, couldn't explain. Seldom had the calling taken her so viciously. It crippled with its measure of urgency, driving her to haste.

Something was very, very wrong. "Go to your apartment, Goddamn it!"

He turned and ran up the stairs, leaving Gaby free to do what she must.

She stumbled up behind him, went through the door and outside into the sizzling evening air. Free of Mort's

scrutiny, she allowed the summons to guide her down the
block toward where Luther had left . . .

And realization hit her.

Luther.

The moment the thought exploded in her brain, she understood the extreme urgency, the grinding pain.

Luther was in trouble.

Chapter 10

With a cry of denial at the inevitable, Gaby gave the summons free rein. If someone saw her, fuck it. This was no time for subterfuge, not with Luther at risk.

Strength surged through her body. Her legs took over, racing her through the night, past two drugged whores, a homeless man passed out on the sidewalk. She went between parked cars, down an alley . . . and there it was, blinding in its dominance, crawling black and blistering red, popping and crackling.

Through the veiling hues of evil, trouble, and illness, Gaby made out the piles of refuse and the pipe on the ground. She smelled the acrid scent of evil as it raped her nostrils and her brain.

And she saw the large slumped body, partially draped over plastic garbage bags and cardboard boxes. Blood oozed from a head wound. A rat investigated.

She recognized the clothes. Luther. Lying so still and bloody and . . .

No. *Not dead,* Gaby silently screamed.

"Not that," she whimpered.

He groaned, one hand twitching, and so much relief flooded her system that for once, she could see clearly. Even with the auras dancing in frenetic discourse, Gaby knew that she wasn't too late—and that she was being used.

The cardboard box rustled, revealing her target, filling her with glee . . .

"Gaby?"

She whirled around, and there stood Mort.

Before she could deal with him, he looked beyond her—and fell back in revulsion.

Gaby didn't need to know what he saw. She knew it wouldn't be pretty.

"Go home, Mort." She couldn't waste time seeing if he obeyed.

She faced the discarnate.

This one stunk of fear and sickness. Naked, it lumbered toward her, giant tumors bulging around the middle, the breasts, and under the throat. The growths pulsed with a life of their own, like a heartbeat, like living masses of sickness.

As old as the other one, but smaller, this evil mewled, stretched its toothless mouth wide, and vociferated in ear-splitting measure.

Closer and closer it got—until, with divine help, Gaby saw what others couldn't.

This being had once been selfish and manipulative enough to poison three husbands to death. Each time she profited from her murders. Each time she took satisfaction in the suffering she caused.

Pure evil. Rank with it. Alive with it.

Rightfully, the torments of hell waged on her cumbersome body in the form of unsightly and life-draining tumors. She deserved no less, but had also been given a life sentence of loneliness. Like the first evil, this body had been without friend or family.

Unfortunately for her, she hadn't been content to suffer her misery alone.

Behind her, lying in his own blood, Luther gave evidence of further misdeeds. Evil bitch.

Gaby didn't back step at the ghoulish approach. Luther needed medical attention, and the sooner she dispatched the ghoul, the sooner he could get it.

Smiling in relish, Gaby slid the knife free of the sheath. The naked being fell forward, and Gaby went with the momentum, rolling to the ground and in the process sinking the knife deep in several key places, twisting in the stomach, grinding it across the throat, and lastly cutting through the perineum. One sharp turn of her blade—and the body began bleeding out.

Gaby pushed to her knees and shoved the nude form away. Her skin crawled in revulsion, her stomach heaved.

And another form appeared, this one missing half a face. The jaw was gone, one eye eaten away. Purplish welts and scabbed lumps covered the upper body. It came forward, dragging one useless appendage that might have been a leg in better times.

Through her perception, Gaby knew that early abuse had depraved this soul, but that couldn't play into Gaby's actions. The abused often went on to abuse. Someone had to stop the cycle.

She would be the one.

A hard kick took out the only stationary knee, and the body slumped to the ground. Gaby half turned and kicked

again, driving the vision to its back. Another kick and the
body went as flat as something so crippled could.

This soul had perpetuated a different kind of evil. It had
robbed people of their livelihoods through fraud, stealing
their homes and their life savings. And yep, like the others,
it had spent its time alone, without visitors, without caring
or concern from any other living soul.

Appropriate.

Satisfied, Gaby raised her foot—and stomped it down
hard on the throat.

Life drifted away.

"Gaby?"

Oh shit. No time now to puke.

An awful fear rang in Mort's voice.

Had he seen it all?

Why the hell hadn't he gone back as she'd told him to?

"Gaby, do you hear the sirens?" Above the fear, Mort's
tone was oddly gentle. "We need to go. I think Luther
must've called in for help before he got hurt."

Sirens? Yes, in the deepest recesses of her mind, she did
hear them.

Proving an unrecognized courage, Mort carefully took
her arm. "Please, Gaby. We have to go now."

"Luther . . ." It was an odd thing for her to concern herself with a victim. That wasn't her job, never had been,
and she didn't really know *what* to do about it.

"The sirens are coming for him, I'm sure of it. See his
radio out there beside him? He'll be okay."

Yeah, Mort was probably right. But first . . .

She covered her mouth and ran from the alley to hurl.
A garbage can, already filled with vomit, likely from the
drunk she'd passed, served as good a place as any.

Mort stood beside her, impatient but stoic. When her
head cleared, he again took her arm. "We have to get rid of

these clothes. And you'll need to hide that knife somewhere just in case anyone saw you."

"The knife stays with me." Confused and sick, Gaby
focused on him. "Just what the hell are you doing?"

"Helping you." He looked around to make sure no one
noticed them, then started her on her way. "It's okay, Gaby."

Okay? How the hell could anything ever be okay?
"Yeah? I'd like to know why you think so."

He put an arm around her, and a small smile appeared on
his sallow face. "Because I finally understand. That's why."

Rubbery knees refused to support her. Churning acid continu-
ally tried to forge a path from her stomach out her mouth.
She wanted to cry—but wouldn't.

"You should get away from me, Morty."

"With those creepy things running around? Forget it.
It's safer by you."

He couldn't start thinking of her as his hero. "You're
dumber than I thought, Mort."

"I know."

She pierced him with her gaze, but he only looked around,
worried and nervous. "We should probably get going."

The enervating effect of the kill waned, but she remained shaky and sick at her stomach. "If you stick by me,
and either of us is seen, you're fucked."

"It'd be tough to explain, that's for sure." He peered down
a dark alley, then turned back toward her. "Come on. If we
go home this way, we're less likely to be seen by the cops."

No one in his right mind traveled the area along the
back alleys.

Not if he wanted to live.

"Fine."

Together, they ventured along the rough brick wall to

the very back of the narrow way, then traversed a low concrete wall. A skinny lane stretched along the backs of closed or empty businesses. This time of night, with only the muted drone of street noises out front and the occasional scratching of creatures that feasted off refuse, each footstep echoed a hollowed heartbeat.

More buildings, in worse, more decrepit shape, lurked behind the lane. Ahead of them, yellowed rats' eyes gleamed; druggies shot up; in the worst of the structures, homeless camped out.

It'd be easy to get cornered. It'd be easy for someone to hurt Mort.

If he was alone.

Determined to protect him, Gaby got herself together and took the lead. "Try to be quiet." Obsidian darkness swallowed the sight of doorways and blanketed all sound. Moonlight couldn't find its way between the tall block walls and shingled roofs.

They'd walked in silence for several minutes when Mort asked, his voice shivering, "Do you think more of those things are out here?"

"No." Broken glass crunched under her feet, nearly penetrating her flimsy soles. Something squishy found its way into the sandal and between her toes. With every nerve in her body drawn painfully taut, Gaby continued on. "But there are worse things."

"Worse than those freaks?"

Enraged beyond rational reason, she turned on Mort and slammed him into the nearest brick wall. "They're *people*," she said from between her teeth. She choked on her impotence, the impossibility of the situation. "Damaged, sick, broken by the foulest disease. But still humans who, if they weren't already tainted by a mangled past, would need our help."

"All right, Gaby."

The soft plea of his voice worked better than a sharp blow. She released him to rub the heels of her palms against her burning eye sockets. Salty tears would ease the pain. And make it worse. *"They're sick."*

Mort's hand touched her shoulder. "I know, and I'm sorry."

She shook her head and slapped away his hand. "Christ, don't apologize to me when I'm the one attacking you!"

"You've been through a lot."

So had he.

Because of her.

Unbearable. It was all becoming so unbearable.

She turned and started on her way again. But now that he'd touched her with his sympathy, she couldn't contain herself. So low that she could barely hear herself, she whispered, "I've fought monsters, Mort."

"I know."

He had no idea. "The problem now is that . . ." How to word it? "I killed, and yet, it wasn't the monster I killed. There's a creature, a real fiend, creating these beings and somehow forcing them to act. Or . . ." As she recalled the first evil being, the way he'd looked at that child, the mingling of pain and lust in his eyes, her thoughts tried to sort it out. "Maybe they're just being allowed to act. Maybe the pain of the sickness has distorted their brains, unleashing something they'd once buried."

"I don't know what you mean, Gaby."

She didn't want to stop again. Whether he comprehended or not, talking eased the conflagration of emotions.

And so she talked on. "Some beings, some . . . *afflictions*, can bury their black ways. In the next life, they can't escape retribution, but for this world it helps them survive, to avoid arrest and conviction. No true corruption can ever be fully sequestered, so pain, sickness, can bring out those dormant propensities."

"You think the people you . . . dealt with tonight, had hidden evil?"

"I know they did. So did that grisly specter that Luther found a few days ago."

"Luther said the body was mangled."

"Yeah."

"That was you?"

She heard no denouncement from him, only curiosity.

"When I'm in the zone, I can't control it. I do what feels right, what I can do, and sometimes it's so bad that the body isn't recognizable."

"You're talking about when that strange thing happens to you?"

When her features contort. The reality of that struck another blow, but Gaby fended it off. So she wasn't as different from the bane of immorality as she'd thought. She'd deal with that as she'd dealt with everything else—the best way she knew how. "I thought that I'd removed the evil, but that was just a creature made by the evil. This isn't something I've dealt with before. I don't know where the next one might be—"

"You're sure there'll be more?"

Gaby nodded. "I don't know where they originate, and that's the key. But there are more."

Though she didn't know how to reassure him, she could feel Mort's fear. "I have to find the maker. I have to find the core of the degeneration."

Mort sidled closer to her, so close she could feel his nervous breath on her nape. "Do you know how to do that? How to hunt it?"

"Not really. I've never had to before. Usually I'm sent to the evil. I don't understand why I'm not being sent now."

Mort fell silent, but not for long. "Maybe the person doing all this is confused, and if *he* doesn't know what he's going to do, how could you know?"

She said only, "God would know." The raw edge of an exposed, broken pipe gouged the tender flesh above her elbow. Her skin tore; warm blood spilled.

The injury burned, but not enough to distract her. "Careful." She guided Mort around the obstruction, then used her sleeve to mop away the blood.

"Thanks." Mort bumped into her twice before they found another companionable rhythm. "Gaby? Is it at all possible that the people you killed aren't evil? I mean, they were messed up for sure. But maybe they weren't as evil as you're talking about."

"They were." Her thoughts wandered back through time. "Once, when I was younger—"

"You're young now."

If you went by experience, she was older than anybody should ever be. "I was in my late teens, I think, living in this rundown apartment. A woman next door to me killed her husband, and I didn't know it."

"But I thought . . ."

"I know. You think I'm some superhero or some such crazy shit. But I'm not, Mort, so don't get yourself confused. That woman? She shot her husband for cheating on her. I overheard her telling the police that he'd come home drunk, and he told her she was looking old, that she turned him off. He told her he'd been fooling around with a younger woman. So she got their old thirty-eight pistol and she shot him in the head."

"A woman scorned, huh?"

"I stood there, stunned because I hadn't realized anything was happening. There'd been no pain, no calling. Later I realized it was because what happened was normal."

"You think so?"

"She wasn't evil incarnate. She was just a woman in love who had her pride hurt bad enough that she showed poor judgment. Before the cops took her away, she was already crying for her loss, wishing she hadn't done it."

"So . . ." He trailed off, then regrouped. "If what you're saying is that you only get that awful way when something truly evil is happening, then that means . . ."

Gaby glanced back at him.

He swallowed audibly. "Whatever that was after Luther was—"

"The basest of evils. A true depravity."

"Like . . ." Eyes wide, he whispered, "The devil or something?"

"Worse. A demonic being here on earth." Thanks to the broken pipe, Gaby's arm started a steady ache.

"Then Luther is in real trouble."

"Yeah, I think so. But I'll look out for him."

"How?" Mort practically screeched. "You can't be with him every minute. You can't stand guard over him. Luther isn't the type of man who'd ever allow it, but he's also not a man to believe in—"

"Bogeymen? He's learning."

"He's my friend, Gaby," Mort said with grave depression. "I don't want anything to happen to him."

"Nothing will," Gaby vowed, both to Mort and to herself. "Like I told you, if something really bad comes after him, I'll know and I'll . . . go to him. Wherever he is. And no, don't ask me how. That's just how it works."

"You instinctively know where to go?"

"Sort of. Somehow, I just get there."

Given the silence, Gaby knew Mort didn't understand, and was starting to ponder her sanity again.

"Look. It's like this. Information gets channeled

through me. My body is just a conduit for the purpose. I end up where I need to be, and I do what needs to be done, and then I'm me again. End of story."

"I trust you."

He was such a dupe. "Great. Now take a deep breath. We'll be home soon," she reassured Mort, because she didn't dare reassure herself. "You'll be able to relax then."

"After tonight, I don't think I'll ever relax again."

His voice no sooner faded than they heard an odd but human sound. Flattening back against the wall, her hand already over Mort's mouth, Gaby waited.

A whimper.

Slurping. Silent tears.

Rank commands and foul enjoyment.

She heard it all, and she understood.

Rage, not God's command, stirred her blood. Her eyes narrowed, and she stared through the abyss. "Stay here, Mort."

"Gaby, no, please." Mort's hands grasped at her shirt. "You don't know who it is, if it might be the cops or another of those crazy people—"

"Get a grip," she hissed at Mort, impatient to intercede. "I'll be right back." She brushed him off and crept away, her knife in her hand, the injury in her arm forgotten. Up ahead, a dim glow shone from one building.

The end of the alley.

They'd be close to home, but she had work to do yet. No, God hadn't called her for this one.

But damn it, He should have.

As Gaby stepped into the light, she saw a couple at the edge of the alley, in the shadows, but not really hidden. The woman knelt on the rough ground, her blouse mostly torn off, her face and upper arms red, scratched, and bruised.

She was held captive close to the man's body, her face

shoved against his belly. Her cheeks hollowed out, her head bobbed.

She sobbed again.

As Gaby took in the scene, the man closed his eyes in release.

Moaning in what Gaby interpreted as harsh pleasure, his body jerked obscenely. The woman tried to pull back, but he cruelly twisted his hand in her ponytail, using the hold like a leash, forcing her to perform on him.

To swallow.

The sight of it all, her comprehension, froze Gaby to the spot.

The man slumped against the wall, his body lax. Released, the woman quickly scampered back.

Tears tracked her cheeks. Her nose bled.

Torn from her stupor, Gaby didn't even stop to think about it; she allowed herself to react.

In an instant, her knife whistled through the air—and sank with satisfying accuracy into the bastard's shoulder.

He contorted on a yelp of surprise, followed by a shout of outrage. He looked at the girl on her knees first, and seeing she wasn't a threat, his gaze swung around until he found Gaby striding toward him. She wasn't done with him, not by a long shot, and he must have sensed that.

Ignoring her knife in his flesh, he tried to charge her.

Good. Even though he was a miserable bully and rapist, he had strength and he wasn't a coward.

She wanted a fight. She wanted this fight.

It felt right. It felt purposeful.

For this, she could *almost* smile.

"That's right," Gaby taunted. "Tangle with someone who *isn't* cowed by you."

"Stupid bitch," he thundered. "You'll be damn sorry you—"

He was in midthreat when Gaby's heel connected with his chin. When his head snapped back, her elbow jammed into his throat. As he gurgled and gagged, she retrieved her knife, sliding it out of his dense flesh to press it tight, tight enough to cut, where he'd feel it most.

The girl screamed, scrambling backward on hands and heels like a tipsy crab.

Mort rushed out of the alley. "Gaby!"

With so much fanfare, she wouldn't have been surprised if a spotlight had suddenly shone down on her wretched head.

Face close to the man's, her fist keeping the knife blade snug against his groin, Gaby whispered, "You deserve to lose this, don't you?" She pressed in enough to nick him, making certain he understood.

"You're insane," he garbled, still suffering from the trauma to his throat.

"You betcha. Insane enough that I'll haunt your dreams for the rest of your life."

He looked into her eyes and shriveled back in fear.

His impaired esophagus made him gasp for each shallow breath. Distress for his precious jewels kept his eyes wide and wild. Drool trickled from the side of his trembling mouth.

Gaby enjoyed his reaction.

She enjoyed herself in this role.

"I'll know what you do," she told him. "What you think and what you want. If you ever again use force on anyone or anything, I swear to God, I'll castrate you."

The man prayed, which amused Gaby. God wouldn't help him. Not tonight.

But then Mort grabbed her arm. "Gaby, please. You cut him bad and he's bleeding. He could die."

A fog lifted, and Gaby became aware of everything.

The sobs of the man, the worst sobs of the girl, Mort's palpitating fear.

"He deserves death." But she jerked her knife away from him.

It was really bloody now. And so was she.

"Maybe he does," Mort said, "but you don't deserve his death on your hands."

Gaby caught her breath. Mort had stopped her for *her* sake?

The man crumpled to the ground, drenched in a combination of sweat, blood, and more disgusting body fluids.

Foul bastard.

Repulsed, Gaby turned to look at the girl.

Homely little thing, with ruined makeup smeared everywhere and a red, snotty nose. "How old are you?"

Her lips quivered. "Twenty."

"Liar." She looked to be in her midteens, maybe seventeen on a stretch. "Go home."

"I . . . I can't."

Of course not. If she could, she wouldn't be here now, tonight, in this hopeless place. The futility of it all settled in once again, evaporating the elation of triumph. "Then at least get away from here."

The girl nodded, lumbered to her feet, and wiped her mouth. More tears leaked out. She pushed hair away from her bruised and dirty face. "Thank you so much."

Fingers curling around her knife hilt, Gaby snarled, "I was too late. He'd already used you."

"No." She shook her head. "You wasn't too late. He wasn't done with me. He would have . . . he woulda done more. Worse stuff. He told me so. So, thank you."

Hoping she had made a difference, Gaby nodded.

Waiting until after the girl had run off, Gaby dropped to one knee by the man.

Mort panicked again. "What are you doing?"

"Well I'm not going to stick him again, if that's what you're thinking. What would be the point?" She set her knife to the side. "I'm seeing if he has a cell phone."

"But . . . why?"

"So we can get him some help." She found a phone in his loose, drooping pants pocket, but had to wipe the blood away before she could see the numbers. "Like you said, Mort. I don't need his death on my hands. Not if I can help it."

Holding the phone away from her face, Gaby called 911 and calmly gave the address and situation.

"The cops'll get you, bitch," the man muttered in faint aggression. He barely kept himself sitting upright and kept swaying as if ready to topple. One arm hung useless at his side, his hand in his lap over his crotch, and with the opposite hand he tried to stem the sluggish flow of blood from his shoulder.

"Shut up, stupid. You're almost dead, and the cops would be more interested in arresting you than me." She withdrew his wallet and read his name, his address. She leaned down and held the open wallet in front of his face. "Besides, I know you now, who you are and where you live. If you rat me out, or even try to rat me out, you'll regret it. I can promise you that."

New fear smothered his hostility and rendered him mute.

Attention darting this way and that, Mort wrung his hands over Gaby until she'd again wiped the phone—this time to remove her prints—and shoved it back in the man's pocket.

"All right, Mort." Against the man's hair, she wiped the blood from her knife and returned it to its sheath. "Let's go."

Mort hurried after her. "You're okay now?"

"Yeah, I'm fine. Better than fine." Damn it, she felt good. Strong. Altruistic. She'd stopped a crime and, maybe, hadn't killed anyone. Until an ambulance reached that clown, she wouldn't place any bets, though. Not that she'd waste pity or regret on any man who'd rape a woman in any way.

Her stride longer and more sure, she headed for the apartment building. "Mort?"

He hustled along beside her, breathing fast from exertion. "Yeah?"

"I get the overall picture, but specifically, what was he doing to her?"

Mort stumbled over his own feet and then had to rush to catch back up with her. "You're kidding."

"No. I mean, I get that it was sexual. But I'm not sure I understand. Spell it out for me, okay?"

"Oh God." He shook his head hard. "Gaby, please, don't ask me stuff like that."

She slanted him a glance. He looked . . . ill. More so than usual. "Why not?"

"Because I can't answer you, that's why!"

His raised voice was enough to alert the National Guard. "There's no reason to get hysterical about it."

"Hysterical? Of course I'm hysterical! You've got the blood of three people on you. I can hear the sirens of at least two different police cars. We left a man half dead back there." He put both hands in his hair. "I've got good reason to be hysterical."

"Shhh. Calm down, Mort. I'll clean up and it'll all be okay."

"Clean up? Have you looked at yourself?" He took his hands out of his hair so he could wring them together. "You're a mess."

"Peroxide gets blood out, and even if it doesn't, we had animal blood in the stairs today. Anyone will believe it's from that."

"Not if they do all that fancy forensics stuff—"

Dolt. Not that she could blame him for being unfamiliar with police priorities. "The guy in the alley will say he was jumped, and that he doesn't know who did it."

"You're sure?"

"What else can he say? That he was raping a minor and someone defended her?" Gaby snorted. "But even if he didn't, it won't matter. Contrary to popular fiction, the cops don't pull out the expensive tests for every crime going. Not unless they have a murder victim, and reasonable suspicion on someone, and a lot of other stuff. And before you tell me they'll have a murder victim, let's wait to borrow trouble, okay? Those creatures in the alley might be written off as lunatics or something, and that other jerk might live."

"Three bodies. Three. Oh God." He appeared ready to cry. "We have to hurry."

His attitude nettled. That last thing they did . . . well, that was right and proper, what any good citizen should do.

Wasn't it?

And just what the hell did she know about good citizens, being a freak and all?

Sullen now, thanks to Mort, Gaby said, "I told you not to get involved."

"It's too late for that, so save it."

A command from Mort?

For her?

Miffed, Gaby stopped at the apartment entrance and leveled a mean look on Mort. He stared back, defiant and nervous, and oddly protective.

Damn it, for such a weaselly little creep, he really got to her sometimes. "All right, Mort. Make yourself useful. Go get me a towel. I'll head straight to the basement and throw my stuff in the laundry. Bring any peroxide you might have. I'll wash up down there, then go upstairs to dress again."

With something constructive to do, Mort was motivated. "Right. Got it. Let's go."

To see Mort like this, almost as a sidekick, as a . . . friend, left her soft inside. He could be a pain in the ass, but right now, she was glad she had him.

Luther, on the other hand . . . well, she didn't know what to think about Luther.

Was he, like Mort, an ally, a person she could trust, maybe even confide in?

Or would Detective Luther Cross be the man who finally brought her to an end?

Chapter 11

Luther lay in the hospital bed, his head pounding, his eyes red, and his thoughts churning.

The past few hours were there, but they lacked clarity. It was after he'd left Gaby at the apartment with Mort that things got cloudy. He remembered heading to the butcher's. Then he'd heard a sound, had surely investigated. He recalled a deformed person, so pathetic and sad that shame smothered him whenever he recalled his reaction to . . . it.

For the life of him, he still couldn't say if the person had been female or male.

In the deepest recesses of his mind, another vague memory stirred.

Gaby's voice.

And Mort's.

But he couldn't get a grasp on it, and when he tried to explain his vague perceptions of violence and retribution, the other detectives looked at him like he was nuts. Or delirious. Or suffering something worse than a concussion.

Where the hell were the docs? He wanted to go home.

He wanted to check on Gaby. To ask her . . . what? If she'd been nearby when a grossly disfigured asexual being attacked him, and then disappeared?

Luther could easily imagine her reaction to that.

As if he'd summoned her, she stuck her head around the curtain. Their gazes met, his shocked at her appearance, hers challenging, and then she came on around, full of bravado and that habitual mordancy.

"Just as I figured. You're lying in here faking it, soaking up all the attention, huh?"

"Do you see anyone doting on me?"

Gaby didn't smile. No, never that. But she shrugged and dropped her skinny ass onto the side of his bed. "You probably chased everyone off with your piss-into-the-wind attitude."

Damn, it was good to see her, to know she was okay and as ornery as ever. She smelled fresh, as if she'd just showered. Her cheeks were rosy, her dark hair glossy and sleek. "Is it necessary for me to point out that your insult is somewhat like the pot calling the kettle black?"

"Maybe." She looked him over, her gaze lingering on the bandage around his head until her brows pinched together. "Don't you think you should get back out there on the streets and figure out who waylaid you?"

Suspicion blunted his pleasure at seeing her, but he kept his tone even with mere curiosity. "What makes you think anyone waylaid me?"

With a roll of her eyes, she ticked off reasons on her long, slender fingers. "You're in a hospital. There's a bandage around your head. You're white faced. If I'm not missing my guess, you're bare-assed beneath that ugly hospital gown, and—"

"Soon as the doc releases me," Luther cut in, "I'll be out of here." He wanted to take her hand, but didn't dare. "How did you know to find me here, Gaby?"

"The streets talk. Being a cop and all, you should know that." She tilted her head, frowned again, then looked behind her. "Mort? Where did you go?"

And around the curtain came Mort. "Hi, Luther."

"Mort. So Gaby dragged you along?"

His thin shoulders rolled forward. "We were worried. Wanted to make sure you were okay." He cleared his throat. "We heard someone jumped you?"

"I assume so. I really don't remember too much about it."

"Amnesia?" Mort shuffled closer. "No way. Really?"

"Just a lack of clear details." Luther looked at Gaby, but she avoided his gaze by peering at the blinking dials behind him.

Mort again cleared his throat. "So . . . you got hurt and called your friends. Other cops, I mean. Did they catch anybody yet?"

"No. It's weird, but whoever was in the alley with me up and disappeared."

That got Gaby's interest. "Disappeared? How?"

"I have no idea. Thanks to a whack on the head, I was out of it. I didn't come to until the ambulance got to me." Thinking about it kicked up the throbbing of Luther's headache another notch. "I've never been knocked out before."

"No wonder." Gaby gave him the once-over. "You are a big cuss for anyone to mess with."

Defending himself, he explained, "I got hit from behind." He put his fingers to the exact spot over the back of his skull where he now lacked a two-inch square of hair, but had gained several stitches. "Most people who get knocked out are only out for a few seconds, but the bastard really brained me."

"That's why your sorry ass is still in bed?" Gaby asked. "The docs are worried about you being unconscious for too long?"

"They took some tests, yeah."

Eyes dark with worry, she caught her lush bottom lip in sharp white teeth. Her voice lowered in commiseration. "Does it hurt?"

His voice lowered, too—from awareness. "Yeah, like a son of a bitch." Ignoring Mort's fascinated presence, Luther added, "Wanna kiss it and make it better?"

Just that easily, Gaby shook off her tenderness. "Hell no. But Mort might." She turned to her landlord. "What about it, Mort? You feel like puckering up?"

"Uh . . . No. That's okay."

"Worried about diseases, huh? Not that I blame you. He's mean enough to be rabid."

Luther chuckled—and paid for it with a lightning shaft of pain.

Gaby lifted off the bed. "We should go and let you rest."

"Wait." This time he went ahead and took her hand and if she didn't like it, tough shit. That's when he noticed the bandage around her arm. More suspicions crowded in, adding to the strain in his cranium. "What happened to you?"

"A broken pipe bit me. But don't worry about that now."

"What broken pipe?"

Expression aggrieved, she said, "How about I share the whole sordid story with you when you're up and about?"

"I'll be up as soon as the docs get back in here."

"Tomorrow then."

It'd be an excuse to see her. "You promise?"

Her head tilted; mystifying emotion shone in her light blue eyes. "Yeah, cop. I promise."

Luther couldn't put a name on it, but he felt that something monumental had just occurred between them. Gaby had committed to him somehow. She'd decided to trust him in some indefinable way.

He felt like a newly appointed king. Like a triumphant warrior. He had to tamp down those bizarre emotions to deal with her here and now. "You said the streets talk."

"Chatter, chatter, chatter. It's nonstop."

He looked from Gaby to Mort and back again. "So what did you hear?"

Hedging, Mort shifted from foot to foot. "Um . . ."

Gaby's manner became impassive. "Give us a minute, Mort, okay?"

"Sure." With grateful haste, Mort darted back around the curtain.

Putting a hand on either side of his pillow, Gaby leaned down and loomed over him. She looked deadly serious, and so sweet that Luther wished he were up to snuff so he could haul her down and kiss her.

He waited.

She looked at his injury, at his mouth, and then finally into his eyes. "Just between us, okay?"

Now that piqued his interest. "Okay."

"Your word, Luther?"

God, he loved it when she broke down and said his name. He couldn't define what it was about her, but each concession felt like a precious gift.

Giving his word before he knew the details was risky, but curiosity got the better of him. "All right, Gaby. You have it."

"I think you were attacked by another of those cancerous things. Like the thing you were first investigating."

Thing? "You mean the filleted man from the other side of town?"

"Yeah." She nodded. "The cops didn't find anyone there with you?"

"No. They say I was alone."

"But you didn't hit yourself in the head."

"No."

She considered that. "There was blood around the area, right?"

"My own, yes. And there were scraps from the butcher that a stray dog had gotten into. Besides that, I don't know. Blood darkens pretty quickly." Luther watched her scowl and wondered why she didn't have frown wrinkles, given all the stewing she did.

"I guess if the cops found you alone, they figured you were just mugged or something, right? No reason to go over the area in detail, checking for forensics."

"That's the assumption. Except nothing was taken off me. Not my wallet, my gun, my radio."

"Right." As she pieced things together, her mouth pinched in displeasure at what she obviously considered a sign of ignorance. "So the next assumption is that backup came too quickly and the crime was thwarted."

Fascinating. "Something like that."

Her gaze locked on his. "The lock was broken on a window in Mort's basement. It faces the back alley. I found it wide open. That's probably how someone got in to hang that carcass, and again to dump the blood."

"I see." He hadn't even thought about windows in the basement. What the hell kind of detective was he?

The kind thrown off-kilter by Gabrielle Cody, apparently.

"It's also how someone likely knew you'd be near the butcher's. They could have overheard us talking."

She looked as simply dressed as ever in her loose dark

T-shirt and worn jeans. But this close, Luther could see the blue striations in her irises and the way her long lashes left feathery shadows on her smooth cheeks. "Let me guess. You don't want me to investigate the break-in?"

"It'd be safer for Mort if you stop coming around his place so often."

As Luther studied her, he noted something in her expression, something close to honesty that proved she did worry for Mort. But something more, too, something vague and mysterious. "If I don't come around, how will I get in touch with you?"

The blue of her eyes darkened to midnight. "Why would you want to?"

Luther said nothing.

She already knew why.

Ill grace accompanied her surrender. "All right, fine. Be a jerk. You can come one more time, and we'll figure out how to stay in touch. But after that, you'll have to stay away. You got me?"

Instead of agreeing, he asked a question of his own. "Who do you think attacked me, Gaby?"

"I don't know."

Liar. "Take a guess."

"All right." She leaned closer and her cool hair, even cut so short, brushed against his forehead in a teasing caress. "When I first met you, you said there weren't any bogeymen."

"I remember."

Shocking Luther, her mouth touched his forehead, so gentle, barely there.

A kiss of healing.

To make it better.

She sat up and away. "The bogeymen gotcha, Luther." She stood, and nodded at his head. "You've got the proof on your noggin. It's time to admit you're wrong. That's the only way you'll ever be able to defeat them."

She started out of the room.

"Gaby?"

Pausing, she said, "Yeah?"

"If you had to start looking for the bogeymen in one place, where would you start?"

Keeping her back to him, her shoulders straight and proud, she said, "Where I'd start is my business, cop." Over her shoulder, her blue-eyed gaze struck with laser accuracy. "But you should start in the hospital."

"This hospital?"

"Yeah." Her gaze never faltered. "Try the cancer ward and go from there."

Letting that go for now, he asked, "If bogeymen got me, then why aren't I dead?"

"That's an easy one, cop. Someone saved you."

With that niggling memory of Gaby's voice at the scene, Luther pushed up to one elbow. *"You?"*

Pain marred her features before her countenance turned sardonic. "Yeah, right. That knock on the head really rattled what little brains you had, didn't it?"

Luther would not let her throw him off with insults. "I was the only one there when backup arrived." He watched her closely. "Where did the bogeymen go?"

Wearing no expression at all, she shrugged. "Where they all go, Luther." She turned away, and he barely heard her whisper, "Straight to hell."

Before he could call her back, she was gone.

Luther shoved the sheet aside. The pain in his head mushroomed, but he couldn't stay idle in the bed while Gaby stuck her stubborn little nose into dangerous police business.

If he didn't find the bogeymen, she would. He knew it down deep in the pit of his soul.

Five minutes later, when the doc walked in, Luther was dressed and anxious to be on his way. The attending physician tried to insist he couldn't drive and shouldn't be alone. Luther didn't need to do either one. He had another officer who could pick him up, but in the meantime, trolling the halls of the hospital would keep him in plain view of plenty of people.

He needed to follow what few clues Gaby had given him. He had to keep her safe.

Damn it all, he had to find a bogeyman.

Knowing Luther wouldn't be far behind her, Gaby dragged Morty along the white halls of the cancer ward. She shouldn't have told Mort anything.

She shouldn't have . . . well, more or less asked for his help.

She worked alone, damn it. Always had.

That's how God had designed it.

So why the hell did she still have Mort in tow?

"What are we looking for, Gaby?"

For some lame reason, Mort's presence brought her comfort in the memory-laden section of the hospital. Her body, her mind, recognized the smells, the sights, the auras and the emotions. Mort, with all his newfound gallantry, blunted the cutting edges of desolation.

She wore the yoke of his friendship, accomplishing much, and bearing the burden. "I'll let you know when I see it."

Ambling along, Gaby peered into each room, and eavesdropped on each conversation. Every nurse, doctor, and patient received her sharp appraisal.

"What are we doing here, Gaby?

Pausing near a nurses' station, Gaby waited as two doctors approached. Voice low, she explained to Mort, "There's a thick tide of sickness caged in here, ebbing and flowing with no place to go. There's choking depression and a dark, heavy emanation because of it."

Mort stared at her wide-eyed.

Disgusted, Gaby said, "Don't let it spook you."

"It's not. But you're freaking me out."

He *looked* freaked, causing her to lock her teeth. "You weren't afraid of me earlier."

"I'm not afraid now. Just worried. But this isn't anything like earlier. You were hurting then. I could tell." He chewed his lower lip. "Can you tell me now what was wrong, what happened to you? I think I understand most of it. But you . . . you looked so different—"

"I didn't!"

At her angry retort, Mort jumped a foot. "Okay, okay," he soothed. "You looked the same—"

Sickened at herself and the growing stain of reality, Gaby dropped back against the wall. "Did I?" She turned her head toward him. "Did I look the same, Mort?"

Apologetic, Mort shook his head. "No."

"Fuck."

"Shhh. The nurses will hear you."

Reminded of her purpose, Gaby turned her body to face Mort as if in close conversation. "Be quiet so I can listen in."

"Listen in on what?"

To him, to a plain, mortal of a guy like Mort, the low voices of the doctors and nurses would be insubstantial. But for Gaby . . . "Just hush."

"Okay."

The conversation was a mere drone at first.

Until Gaby concentrated.

Then she heard them as clearly as if they addressed her personally from only a foot away. Another God-given talent.

Super ears—when need be.

"Ms. Davies has taken a turn for the worse. When I visited with her this morning, I couldn't get any response at all. Her vitals are weak. I don't think she's going to make it much longer. She's barely hanging on."

A female voice said, "I thought she was better yesterday."

"She's dying," said a male voice. "How much better did you think she'd get?"

Annoyed but attempting to hide it, the female said, "I'll check in on her now, to see if I can ease her in some way."

Gruffer and filled with impatience, the man growled, "It's a waste of time, Dr. Chiles. You're here to doctor her. Her family and friends should be soothing her."

"She has none."

"Perfect. So we're supposed to pick up the slack?"

"I thought—"

"I know what you thought. But you have other patients to see today, patients who are coherent, who have a chance. They need your care. Let Ms. Davies pass. We're short on beds anyway."

"I'll see to all my patients, Dr. Marton. But I won't let Ms. Davies suffer needlessly."

"If there's no response, what makes you think she's suffering?"

"Cancer has taken her, and it seldom does so without a great deal of pain."

"Hell." Gaby heard the pause, and then: "Fine. Do what you want. But she'll hardly know, now will she?"

Out of the corner of her eye, Gaby watched as the male doctor, Dr. Marton, stormed past. He was big, and though he tried to conceal it, he was furious.

At himself? At Dr. Chiles? Or at the hopeless situation in the cancer ward?

Behind Gaby, the nurses held silent, but Dr. Chiles said, "He's tired. Too many long hours and too little hope."

Then she too, walked away, releasing the nurses to gossip freely.

"God, he's a coldhearted bastard."

"I'm surprised he didn't have Ms. Davies moved out of here as he usually does with the indigent patients who can't pay for hospice."

"That horrible place where he sends them . . ." A shudder of revulsion broke the voice. "Can you imagine dwindling away in that cold, dreadful place, all alone and in so much pain?"

"At least he makes routine visits there to help treat them."

"If you call his brand of doctoring real treatment."

Like magnetized puzzle pieces clicking together, awareness, realization, and suspicion all formed an image of possibilities.

Dr. Marton.

Terminal cancer patients.

Indigent patients, all alone, without family or friends.

Each abomination Gaby had faced had an evil past, a past that had alienated them from family and friends, leaving them alone with their tragic fates.

Dr. Marton sent them somewhere, and then treated them there.

Where?

"Come on, Mort." In a hurry to investigate, Gaby had taken three steps before she realized Mort didn't follow. She turned back and saw him staring into Ms. Davies's room.

Retracing her steps, she paused beside Mort and followed

his gaze into the room. The nurses and Dr. Chiles congregated around the sick bed.

Voice stricken, Mort whispered, "What's going on do you think?"

"She's dead."

He fell back a step, but couldn't alter his stare from the scene. "But . . . how can you tell for sure? She could be sleeping . . ."

"She's not."

"Maybe . . ."

"No." Anxious to drag him away, Gaby took his hand. His fingers curled around hers, warm and secure and again, comforting. "Trust me, Mort. She's gone."

If he saw enough dead people, he'd learn to tell the difference between a sleeping body and a hollow shell. After death, the remaining flesh and bones held only a dark chasm instead of a vibrant soul.

She didn't want Mort to learn about that. She didn't want him to become familiar with death.

Not the way she had.

He grew winded trying to keep up with her. "Where are we going now?"

"Out of here. I can't breathe in here."

His hand tightened on hers, slowing her down. "You know something, don't you?"

"No." What she knew, she couldn't share. Not with a simple fellow like Mort. Regardless of his recent stoicism, he'd never understand what she did.

He'd never understand who she was.

"You can trust me, Gaby."

That deserved no more than a snort.

"C'mon. Tell me. Before I noticed everyone going into that poor old lady's room, I saw you . . ."

With the suddenness of a stroke, his voice died.

"I what?" Gaby asked.

"Nothing."

He stayed silent, and Gaby stopped, jerking around to face him. "What, damn it?"

She watched as he resigned himself to giving her a straight answer. "You looked funny again. Not as much as in the alley, but . . . sharper." His gaze searched hers. "More dangerous."

It had happened again, and over something so simple, something so ordinary? Jesus, did she run around shifting all the time?

Maybe.

For two heartbeats, Gaby could do nothing. Then she exploded. "Fuck, fuck, *fuck*."

And from behind her, Luther *tsked*. "Gabrielle Cody. You really do need to learn to curb that foul mouth of yours."

Hands fisted and teeth sawing together, she pivoted around to face her newest nemesis. "So, cop, you *were* faking?"

"Nah. But I do feel a lot better." He daringly reached out and touched her bottom lip with one finger. "Maybe your kiss healed me after all."

Gaby jerked back out of his reach. She and God both knew that her job wasn't to heal.

It was to destroy.

To Mort, she said, *"Stay."*

He blinked at her hard and fast, but didn't question her, or object.

Knowing he would do as told, Gaby grabbed Luther by the front of his shirt and dragged him toward a quieter corner. Using anomalous strength that came when she needed it, she shoved his broad back up against the wall.

Luther allowed her manhandling with an amused male smile.

"*Don't* start questioning me and don't you *dare* touch me again. I have a few things to tell you and you're going to listen. Then I'm outta here."

"All right."

"First, you might as well stop grinning like a fool right now because you won't find any of this funny." She sucked up a fortifying breath and strived to calm her anger. "You need to do a background check or whatever it is detectives do with suspicious people, on a physician here. A Dr. Marton."

"Why is Dr. Marton suspicious?"

"Try listening, Luther—I said no questions, remember? I don't have the time or the patience for it! You'll just have to trust me for now."

Wearing a speculative expression, Luther relaxed against the wall. Finally, he nodded. "Okay." But he made it clear, "For now."

Gaby could tell that he wasn't taking her seriously, that he merely indulged her, and more than anything, even more than she wanted to investigate the strange emotions he evoked, she wanted to flatten him.

He deserved no less for the dirty trick he'd pulled on her.

"Since you're being so agreeable, cop, you might as well find out where the indigent cancer patients are sent when they don't have family to look out for them. It's probably a government facility of some sort. You know the type—looks pretty on the outside, but inside it not only lacks proper care but also borders on abuse and neglect. Sort of like the old-folks' homes that are forever getting busted."

Luther started to speak, and Gaby slashed a hand through the air, silencing him.

"After that, you can make damn sure that a just-deceased patient by the name of Ms. Davies is properly put to rest."

Going as high as the bandage on his head would allow, Luther's brows lifted. "Let me guess. You're worried about a zombie now?"

Maintaining her grip on his shirt, Gaby jerked him down closer to her. He winced in pain, but she'd already used up her meager well of sympathy on him.

"No, you smart-ass. I'm worried about a doctor clever enough to make it look like someone has died when she hasn't."

Abrupt comprehension honed Luther's features. Finally, finally, he put stock in what she said.

His brows crunched back down. "Dr. Marton?"

"You really do have a problem remembering that no-questions rule, huh?"

"Fuck your rule. Why do you suspect Dr. Marton?"

"He treats cancer patients."

"So?"

Now that he was riled, Gaby relaxed a little. "I don't know of anything specific, but I imagine there are all types of drugs that could cause the illusion of death. Then maybe that same doctor could have the body moved—"

"Jesus."

"—to a place where he can let the cancer take over. Maybe even cultivate it."

Luther stared at her as if she'd grown two heads. "Why on earth would *anyone*, but especially a doctor, do something that gruesome?"

"How should I know? There are sick fucks everywhere—but maybe a doctor with a twisted mind would do it for science or some such shit." For emphasis, to make sure that he got the whole picture, Gaby went up on her toes so that their noses almost touched. "Think about it, Luther. What else would explain these strange tumors you described?"

Luther's mouth opened in shock, and then closed again. "I don't know. But Gaby . . . what you're suggesting, well . . . You're serious about this?"

"Yup, sorry, cop, but I am. Whether or not you believe me, whether you do anything about it or not, that's totally up to you. I don't have the time or the inclination to try to convince you."

She released him with a shove, but took only one step before coming back around and shoving her face up to his again. "And by the way, it was pretty damn cruel of you to make me sexually aware of stuff when I can't do jack shit about it. I don't know what you were thinking, but let me tell you, it flat-out sucks."

Her charge tipped his composure. His voice dropped and his harsh appearance softened. "Gaby—"

Now that she'd had her say, no way in hell would she stick around to discuss it with him. "Come on, Mort. Get a move on."

With a long stride and fast feet, she made her way down the corridor, not caring if Mort followed or not, and sure as certain not about to look back to see Luther's reaction.

He *was* cruel.

Cruel, and confusing, and now in the middle of trying to expose a madman bent on unleashing monsters demented from cancerous afflictions on the unsuspecting public, she couldn't stop thinking about sex.

With Luther.

She wasn't at all certain exactly how it'd work, but she knew it'd probably be real nice. Maybe the nicest thing to ever happen to her miserable life.

The painful truth was, she'd never know for sure.

She couldn't know.

Paladins didn't have sex. They obeyed God's command. And so far, God hadn't told her to do the nasty with a detective, and definitely not with Luther Cross. Somehow, Gaby didn't think He ever would.

And that was the cruelest truth of all.

Chapter 12

"Gaby?"

Anger kept her stewing in silence.

Anger at cancer for being so ugly, so devastating; at Luther for making her curious about things; at God, for making her who she was.

And at herself, for being too weak to change her untenable circumstances.

But she wasn't angry at Mort, so as they exited the air-conditioned hospital and walked out into the balmy night, she swallowed her ire and gave in to him. "What is it?"

"Why were you so upset in the hospital?"

"It's a long story, Mort, but I've known cancer and the damage it does. Being around it, feeling all that malignant evil just makes me ill."

"You felt evil there?"

Through the impenetrable darkness, Gaby gaped at him. "How could you *not* feel it?"

They reached his beat-up, aged sedan and got inside. Mort started the engine, but didn't drive away. Tall security lamps sent elongated fingers of light through the windshield. Gaby could just see the faint outline of Mort's smile.

"I guess I couldn't feel anything bad because I felt so much good stuff instead."

Good stuff? Had he flipped? "What the hell are you talking about now? Everyone in there has both feet in the friggin' grave. Jesus, Mort, they're all *dying*."

"Not the people who cared for them. They were alive and busy and they all sounded so concerned for that poor Ms. Davies." His hands flexed on the steering wheel. "That can't be an easy job, Gaby."

It'd be more of a hell than what she already did. "I couldn't do it."

"Me, either. Those people are angels."

Angels on earth? Maybe. She'd never really concerned herself with them. Her purpose centered on evil, not good. "That's my point. It's depressing."

"But they give comfort and hope—"

"Hope for what? A quicker death? A less painful death? Doesn't matter, they're still dead." Why the hell did he want to argue this with her? "I could smell it. The only thing that smelled worse was antiseptic."

"I thought it smelled sterile, to protect the patients from germs." He put the car in gear and pulled out of his parking spot. "I'll tell you what. It smelled a whole lot better than that carcass that got hung in the foyer, or the blood on the stairs. It smelled better than the garbage cans that sit in the sun and bake." He glanced her way. "It smells better than the basement we use to clean our laundry."

Propping her feet on the dash and slumping into her seat, Gaby considered his words—and had to agree. "I guess you're right."

Her concession must've given him courage, because Mort didn't let it go there. "But you picked up on more than the people dying, the nurses, and the smells of the place, didn't you, Gaby?"

She was just tired enough, just fed up enough, to say, "Yeah."

"You know someone there is doing something evil, huh?"

"Someone is always doing something evil, Mort. It's the way of the world. Get used to it."

"But like you said, some stuff is normal evil, and some isn't. When you change, it's to make you better able to deal with the abnormal stuff, huh?" This time, he didn't even give her time to reply. "In the alley, when you fought those . . . things. You were awesome. Like an avenging angel. Even in movies, I haven't seen anyone move like that. And you didn't look so much like you. It was . . . well, not weird, so don't get offended again. Just sort of amazing."

Gaby groaned. All her life, she'd assumed if anyone knew the truth of her, they'd call her a freak.

Instead, Mort damn near idolized her.

"There are no superheroes, Mort."

"You saved Luther. You saved that poor girl from more humiliation and worse. Against you, no one stands a chance, not a rapist and not a ghoul."

"Those things after Luther weren't ghouls. They were evil people punished by God, and tormented by a human. Odds are they didn't even know what they were doing. So much suffering would have to affect someone mentally."

"They were attacking Luther!"

"I don't know about that. Neither of them was agile enough or strong enough to do any damage to a big man like him."

"He was hit in the head. Hurt."

"Yeah, but did they do it? I dunno." She put her head back and watched passing shadows out the window. "The one thing had a useless leg. It was there, but the appendage didn't work, so if anything, that would have slowed him down. And that woman . . . her throat had been eaten away with disease. She only wanted help." Gaby closed her eyes. "Unfortunately for all of us, she was beyond help, in life and death."

"What do you mean?"

"Her body was too deteriorated with disease to ever recover. And her past was too tainted for her to get any type of afterlife. God wouldn't have—"

Catching herself, Gaby clamped her lips together.

Too late; Mort caught her misstep. "God wouldn't have what?"

He wouldn't have sent Gaby to demolish the creature if she'd had any redemption at all. "Nothing."

"Did He send you after her?"

She kept her lips firmly sealed. Anything she said would only make it worse. She'd turned into a damned blabbermouth and that just wouldn't do.

"I saw you, Gaby. I know something happened to you. That's why I followed you. After I saw what you did, well, I want to keep helping."

"You've done enough. But . . . thanks."

"Could you maybe do an exorcism?"

The absurdity of that almost brought a laugh from the humorless well of her soul. "No."

"But if evil possesses those beings, then maybe an exorcism could—"

"It's not like that, Mort. I wish it were that easy. Evil doesn't come from hell to possess people. It *is* people. Some people, anyway."

He drove on in silence, rendering Gaby rigid with guilt for stifling his small hope.

Then it struck her, what she wanted to do next. Mort would feel useful, and she could gain more clues. "Hey."

He glanced at her.

"Feel like a drive?"

"Uh . . . I am driving."

"Yeah, but not in the direction I want." She instructed him toward the section of town where she destroyed the first creature. Rather than go the usual route, she took him past the abandoned Cancer Research Center that she remembered was visible from the road. The broad face of the building stood as an eerie specter in the darkness.

Mort shivered. "Now that feels creepy."

"I know." She opened her door. "You want to help, Mort?"

His uneasy gaze went past her to look again at that imposing structure. "Yeah."

"Then I need you to stay here, with the doors locked and the engine running. No, don't argue."

He closed his mouth against the automatic protests.

"If anyone shows up, anyone suspicious, drive away, but only go around the block and then come back. If you aren't here when I come back out of the woods, I'll hide and wait for you, okay?"

"This isn't a very nice part of town."

So much for him playing sidekick. "No shit, but you'll be safe enough. I promise."

Big eyes turned to her. "You'd feel it if anyone tried to hurt me?"

Hell, she honestly didn't know. It came down to that contrast of commonplace evil versus the deviant, preternatural evil. If a bully came after Mort, a drug dealer or a punk from a gang, that'd be an everyday type of crime, and she might not have a clue. "Look, just keep the doors locked and pay attention, and nothing can hurt you, right?"

His bony shoulders straightened. "Right. I'll be here, Gaby. I won't let you down."

She did *not* want him to take any stupid chances. "Stow the melodrama and keep alert. I'll be back in fifteen minutes." She slammed the door, waited while Mort secured all the locks, and then faced the anomalistic presence that hid in aged brick and mortar.

This, she decided, was where the core of malevolence issued forth. She would find her answers here.

Uneasily, Gaby moved forward. She remembered that the research hospital hid the smaller buildings behind it, especially the isolation hospital. That's where the auras had been most frenetic and disjointed, as if many discontented souls had coalesced into one excruciating, violent emanation.

She felt it now.

Drawing her. Pulling her in.

Being receptive to the energy of others had its drawbacks; Gaby sensed it wasn't only evil spirits at play. The emanations could also be coming from those who had led desperately unhappy lives—or those who faced terrible deaths.

The grip of so many forces had the ability to bleed her of her own resources. In the normal course of things, she'd withdraw from the area, from the person or people depleting her.

But this wasn't normal.

This was her mission, not God's. She wasn't His conduit, as was usually the case when she faced evil, and that alone made it exceedingly dangerous. If she didn't fight the allure, it might consume her. And if that happened, who would look after Mort?

Who would protect Luther?

Uncaring whether curious eyes might notice, Gaby withdrew her knife. Having it in her hand amped up her courage. High weeds and prickly scrub shrubs knicked the skin on her feet and snagged in her jeans. Gaby pressed forward, past the looming structure, into the woods, and beyond.

With each step, her heart beat harder and faster until it pained her. "Fuck," she whispered, just to hear her own voice. "Fuck, fuck, fuck. Who are you?"

Far ahead, she saw a faint illumination through the shrouding woods.

Fear evaporated in the face of discovery.

Hunkering down behind a broken tree trunk, Gaby watched. Weaving with the cadence of footsteps, the light shifted, dimmed, and grew brighter.

Ah. Someone carried a flashlight and the uneven ground made the light bounce and shudder. Who? And why be in the woods this late at night?

Sounds reached her attuned ears—footsteps, crunching leaves, soft crooning.

She also heard great suffering.

Then . . . coercion. And joy.

Horror at those combined murmurings kept Gaby still. She saw it all as a human, and hated the view. Why did God do this to her? Why now, and why with this particular wickedness?

There were no answers, and she strained her ears to hear more. A small brook, relaxing in its monotone flow. Bubbling. Gurgling . . .

Choking.

Comprehension brought Gaby to her feet. No! That wasn't water; it was . . . spittle. Life.

Being *crushed* out of another.

Unthinking of her own possible peril, of where to go or what to do, Gaby charged forward. She tripped over fallen branches and rocks, rushed back to her feet only to be snagged in dead foliage and grabbed by thorny weeds. She fought wildly to free herself.

All in vain.

With the first thundering rush of her footsteps, the light went out and the woods fell dead silent.

Oh please. She searched, but there was nothing, no life and no death and no noise, movement, or light of any kind.

It was so silent that she knew it wasn't natural. The night breathed and shifted; it made its presence known. But not tonight. This night was utterly still.

She couldn't do anything about it. Not in the darkness, alone.

In the daylight, she'd come back.

In the daylight, she'd make someone, or something, very sorry.

Defeat left a bitter taste in her mouth and filled her heart with heavy stones. Her weakness had allowed someone to die.

Someone to murder.

She found Mort where she'd left him, and he was so relieved to see her that at first he asked no questions. Anxious to be out of the area, he just drove.

It wasn't until a few minutes later, when they'd reached the apartment, that he said, "Well?"

"Nothing," she lied. "A dead end." She wouldn't take Mort back there with her. She wouldn't involve him. Never again. Her skin still crawled with the taint of iniquitous depravity. She would destroy the evil, but she'd do so while protecting Mort, whatever it took.

It struck Gaby that she'd once thought her life complicated, when in fact, it was absurdly simple. But now, the more she interacted with regular, normal people, the more twisted and gnarled it made her life, and she feared she'd never get it unraveled again.

One thing was certain: having a friend was a real pain in the ass.

❦

Midafternoon on the next day, Gaby found Luther on a basket-ball court. A much smaller bandage had replaced the wrapping around his head.

Hell of a way for a man with a concussion to behave, Gaby thought. He didn't exert himself overly, but he didn't sit on the sidelines either.

Rather than call out to him, she sat cross-legged on the lawn beneath the shade of a tall tree, and just observed. He played with a bunch of inner-city kids in a rainbow of colors: ebony, pink, beige, brown, caramel. Boys and girls. Some barefoot, most stick-thin. They looked to be around nine or ten.

They enjoyed themselves.

So did Luther.

It felt odd to see someone so carefree and happy, someone who knew about the cancer, and the malevolence, and the doctor . . .

Had he even checked into it all, as she'd asked?

Or had he blown off her directions to play instead? That is, if you could call civic duty on a hot afternoon "play."

Gaby looked up at the blistering sun. It had to be eighty-five, which was cooler than they'd had lately, but under a cloudless sky was still hot enough to roast. The blacktop court would amplify the heat. A concussion would amplify the discomfort.

Luther didn't seem to mind.

He looked good in dirty white sneakers, gray sweatpants,

and nothing else. Gaby had seen men without shirts before, but none like Luther. He had a naturally strong body, not muscles carved in a gym. Sweat gleamed on his sleek shoulders and darkened his chest hair. Gaby visually followed the path of that hair as it narrowed to a line running down his abdomen to his navel, and into his sweats.

He turned, feigned a shot, and then allowed a kid to steal the ball from him.

Her heart skipped at the sight of his smile.

Hands on his knees, head hanging and blond hair sweaty, he called it quits. "That's it, kids. I'm beat. You've done me in."

A chorus of complaints rang out, but Luther just straightened on a laugh, ruffled hair, patted backs, and walked to a bench to get a towel. Another cop, this one a shapely female, took his place.

As she passed Luther, he said, "Thanks, Ann. I appreciate it."

"No problem, sweetheart. This is my chance to prove I'm more than a pretty face."

"I never doubted it."

Gaby took in the exchange with a scowl. The woman flirted with him, but Luther took it in stride.

Without seeing Gaby, he used the towel to dry his chest and shoulders and started in her direction. Arm raised, he rubbed the back of his neck and Gaby could see his armpit, the bulge of an impressive biceps, and . . .

A gold cross hanging around his neck.

She was on her feet before he reached her.

He drew up short. "Gaby?" After glancing around to see if anyone had noticed her, he moved closer. "What are you doing here?"

She snatched up the cross hanging from the short chain. "What the hell is this?"

The backs of her fingers touched against his damp, heated chest. She felt his body hair, crisp but also soft. She could smell him—man and sweat and . . . Luther. Her heart thumped harder.

Sneering, she said, "You're kidding, right? You think this will help anything?"

He studied her, and without her realizing it, he'd curled his big hand over hers. "Come here, Gaby." He pulled her hand from his cross and led her away from the basketball court to the other side of the street. "Sit down."

The hell she would. "Don't give me orders."

He eyed her. "Are you pissed for any particular reason, or just as a way of life?"

Damn it. She hadn't been pissed. Not until she saw the woman with him. And the cross.

But mostly the woman.

Not that she'd ever tell him so. If she did, she'd really feel like a moron.

Changing the subject from her mood to his bling seemed a good idea. "That's nothing more than an icon, you know. It's not going to ward off evil."

"It was a gift from my grandmother, who has since passed away. I loved her, so I wear it."

How dare he continue to sound so levelheaded and calm in the face of her growing ire? "That's all there is to it?"

"I'm not worried about vampires, if that's what you mean."

Her shoulders straightened, but still she felt about two feet tall. "Sorry."

"Wow." A smile teased his firm mouth. "You almost said that like you meant it."

Pressing her fingers under her sunglasses, Gaby rubbed at her eyes. "Look, I didn't hunt you down to argue with you."

"Could have fooled me." He slung the towel around his neck. "How did you hunt me down?"

"I went to the station, and was told it was your day off. I asked if anyone knew where I could find you, and someone sitting in there—not a cop, but someone else—"

"Gary Webb? Twenty-one-year-old kid with too much energy?"

"Maybe. He told me to check here."

"All right. And you hunted me down because . . . ?"

Gaby looked around the area. "Is there someplace I can buy you a Coke?"

"No." He folded his arms over his chest. "But I can buy you one if you feel like walking a block."

"I can walk."

In strained and silent agreement, she went with Luther to his car where he stowed the towel and then dug out a white T-shirt and slipped it on. He finger-combed his sweaty hair away from his face and retrieved his sunglasses. "Ready?"

"Sure." They started down the street.

At a convenience store, he went inside, and Gaby followed. There was no air conditioning, but a squeaky fan stirred the humid air, offering a modicum of relief.

"Get what you want," he told her, so she chose a cola and a candy bar. He grabbed a sport drink and two traveler's packs of aspirin.

"Head still hurting?"

"A little. I'm fine." But he opened both packs and popped them into his mouth, washing them down with the cold green drink.

"You were probably supposed to take it easy today, huh?"

"I had other things to do besides taking it easy." He paid and they went back outside. "This way."

There were no benches nearby, so he led her to a grassy spot beneath a tree, and together they sat.

With each passing second, Gaby felt more like an idiot. The man had barely had time to sleep, much less do as she'd asked. And he was hurt, so probably shouldn't have done anything at all anyway.

Luther stared at her, waiting.

"I wanted to talk to you for a couple of reasons. I was going to tell you how I cut my arm—"

"Let's start with that."

She shook her head. "In a minute." She indulged in a long drink of her cold soda, and then on impulse she stretched out on her back in the grass. "I guess you've been too laid up to check into the hospital stuff like I asked, huh?"

He stretched out, too, but on his side, propping himself up on an elbow so he could watch her. "Actually, I did that before I left the hospital."

She turned her head toward him. "Really?" Wow, so maybe he'd listened to her after all.

"They've lost twenty patients over the last two years."

"Is that a lot?"

"Not according to them. Not for the cancer ward."

Gaby put an arm behind her head and stared up at the sky. "Doctors usually visit more than one hospital. Check the other ones that Dr. Marton goes to, too."

"Okay."

She scrutinized him. "Did you check on that place where the indigent patients go?"

"I got an address, but I haven't been there yet. I did some research, though, and nothing fishy turned up."

Gaby nodded. "Visit it anyway."

"I planned to."

He was so agreeable, so easy, that somehow the words just slipped out. "I stabbed a man last night."

In the middle of taking another drink, Luther halted. He didn't blink. He didn't say anything. He just froze.

Gaby rolled her lips in, worked the words around in her mind, and then plunged on. "He'll live, I think. Without giving my name, I called the cops so they could take him to a hospital or whatever. You'll probably hear about it at the station, and I didn't want you to start suspecting me of anything."

Plus she figured half-truths would throw him off a more dangerous course of supposition. And she had some questions for him, questions that Mort had refused to answer.

Still Luther said nothing.

His silence spurred her to say more. "See, Mort and I were out and about . . . just walking. He was sort of shook up after that blood in the stairwell, and even after we cleaned it, the smell was awful, so we took in some fresh air." She'd already cued Mort, and if Luther questioned him, he damn well better lie convincingly.

"When we were heading home, we saw this man assaulting a girl in an alley."

"A hooker?"

Gaby gave him a sharp look. "Does it matter?"

"Not to me. But I want details."

After taking off her sunglasses, Gaby turned her face toward Luther. "She might have been a hooker, but she was still a kid and the guy was forcing her."

"And?"

"I stopped him."

Luther sat the sport drink aside. "With your knife?"

She nodded. "I told him if he ever hurt her again, I'd castrate him."

Small muscles flexed in Luther's face, taking him from fear to anger to rage and back again. "Where did you stab him, Gaby?"

"In the shoulder. I threw my knife first, to stop him." She felt compelled to honesty. "I have very good aim."

A big breath expanded Luther's already impressive chest.

"But then he tried to charge me, so I sort of pulled it out of him and put it to his balls and told him what would happen if he didn't change his ways."

Luther twitched.

Gaby felt the need to rush through the rest of her explanation. "He was making her do stuff to him, Luther. Really ugly stuff. She was crying and she was sort of beat up—"

"Where is she now?"

That his first thought would be concern for the girl warmed Gaby. More than ever, she saw the white aura surrounding him. "I don't know. She ran off after I stopped the attack."

Luther fell to his back. "I don't fucking believe this."

"I didn't tell the cops who I am and I don't think that guy will, either."

"If he lived."

"Well, yeah. But I think he will. I mean, sure, he was bleeding a lot and everything, but it was just a shoulder wound."

"Unless you nicked something else."

Did he have to sound so morbid? "I guess."

"I'll ask around about the incident. I can find out who was on call last night, see how the man fared after your unique sense of justice."

Gaby didn't like the accusation in his tone. "He deserved it, Luther."

"From what you said, I'm sure he did. But you should have called the police, not taken it on yourself to deal with him."

"By the time the cops got there, who knows what else he might have done to that poor girl?"

"Who knows what he might have done to *you*, Gaby, if your aim had faltered a little. Did you ever think of that?"

"No, because my aim doesn't falter."

He muttered several steaming curses before saying, "I can't believe you're bragging about this."

He looked really put out, ready to shut down on her, but tough. She had questions and he most likely had answers. Mort sure as hell hadn't wanted to talk to her about it. "I suppose now isn't a very good time to ask you stuff?"

To her surprise, he put an arm over his eyes and appeared to relax. He took two deep breaths and let out the last one in a long, slow exhalation. "All right. What stuff?"

Well, that was better. Calmer anyway. "The man had the woman on her knees and he kept pushing her face into his crotch."

Luther froze again.

"It was like he was screwing her, but not where he should be."

"Gaby," Luther choked out. "Shush."

"I know there's a lot of deviant stuff out there and that men pay women to do a lot of weird things. But like I told you, I don't watch television, and whenever I hear music playing on the street, I don't really pay much attention to the words. I don't really know what's normal and what isn't. What that guy did didn't look normal, but I wanted to know—"

"Give me a minute here, okay?"

"Just tell me what he was doing and if it's acceptable or not. The girl sure didn't seem to think so. She hated it. Hell, he'd had to beat her up to make her do it."

"I don't believe this."

"The thing is, Mort was upset that she was hurt, but he didn't seem confused about what the jerk did or anything."

In one swift movement, Luther was over her. *Now* he looked angry. "Are you playing with me?"

Flat on her back? In the sun? In the middle of the community?

"No." His blond hair, still damp from his exertions, went wavy in places. That seemed very at odds with such a rugged male. "I never have time for playing. You should know that by now."

"Don't start with the confusing talk, Gaby. I want a straight answer." His hands gripped her shoulders. "You honestly don't know what oral sex is?"

"Oral sex." She supposed that sounded right for what she'd seen. It was definitely sex of some sort. "You want plain speaking? Fine. I've seen the prostitutes jerk guys off. I've seen them bend over stuff and let johns do them from the back, like a dog."

Luther's eyes widened a little more with every word she spoke.

"I've even seen them—"

His hand smashed over her mouth. "Jesus, woman." Additional heat darkened his high cheekbones. "Do you spend all your time watching hookers at work?"

He'd silenced her, so she shrugged. She'd have a tough time avoiding seeing it where she lived. Every time she stepped out of the apartment, the whores were there, sometimes doing their business in a parked car, sometimes in an alley.

Sometimes in plain sight, if that's what the john wanted.

Luther's hand shifted. His fingers touched her mouth. Lightly. Caressing. With one finger, he parted her lips.

"Gaby, I want to kiss you."

Could have fooled her. "You look more like you want to strangle me."

"That too." He continued touching her mouth. "Do you think it'd be okay if I kissed you?"

She had to think about it. It wouldn't be smart, would in fact be idiotic—"Yeah."

Luther bent down, hesitated, then came closer. He brushed his mouth over hers. He didn't do much, just hovered there, teasing her. His mouth barely touching hers.

Gaby felt his hot breath as it accelerated. She felt his building tension and her own anticipation.

Then she felt Luther's absence.

She opened her eyes and saw him sitting up beside her. She waited, and he looked down at her with accusation, need, and so much more. "You are one dangerous little girl, Gabrielle Cody."

Chapter 13

"You just figured that out?"

He plucked a blade of grass, then another. Looking away, he said, "I haven't figured out anything. Around you, nothing is clear."

"I know." She was an abnormality of the first order. How could a nice, normal cop like Luther Cross ever understand her, when she didn't entirely understand herself?

"So." He tossed the blades of grass aside. "Rather than splurge on a cheap radio, you watch the local streetwalkers for entertainment." He looked at her. "Or is it edification?"

If he wanted to snipe, she could snipe right back. "Given your pinched-up look and the way Mort dodged the topic, it's pretty obvious that if I don't watch the hookers on occasion, I'm not going to learn much."

He turned coldly austere. "Anything you need to know, you can't learn from them."

"Can't learn it from you either, apparently." She sat up

and brushed dried grass and dirt from her hair. Luther hadn't moved that far away, but she now felt a definite distance between them that hadn't been there a few moments ago. "I'm so dangerous, you're suddenly afraid of me?"

Luther pulled up one knee and crossed his arms over it. "Truth is, Gaby, I'm more afraid for you than of you. You're the strangest girl I've ever met. At times, there's this awful vulnerability about you that makes me damn near want to cry. Then you make me so hot that I can't breathe. Then you calmly tell me, a detective, that you played vigilante and stabbed someone."

Hurt, Gaby pushed to her feet. "I guess you would rather I hadn't helped her." Why had she hoped that, like Mort, he'd be impressed?

Stupid.

Mort was sad and lonely. Luther Cross was a shining advocate who likely had an abundance of close friends and family backing him.

He stood, too, and though he was only three inches taller, he seemed much bigger in every way. One shaky hand reached out to cup her face. "I'd rather you didn't put yourself in danger."

Yeah, she'd rather that, too. But more often than not, she had no choice. "Sorry."

His mouth lifted. "Now that sounded sincere." His thumb brushed her cheek. He dropped his hand from her face to lace his fingers with hers. "Come here."

"Where are we going?"

"Someplace more private." He started walking, his pace urgent, towing her along. "Someplace where I can explain a few things to you."

"Like?"

"Oral sex. The difference between what hookers do and what I'd like to do with you."

"Me? And *you*?" Her heart started that odd staccato thumping again. "Forget about it. I already told you that I can't—"

"I know. One of these days, you'll tell me why. But I would never force you, Gaby."

Obnoxious jerk. "I wouldn't *let* you."

"I'd never even try."

He towed her into a smelly alley and backed her up against a damp brick wall. Her thin T-shirt did nothing to protect her shoulders from the rough face of the broken bricks.

But Gaby didn't care.

"Hookers do what they do for money, without emotion and without experiencing a single pleasure. Not because they want to, but because they have a habit to feed, or an empty stomach, or an insistent pimp."

As if he'd been running, Luther breathed hard and fast. His fingers caught her wrists and raised her hands to his shoulders. "Because they consent, it's different from actual rape, and from what you say you saw last night. But in my view, not by a whole lot. Any man who uses a woman, who takes advantage of her desperation, isn't much of a man."

"It looked ugly," Gaby agreed, glad to have some real light shed on it all. "Like evil."

"And to you, evil, like cancer, is a live entity?"

She hated to tell him, but . . . "It is, Luther. Very alive."

He didn't laugh at her, didn't argue or try to dissuade her. "Rape is both ugly and evil." He looked at her mouth. "But when two people are willing, anything goes, and what might look unpleasant otherwise becomes . . . very nice."

"You'll understand if I have my doubts." But that wasn't entirely true. With Luther, she could imagine most things would be nice. Even being pinned against a dirty brick wall.

"Now, Gaby, I'm going to kiss you, and I want you to open your mouth for me."

"Why?"

"Consider it an exercise in oral sex, why it's pleasurable and why men and women do it."

Her skin went all tingly. And deeper down, inside herself. "Yeah, okay."

"Wait." He touched her lips. "Promise you won't bite me."

Bite him?

"Just promise me, Gaby. Your reactions are not all that trustworthy and I don't want to lose my tongue."

His tongue. The tingling turned to a warm energy filling her whole body. "I won't bite you."

The second the words left her, his mouth covered hers. When his tongue touched her lips, Gaby remembered to part them. He dipped in, just a little, and the slick feel of his tongue, the *taste* of him, did crazy things to her.

She liked it. A lot.

Her hands clenched on his shoulders.

Continuing to tease her, he licked his tongue over her lips, her tongue, her teeth.

Deeper.

They were both breathing hard when he drew back and whispered, "Now, when I put my tongue in your mouth, I want you to suck on it."

Wow. Gaby nodded, and gladly accepted his tongue back. As instructed, she sucked—and it was wildly exciting. For both of them.

Who knew?

The kissing grew hotter, deeper. Both of Luther's hands held her face. He pulled back yet again. Eyes dark and hot, he stared at her, studied her.

Oh no. Did she look different again? Had she changed, as both he and Mort claimed she did?

The panic had just started when, voice rough, Luther instructed, "Don't think, Gaby. Give me your tongue. I'm going to suck on it so you can see how it feels."

At his instruction, worrisome thoughts scattered.

She didn't need any more encouragement than that. Gaby plastered herself to him and mimicked what he'd done to her.

Luther moved closer so that his whole body pressed hers. But, oddly, he didn't touch her with his hands. He kept them flattened on the brick wall at either side of her head.

He freed his mouth with a groan. "Gaby?" He kissed her chin, her jaw. "I'm sorry, but we have to stop or I'm going to lose it."

For one of the few times in her life, she couldn't think of a single smart retort.

"Here's the thing." Putting his cheek to hers, he whispered directly into her ear. "As good as that feels to us both, it's so much better when it's not just a tongue you're sucking on."

Oral sex. Images worked through her mind, vivid and sensual, making her acutely aware of Luther's body against hers. "You're hard."

"I keep imagining your mouth on me, and hell yeah, I'm hard."

She could see why. The idea excited her, too. "As long as you're being so talkative and honest, I have another question."

"God help me."

Because she had to know, Gaby asked with tentative uncertainty, "Do I look different right now?"

Luther kissed the bridge of her nose, her forehead, her chin. "You look sexy. Turned on. But also a little afraid." His warm smile took the insult from the words. "All reasonable reactions from a virgin."

"But I don't look . . . weird?"

He smoothed back her hair—and measured his words. "I'll admit that you change so much, I can't keep up. And yes, you look different from how you normally look." The smile evaporated, replaced by concern and reassurance. "But never would I use the word *weird*. Just different, Gaby."

Shit. Ashamed, she turned her face away, and Luther brought it back around.

"Your features are sharper, more defined. Stronger. But you're still you, Gaby. No doubt about it. And I like you. A lot. So whatever affliction alters your appearance, please don't let it add to your sadness."

Her sadness. Gaby frowned. Luther saw too much, and made her care far too easily.

Recognizing her expression, he said, "Here we go," with a lot of resignation.

"I'm not afraid, smart-ass, just curious and a little confused."

He widened his stance and looked down his nose at her. "About what?"

"All this sucking business. I mean . . ." She nudged her belly against his erection. "I might be unschooled on sexual things, but I understand anatomy, so I see how it'd work on you. But for a woman . . ."

The sound he made was half laugh, half groan. "You'll have to trust me on this. Women have other places that are equally . . . receptive to a tongue, or a soft suck."

"Where?"

He groaned again. "I can't talk about this anymore." Leaning back to look at her, he whispered, "But one of these days, I'd like to show you."

"Yeah, well, don't hold your breath. What either of us wants won't matter in the long run. Sex for me isn't likely."

She couldn't see it anywhere in her immediate future, for sure.

Though she'd like to.

Especially now, after this little demonstration from Luther. "That's why I shouldn't have asked you about this, I guess. But Mort wouldn't tell me—"

"I'd have punched him if he had."

Gaby shoved Luther back the length of her arms. "Mort is my friend now. Don't hurt him."

"I was kidding. He's my friend, too." He put his forehead to hers. "But I'd rather you come to me with those types of questions. Okay?"

"I don't know. I don't like feeling this way. I meant it when I told you it was cruel to get all this started. There's so much that we still have to do. Those cancerous things are still loose and someone hit you in the head, and Dr. Marton—"

Yet again, his hand covered her mouth. "I'm sorry if I've frustrated you, Gaby, if I've made you more aware of things you wanted to pretend didn't exist. But I don't want you involved with any of my police work."

She fried him with her gaze.

Disgruntled, Luther sighed. "I can handle it, I swear."

She shook her head. He couldn't, and that was the plain simple truth.

Just that easily, Luther turned back into a cop instead of a lover. He released her and took a step away. "Damn it, Gaby, promise me you won't get involved."

"I can promise you I will." She sidled out from between the wall and his bricklike body. "And before you start threatening to arrest me again, remember that you gave me your word, too."

"Only to keep our conversation last night between the two of us."

Anger sent the lust away. "Fine. So I could trust you last night, but not today? I should have realized that. I won't make the mistake again."

She turned to walk away, and Luther caught her arm.

Bad temper had her swinging before she thought better of it. Luckily, given his concussion, he twisted enough that her fist landed on his shoulder and not his already injured head.

"Enough."

His blustering didn't faze her. She lowered her fists and curled her lip. "Let me guess. Horniness makes you meaner than usual."

Left eye twitching, Luther stared at her. His eyes narrowed more. Then he nodded. "I suppose it does."

That reply so took her by surprise, Gaby almost grinned. The lighthearted feeling was so alien to her that it left her disconcerted. "And you call me dangerous."

"Gaby, wait."

"For what? You want to tease me more?"

"No, actually . . ." He straightened to his full height. "I want to ask you out on a date."

"Are you out of your fucking mind?"

Well, Luther thought, he should have expected just such a reaction. On some topics, Gaby could be very predictable.

Especially when she made cavalier confessions about stabbing rapists in the dead of the night.

It wasn't easy, but Luther tamped down his temper again. The best way to protect Gaby and to learn all her secrets—secrets he felt certain would help unravel his current mystery—was to get closer to her.

He liked that idea on several levels, only one of them being personal interest.

If it turned out she really was just a confused, mixed-up product of her upbringing, great. But if she was somehow involved with the murder of that man, and his attack, he'd prosecute her just as he would any other criminal.

Regardless of how it'd hurt him to do so.

He'd thought about it, and he knew how to counter the many arguments she'd have against a growing relationship. "No, I'm sane enough. I think."

He eyed her head to toe. The mysterious shifting of her features had faded away. She once again looked like regular Gaby Cody, tall, thin, mean-tempered, too sensitive and too guarded, and far too alone.

"Forget it." She started out of the alley.

"No."

Going rigid with disbelief, she jerked around to face him. "What do you mean, *no*?"

"No, I won't forget about it. Don't be a coward, Gaby. Give me a chance."

Her chin tucked in and her eyes narrowed to furious slits. "Coward?"

"It's not a big deal. I'm not proposing we go to a fancy dinner or anything. In fact, what I have planned is totally casual. You won't even have to change clothes."

"I couldn't if I wanted to, you ass. I don't own anything different!"

That stymied him. So Gaby always dressed in that hideous getup? "You don't own—"

As if regretting that confession, she pressed her mouth together.

"Why?"

Giving nothing away, she said, "I don't have much to spend, and I'm no more interested in fashion than I am in television or music or *playing*."

"So you literally wear the same clothes, day in and day out."

Her chin went up. "Yes."

"Do you at least have colorful pajamas?"

"I sleep naked."

He did not need to know that. Best to get things back on track before he totally lost sight of his purpose. "What you're wearing is perfect for what I have in mind."

"Slumming?"

She could be so defensive. "No, actually, but it is casual. I'll be in jeans, too. So . . . Thursday at six? I'd say tomorrow or the next day, but I have some things to tend to first—"

"Like checking out the treatment center for the indigent?"

Glad that he could accommodate her on that, Luther nodded. "Yes."

"And making sure that Ms. Davies gets a proper burial?"

Because it mattered to her, he said, "Yes, I'll check into that."

"Are you screwing that female cop?"

The rapid-fire change in subject threw Luther. "Who? Ann?"

"I think that was her name. The pretty one who came to play basketball with you."

"No, I'm not."

"How many female cops do you know?"

"Several." He studied Gaby, wondering where her thoughts were taking her. "Women have all the same positions in the police force as men, though I'd say men still outnumber them."

"So which ones are you screwing?"

He should have been used to her language by now. She didn't use it to be deliberately crude or off-putting. Luther honestly thought she knew no other way, and understanding that only increased the mystery surrounding her. "I'm not intimate with any of them."

Gaby scoffed, but otherwise didn't look the least bit concerned about his personal life. "When you first saw me today, you hauled me away because you didn't want your friend Ann to see me, right?"

"Yes." The Inquisition couldn't have been this difficult.

"Why? Were you afraid I'd embarrass you?"

"No." Very little would ever get past Gaby. Luther crossed his arms over his chest and leaned on the brick wall. "The truth is, I'm still uncertain how involved you might be with certain things going on."

"The filleted man?"

While most women would have at least cringed, if not gone hysterical, Gaby acknowledged the gruesome murder with casual disregard.

"Quit calling him that, but yes. That's who I'm talking about." Among other things. "Not that I'm accusing you of anything, Gaby, but if you are involved, the less anyone else knows about you, the better I'll be able to protect you—"

"Protect me?" She turned and strode away, saying, "You're an idiot."

Luther caught up to her. "Because I want to protect you?"

"Because you think you can. Because you think I'm the one who needs protection."

"If not you, Gaby, then who?"

She shook her head—and slanted him a look that made Luther's masculine ego rebel.

"*Me?* You think that I need protection?"

Another look. "You're the one with the fat bandage on his head."

Son of a bitch! "I was jumped from *behind,* Gaby."

"And they say cops are alert. Can't prove it by you,

huh?" She headed back toward his car. "Look, just because I let you kiss me and rub yourself against me a little doesn't make you responsible for me."

The way she put things . . . She was more blunt than a long-practiced porn star, but as innocent as a child. He supposed most of that could be attributed to being raised partially in foster care, and then later by a priest. An odd mix, that.

"How far did you get in school?"

"About eighth grade. Why?"

That helped explain things further. Most kids learned so much just by being with each other. "How come?"

"Father homeschooled me." And then under her breath, she added, "But only in things he found important."

"Like?"

She shook her head. They neared the court and Gaby stared toward Ann. More kids had joined her, and together they made a ruckus.

"She's a nice lady, isn't she?"

"I think so." As they got closer, they could both hear Ann's husky laugh. For some reason, it bothered Luther.

He didn't want Gaby to draw comparisons to herself.

"Thursday, at six o'clock, I'm coming by for you, Gaby."

"It's a free country."

Damn, but she could be so infuriating. "I want you to be there."

"If nothing else comes up, I will be."

Guessing that was the closest he'd get to a promised date, Luther matched his stride to hers. "Can I give you a ride back to your place?"

"I'll take a bus."

"I could drive you."

She stopped beside his car and faced him. "I'd rather

take a bus. I don't want to be around you any more today. You're better in small doses."

Luther propped his hands on his hips. If he didn't have a healthy self-image, he'd be demolished. "All right. But I meant it about Thursday, Gaby. Don't pull out your fists, but there really is no reason to worry about my plans. I promise you'll like it."

She made a face. "Yeah, well, I liked what you did in the alley, too, but it still worries me. A lot. So I'll have to think about Thursday. But I'll try to talk myself into it. I've never been on a date." She let out a breath. "Luther?"

"Yes?"

"Promise me you'll be careful, okay? I know I used too much sarcasm before, taunting you for getting taken off guard. But you really do have someone trying to hurt you, and regardless of any suspicions you might have, it's not me."

"I promise."

"Good." She tipped her head. "You infuriate me, but I'd hate to see anything happen to you."

Luther stood there, without words, and watched her leave him.

He wanted to believe her. He *did* believe her.

And that left him more concerned than anything else could have.

Chapter 14

Setting the ink aside, Gaby looked at her last drawing, a depiction of a crazed ghoul dying a deserving death under her hands. As a reflection of her current foul disposition, everything now appeared more intense, bigger, darker, and meaner.

Desire for Luther, foreboding of the strange new evil that taunted her, and rage over her helplessness in both made a strange elixir that Gaby had trouble swallowing. Her appetite had waned, she couldn't keep still, and she desperately wanted God to call her out, to give her the power to do something, anything, other than fret like an old woman.

But hour after hour, no call came.

Worse, with Morty dogging her every step, Gaby couldn't track down the mutant atrocity as she'd like. Twice, she had tried going back to the woods to investigate further the freakish happenings and turbulent apparitions festering there.

But shaking Mort proved impossible. Like a shadow, where she went, he followed.

Allowing him to befriend her had monumental repercussions. In the name of friendship, Mort now felt free to invade her privacy at will. Several times yesterday, he'd come to her door asking if she'd like a meal, a drink, a walk around the block. Twice today he'd done the same, lingering in the hall even after she'd barked orders for him to get lost.

No matter how she tried to dissuade him, Mort remained immune to her need for solitude.

If she sought peace with her thoughts on the front stoop, he joined her in the way of old familiar friends, with nothing much to say, content just to waste an hour together.

With sturdy locks now on the front door and all the windows, Morty even slept with his apartment door ajar—he claimed because the current circumstances had shaken him and he wanted to feel closer to Gaby.

She knew it was so that he could hear her come and go.

The dolt worried for her, and had some harebrained idea about protecting her, probably more from herself than anything or anyone else.

He suffocated her—but she wasn't hard-hearted enough to tell him so outright.

In fact, if it weren't for so much evil lurking, Gaby might have enjoyed Mort's persistent companionship.

To keep from taking her bad temper out on him more than she already had, she spent long hours at her desk, working on a new story. She wrote out her frustrations and illustrated her worries, and the newest volume in the graphic novel series turned out more powerful than any of the others had.

Being a paladin hadn't obliterated her more selfish vices—like pride. She swelled with it now as each picture and chunk of dialogue came together to create a compelling story of personal struggle, physical conflict, and ultimate triumph.

Writing and drawing throughout the night, she finished the piece of pure fiction in half the time it usually took her.

Having a creative outlet helped—except that Mort and the girl from the alley both showed up in key roles in the story, and the possible ramifications of that wouldn't do. Too many details could give her away, especially since Mort was her biggest fan. If anyone ever connected the stories to her, her goose would be not only cooked but eaten and digested, too.

She needed anonymous depictions, not factual ones.

Yet on top of Mort and the girl, Luther's role in the series also expanded into undeniable proportions.

Not that Gaby made the tough-as-nails angel of justice look anything like Luther Cross. As in most graphic novels, his character took on a larger-than-life appearance, with impossibly broad shoulders and an astonishing handsomeness made cruel by edgy determination and a sharp glint in his eyes.

He protected with one hand and wreaked devastation with the other.

The avenging cop in her series was everything Gaby wished the real Luther Cross could be. He saw the futileness of fighting something that had no real boundaries or moral compass, a mutation that could proliferate across families and into friends, could infest minds and bodies as well as souls.

But Luther wasn't that man. He was merely an above-average servant of the law with keen intuition, overwhelming kindness, and a belief in only what he saw and touched.

He'd never really believe in Gaby, not with the far-fetched realities of her existence.

Looking down at her hands, Gaby noted new calluses on her fingers and messy ink stains beneath her uneven nails. Assuming Mort would soon return with another song and dance about food or fresh air or whatever else the normal people in the world found helpful in times of stress, she stretched her back, rotated her head on her neck to remove a few kinks and, because she couldn't help herself, glanced at the clock.

Five-thirty.

Luther would show up in thirty minutes.

What to do?

Indecision chewed on the edges of Gaby's satisfaction. Finishing the graphic novel no longer sufficed as a freeing accomplishment.

Driven from her seat by self-loathing and the oppressive heat of the room, Gaby left her desk and moved to the wide-open window. No breeze stirred, but at least the exhaust-fumed air from outside didn't smell of ink and dust and disgust from indecision.

Gaby peered at the cloudless sky, the arid leaves on sickly trees, and the passersby milling in the street. Cars moved by in a blur of colors and the noise level rose and faded in an uneven cadence.

Across the street, she spotted a whore making lewd gestures at a passing group of young men. They returned her invitation with vile insults and kept going, uninterested in what she offered.

The whore didn't seem to mind. She walked a little farther and found another man to target.

He seemed more willing.

Curiosity struck a blow, obliterating some of the other disturbing emotions currently plaguing her. She made up her mind.

She had to get outside. Had to walk and think and . . .

investigate. If not the monsters, then something of more interest. Something equally at the forefront of her mind.

If Luther didn't want to wait for her, fine.

Good.

She wasn't at all sure she even wanted him to.

Anxious now that she had a purpose, Gaby went into the
bathroom to scrub her hands, cleaning them the best she
could. Some ink remained under her nails, so she used the
tip of her knife to dig out the stains. Haste made her ruthless and she nicked one fingertip, making it bleed.

Ignoring the small wound, she splashed her face to re-
fresh herself, pushed her hair back, and gave one cursory
glance at her very wrinkled and limp clothes.

So she looked like a used dishrag. Who cared?

She sure as hell didn't.

By the time Gaby finished with her meager ablutions,
the ink on the last pages had dried. She carefully stored
away the story where no one would find it. Tomorrow she'd
look it over, and if it still felt right, she'd get it postmarked
to Mort.

Mailing off a manuscript was the closest Gaby ever got
to eradicating a nightmare.

Mind made up and a lie prepared, she went down the
stairs in her normal noisy way. Mort's head poked out his
door.

Keeping her stony gaze forward, Gaby said, "No."

Smiling, he came out the rest of the way. "Hi to you,
too, Gaby. What are you—"

"No, Mort." Doing her best to block him from her peripheral vision, she kept walking.

"No what?" Barefoot, his hair mangled from an obvious
nap, Mort rushed after her.

"No, I don't need company." Gaby unlocked the door
and pushed it open. "No, you can't come along anyway.

No, I don't need your help." She had one foot out the door.
"No, no, no."

"But—"

"Damn it, Mort!" Impatient to be gone before Luther
showed up, Gaby swung around and backed Mort up to the
wall. "Shouldn't you be running the store?"

"I have a temporary kid helping out today."

Probably so he could keep closer tabs on her. Mort
loved his comic store and usually enjoyed running it.

But today, he didn't. So Gaby would have to use the
lie. "Remember that little girl from the alley?"

"Little girl?" Blinking fast, Mort nodded. "Uh . . . You
mean the lady you saved?"

Gaby hated how he put that, as if she ran around playing
rescuer all the damn time, when nothing could be further
from the truth. "She was a kid, Mort, not a grown lady. I
doubt she's out of her teens."

"Probably not."

"Well, I'm going to see her." Her chin went up, her eyes
narrowed in challenge. "All things considered, I don't
think she'll want any men hanging around."

"You know where she is?"

Gaby had no idea. Course, she had no real notion of
seeing the girl, either. She only needed to escape Mort's
watchful eye. "Not yet, but I'll ask around. I'll find her."

"It's not safe—"

Gaby went nose to nose with Mort. "I. Will be. Fine."
The words came out from between teeth clenched tight
enough to break.

"Okay, okay," he agreed quickly, hoping to mollify her.
"Will you pretty please just tell me how long you'll be
gone?"

Maybe if she'd ever had a mother, Mort's overbearing
nosiness wouldn't have been so annoying. But she'd never

had anyone be so officious, and it left her unglued. "And just how the hell should I know—"

"She won't be long," Luther said from the open doorway.

Gaby swung around to see him. He stared at her, and she felt so guilty she almost shrank away. As promised, he'd dressed casually in jeans and a printed T-shirt that read, THE MEEK SHALL INHERIT THE EARTH—AFTER I'M THROUGH WITH IT.

"Nice shirt," Gaby said.

"She won't be long," Luther said as he stepped into the foyer, "because we have a date. Isn't that right, Gaby?"

Groaning, Gaby seriously considered strangling Mort for holding her up.

Or maybe she'd let him hold her up.

Whatever. The ramifications of her delay sucked. She had Mort chafing behind her, and Luther provoking in front of her.

Without looking at either one, Gaby said to both men, "I'll be back when I'm back," and she shoved her way around Luther.

He let her pass, but damn it, Gaby saw the disappointment on his face, and she saw the damn gift bag in his hand.

A gift. *For her?*

Never in her twenty-one years had anyone given her anything before. What could it be? Gaby racked her brain for gift-type items, but she was as clueless in that as she'd been in other matters that involved normal people. She couldn't see Luther buying her clothes, and the small bag couldn't have held flowers or chocolates.

Even Luther wasn't lame enough to buy her any jewelry. Any fool could see she didn't wear it.

So . . . what?

Not that it mattered; whatever it might be, she couldn't accept it.

She didn't dare.

Legs stiff and stride maddened, Gaby went across the sun-baked blacktop street and down a few blocks until the apartment building was out of sight. The nerves in her face pinched and her eyes burned. They were unfamiliar feelings, and she didn't like them.

Heading toward an empty park bench, Gaby trotted on. She was too antsy to sit, so she dropped her shoulder against the metal lamppost in front of the bench, near the curb, and venomously crossed her arms.

The sun baked against her back, dust blew up on her toes, and she sulked in silence until she spotted a hooker. It was the same one she'd seen from her apartment window. The woman leaned into a car passenger window, and Gaby could see her thong underwear.

Disgusting.

The driver, pulled up beneath the shade of a large elm tree, kept the engine idling. Eventually, the hooker opened the door and climbed into the car. The man driving gave a quick look around, then adjusted himself—and pushed the woman's head down.

Gaby narrowed her eyes and, leaving the lamppost, crept forward. She looked up and down the street, darted around traffic, and gained the opposite sidewalk where the car idled.

Not bothering with discretion, she walked up to the driver's window and looked in.

❧

Irritated, irked, and angry, Luther watched Gaby disappear down the street. He wouldn't chase her down. He'd done that enough already.

Mort came up to stand beside him. "I'm worried about her."

"Don't waste your time."

"Can't help it." Hemming and hawing, his hands in his pockets, Mort said, "She's different, ya know? Most of the stuff she does isn't meant as an insult. It's just . . . she doesn't know any other way."

Luther sighed. "I know."

"You scare her."

Luther grunted.

"I do, too, I think, but I'm not sure. Might just be that I annoy her."

Glancing down at Mort, Luther felt compelled to say, "She's lucky to have your friendship."

"Nah. I'm the lucky one and I know it." He stepped back from the door. "You want something to drink? Some coffee? I can put on fresh. While it's brewing I can check the store to make sure the guy I hired is doing okay. It won't take me long."

"Sure." Luther came in and closed the door behind him. "Do you lock this during the day now?"

"Yep." Rattling a keychain that hung from a belt loop on his pants, Mort added, "Gaby and I have keys, but if she forgot hers, we'll be here when she comes back."

"If she comes back." Luther flipped the deadbolt.

"She will." Mort headed into his apartment. "She hasn't eaten all day. Sooner or later she'll show up for food."

Mort went about rinsing out the carafe and preparing more coffee. Luther drew out a chair. He put the borrowed graphic novel on Mort's table. "I finished it."

After glancing back to see what Luther meant, Mort grinned. "Awesome, huh?"

Interesting plotline and characters, to say the least. It

was a page-turner, an edge-of-your-seat reading adventure. The illustrations were incredible.

But on one level, elements of the novel had disturbed Luther. "I wanted to talk to you about something, but I need your promise you'll keep it private, especially from Gaby."

Mort went still, his hands hovering over the coffee machine, his shoulders stiff. Then he broke into inane chatter and nervous activity. "Yeah. I mean sure. Let me check the store first and we can talk when I come back."

He rushed off before Luther could decipher the crux of his anxiety. Surely keeping a secret from Gaby wouldn't send him into vapors.

And thinking of Gaby, as if he ever did anything else, what the hell was her problem?

While waiting for Mort to return, Luther simmered in his own discontent. How dare she rush off right before he was due to arrive? It couldn't have been more obvious that she wanted to avoid him, that she didn't intend to honor his wish to take her out.

Damned bothersome brat.

He should give her a taste of her own medicine and leave before she returned.

But she'd probably be relieved, not distressed, and damned if he'd do anything to assist her in her efforts to deceive him.

One way or another, he would figure out the elusive Gabrielle Cody.

Mort inched back into the room. "So." He cleared his throat. "Everything's fine at the store. Lots of sales today. Everyone loves a good graphic novel."

"Good. I'm glad your business is doing well."

Tension eased from Mort's shoulders. He went to a

cabinet and retrieved two mugs. "Want a cookie? I bought some at the bakery yesterday. I thought they'd tempt Gaby into eating, but they didn't."

"Tempt her?"

Mort filled the mugs. "She hasn't taken a meal that I know of in two days. I don't know how she stays on her feet."

"That's probably why she's so thin."

"Yeah." Mort set the mugs on the table and opened a drawer to get the cookies. "Probably why she's so surly all the time, too."

Luther indulged a cautious sip of the coffee before looking at Mort over the rim. "That's just her temperament and we both know it."

Grinning, Mort shrugged. "I suppose."

"And that brings us full circle. Can I have your word that you won't share what I have to say with Gaby?"

"Yeah, I guess. That is, I mean, she won't ask me about it anyway, right? She won't know that I know whatever you plan to say?"

Luther took his measure. "What's the matter, Mort? Are you afraid she'll beat it out of you if she knows?"

"She wouldn't have to. I'm a sucky liar. Guilt always shows on my face."

Luther flipped over the *Servant* novel he'd borrowed. "She won't know." He turned the comic toward Mort. "You say you've been reading these for a while now."

"Yeah."

"Haven't you noticed any similarities?"

"To what?"

Suppressing his suffering at Mort's obtuseness, Luther sighed. "To Gaby. The heroine in the graphic novel and Gaby share some unique personality traits."

"No way." Mort looked dumbstruck.

"Yes, way, Mort. Check it out." Luther flipped to a certain page. "I know she doesn't look like Gaby, but haven't you seen that exact expression on her?"

"Actually . . ." Mort drew the novel around and closer. "Yeah. I have."

Going out on a limb, hoping he could trust Mort, Luther ventured, "Do you think it's possible that Gaby emulates the character?"

Mort's jaw went slack.

"Maybe," Luther continued, "given her unconventional upbringing, she didn't have anyone to look up to, so she chose a fictional character."

"A kick-ass invincible character."

"Exactly."

"Geez. I don't know." Going back to the novel, Mort turned a page, then another. Eyes wide, he gazed up at Luther with crestfallen chagrin. "Anything's possible, I suppose.

"It would explain a lot."

Falling back in his seat, Mort slumped. "Yeah, it would." He rubbed at his eyes. "Only thing is, I've never seen Gaby read the series. I've never seen her read anything, really."

"That doesn't mean she hasn't."

"No. She's so damn private."

"So secretive," Luther prompted. "Here's what I want you to do."

"Do?" New alarm drew Mort back upright at the table.

"Relax. It's nothing to unnerve you." Luther cleared the table between them and leaned forward to engage Mort's confidence. "I want you to keep an eye on her, that's all. Especially when the next novel comes out. After you've read it, watch for similarities between the characters and things Gaby says happen in her life and how she reacts. If you notice anything, let me know."

"Oh." Relieved, Mort composed himself. "Yeah, I can do that."

"Great." Luther glanced at his watch. Gaby had been gone only fifteen minutes, but that put her past the time he'd set. He should leave. Just walk out the door and not come back.

But he knew he couldn't.

Some innate incorruptibility beneath Gaby's ballsy, indomitable exterior compelled Luther to keep chipping away at her defenses.

He finished off his coffee and stood. "I have to go, Mort."

"Go?" Mort rose, too. "But where? I thought—"

"I'm going to go find her."

"Oh." Mort followed him to the door. "She won't like that."

Luther grinned. "Yeah, I know."

"But you're going to anyway?"

"That's right." He dug a business card from his pocket. "Do me a favor. If she shows back up before I've returned, give me a call on my cell. But don't tell Gaby."

"If I told her, she wouldn't let me call you."

"Right." Luther clapped him on the shoulder. "Thanks for everything, Mort. You've been a big help."

Morty glowed beneath the praise. "Glad I could lend a hand." He leaned out the door as Luther went down the steps. "Luther?"

Luther turned back. "Yeah?"

"Gaby is a good girl and she has a really enormous heart. It doesn't always show, but it's there." He tapped the business card against his thigh. "To tell you the truth, she's the best person I've ever met."

"I know," Luther said, and oddly enough, he meant it. Then, as much to himself as to Mort, he added, "She's also the saddest. But I plan to change that."

Morty nodded. "Good luck, Luther. I have a feeling you're going to need it."

Chapter 15

The girl whined and sniveled, drawing forth a modicum of sympathy—but not nearly enough to thwart plans already in the works. The doctor tightened latex-covered fingers in her hair. Surgical gloves came in handy for hiding fingerprints, and adding extra traction to a grip.

"Don't you understand? Gaby Cody has to go before she ruins everything. And you're going to help me. Crying about it won't change anything."

Between meager, gasping breaths, the girl pleaded, *"Please . . ."*

The laugh came without humor. "You're beseeching me for pity?" The fist tightened, snapping off hairs, pulling at the scalp so that whimpers turned to hysterical squeals.

But here, deep in the woods, no one would know.

No one would come.

No one would care.

"Stupid child. Your wishes mean nothing to me. There

are grander purposes at play here beyond your pathetic
life."

"Oh God—"

A harsh slap cut off the prayer. "Enough."

As a red-welted handprint rose, the girl gulped down
her noisy pathos.

Uncaring if she understood or not, the doctor verbalized
concerns. "Attempts to get rid of the cop haven't worked—
because of Gaby. Instead of the officer keeping Gaby safe,
it was the other way around."

The doctor paced—and dragged the girl along with
each step.

"I need you to ensure that neither Gaby nor the cop will
breach my dedicated plans. They can't trespass where I
work. They can't hinder my sacred experiments." Stopping, the doctor drew the girl up. "They absolutely cannot
meddle with scientific medicine."

After Gaby had damn near blundered onto a disposal in
the woods, further experiments had been halted. It didn't
matter that the disposal had been necessary and right. Anyone could see that the cancer had run amok and decimated
all functioning brain cells.

But a woman like Gaby Cody wouldn't see it that way.

She wouldn't understand that the host body had become
too unpredictable, too loud and unstable.

Someone like Gaby, a simple woman instead of a brilliant doctor, would never accept that it was best—even
humane—to remove all life from the skeletal remains that
had once been a person.

Remembering infuriated the doctor to a dangerous de-
gree. Both fists tangled in the girl's hair, wrenching her
head back, sending hot salty tears to leak down her blood-
less cheeks.

"No more interference can be tolerated."

Wracking tremors coursed through the girl. "Okay," she whispered. "Please. I'll do whatcha want. I swear I will."

"Of course. I believe you." The grip softened. Fingers brushed the girl's pallid skin, moved over her quivering lips, swollen and damp. She was plump and round, with so much lush flesh to feed, to breed . . . In other circumstances, she'd have made a great addition to the experiments. "Hush now. Hush."

Sobbing, she didn't fight the doctor's embrace, and obediently put her head atop a comforting shoulder when guided to do so. "You're destined for great things, child. You'll be assisting in an exalted scientific breakthrough against diseases, a puissant force in the scheme of future life and death."

But first, Gaby Cody had to go.

"Now, listen carefully to what I want you to do. If you do everything exactly right, I might let you live."

The girl collapsed to her knees, nodding, sniveling.

"If you falter, if you in any way break from my instruction, I'll make you regret it more than you can even imagine."

Gaby watched the byplay in the car with interest. The guy had his eyes closed and his head back—and his slacks around his knees.

Huh. So this was what that rapist had hoped to do to the girl? Only the girl hadn't been willing, and this whore, given her squirming and enthusiastic slurping, categorically was. Her head bobbed and Gaby heard the most obnoxious sounds.

Her stomach lurched.

Then her muscles tightened.

Suddenly the driver opened his eyes and saw her. At

first, he went still with shock, and then in a flurry of motion he shoved the whore away and tried to readjust his pants.

Gaby barely saw him. Drawn inward, she focused on an increasing, familiar pain.

A calling.

Finally.

Just as the last few had, this summons came on her with the force of a tsunami. She needed privacy. She needed time to accept and welcome the anguish that would guide her.

Through the recesses of her mind, she heard the man shouting. "What the fuck is wrong with you, lady?"

Everything.

Gaby shook her head and managed to move her legs enough to back away. She could see, but only in tunnel vision, directly ahead of her, and what she saw was a very angry male who'd had his pleasure interrupted.

Tough. If he didn't back off, and quick, she'd lay him low by habit, and then the poor schmuck would know real agony. When Gaby put a man down, he tended to stay down for a while.

"Get lost," Gaby tried to tell him.

"You interrupted me, bitch. If you wanted to join, you should have asked. Otherwise—"

Gaby took one more step away from the fuming man, ready to brace for an attack

She bumped into something hard.

Something familiar.

Strong arms went around her. *Oh shit.*

"Luther?"

"Shhh. I've got you."

He really did. He had her hook, line, and sinker and she might as well quit fighting it. Even now, with Luther close, the pain became manageable. His effect on her was such that even in the grip of a calling, her vision expanded, her senses opened to her surroundings instead of her inward torment.

Somehow, some way, Luther clarified things.

Into the line of Gaby's vision came Luther's arm, muscles bunched, knuckles white. "You." He pointed at the man in front of Gaby. "Back off right now."

The man didn't. "Just who the hell are you?"

"Detective Luther Cross."

"Oh." The man backpedaled. "Hey, I didn't know. I was minding my own business when—"

His voice a mean snarl, Luther shoved him farther back and said, "Get in your car, *and drive*."

"Right. Sure." The man hesitated, eyeing Gaby with the same fascination he might give a strange animal in the zoo. "Is she fucked up in the head or something?"

Gaby would have flattened the man for that, but Luther reached for him first. Using only his left arm—because his right still held her—he hauled the man up to his tiptoes and rattled his brains.

Poor Luther. He seemed as much in the grip of an overpowering force as Gaby herself. Not wanting him to suffer the same lack of control, Gaby collected herself enough to stop him. "He's not worth it, Luther. You know that."

Luther paused. She heard his deeply indrawn breath, then watched as he shoved the idiot away, sending him to sprawl backward on the sidewalk.

Gaby smirked as the man scuttled up and into his car with prodigious haste. "Jerk."

Luther's hands cupped her face and he looked at her. "You're okay?"

Oddly enough, the pain blanched, then neutralized as if faded away. *Never* had that happened before. "I don't know. I don't understand."

Grim with rage, Luther caught her arm. "Come on."

"No." Gaby meant to shout it, but the word emerged as a breathless whisper. She couldn't just go. Something was happening—or had happened. Why else would she have had the call, only to have the summons ripped away?

Damn it, she wanted to fight. She wanted to be sent after the evil.

Regaining more strength by the moment, she wrenched her arm away from Luther.

He crowded into her and pushed her up against a parked truck. "Do you want to go at it right here, Gaby? Right now? With everyone watching to see? You want to kick my ass? Fine. Let's go, lady."

"What are you talking about?" Gaby didn't give a shit who watched, but surely Luther did. For crying out loud, he was an officer of the law. He couldn't go slugging it out with women in the street.

"I'm talking about me being fed up. With *you*. With all your crazy bullshit and the impossible runaround you put me through."

"I don't put you through anything!"

He leaned close enough that she smelled the coffee on his breath. "Either you come with me now, right now, or we settle it here."

Gaby bristled. "I'd demolish you."

"We'll find out, won't we?"

Damn it, she didn't want to demolish him.

"What's the matter, little girl?" he taunted. "Got something against public displays?"

"Actually, yeah. Someone is watching, someone not nice. Someone—"

"Evil. I know. Your arch nemesis." He half laughed, saying, "A villain of monumental proportions."

Hurt squashed all other comments. He ridiculed her. Finally. Gaby knew it would come, but . . . she had hoped it wouldn't.

"No, Luther. There's no one." Gently, she pressed against his chest. "I'm ready to go if you are."

So frustrated that he shook with it, Luther leaned away.

Gaby stepped around him.

"Where are you going?"

She didn't look at Luther. She didn't dare. If she did, she seriously thought she might cry. "Back to my apartment." She waited for him a few feet away. "That's where you wanted me to go, right?"

"Gaby . . ."

"It's all right." She couldn't bear to hear his excuses. "You don't have to say anything."

"Goddamn it."

That got her frowning. "Don't blame God for your bad behavior."

He was so quiet that Gaby couldn't not look at him. She turned her head—and there stood Luther, his head down, his middle finger and thumb pressed into his eye sockets.

He looked to be in so much pain that Gaby softened. What did it matter if he thought her a joke? That just made him normal. Lucky him. "C'mon, Luther. It's all right."

"No, it's not." He strode up to her. "Here."

He held out the gift bag. How the hell had he hung on to that in the midst of everything else? "What is it?"

"Open it and see."

She looked around, and sure enough, they'd drawn the attention of a few people. Two men stood in front of a liquor store, watching them. The abandoned hooker sat on the curb, gazing in their direction. An old gray-haired lady looked out her second-story window.

"Not here."

"Okay." Luther put his hand at the small of her back and urged her forward. "Let's go."

"Back to my apartment?"

"No. To my car."

Dread slowed her step. "Luther, if you're still wanting that date—"

"Just shut up and walk, Gaby. I have some things to say to you."

"Fine. Whatever."

Luther stopped, put a fist beneath her chin to elevate her face, and kissed her.

That kiss renewed her. The second he pulled away, she missed him.

"Every time you smart off, I'm kissing you."

Regaining her wits, she said, "I wouldn't recommend it."

"I'm on to you, Gaby. You don't want to hurt me."

She snorted.

"Admit it. You boast about all the damage you can do, but you don't really want to do it." He laced his fingers in hers. "Not to me."

"Obnoxious, conceited—"

"Correct. Intuitive. Astute."

"All *right*," she said, cutting him off. "So I don't want to hurt you."

"Thank you."

"But if you push me hard enough, I will."

During their exchange, they'd covered a lot of ground and Gaby found herself in front of the apartment building.

Luther said, "Here's my car," and he opened the passenger door for her.

Feeling like a freakish Cinderella, Gaby climbed in and put the gift bag in her lap. Luther waited, and when she just looked at him, he leaned in and fastened her seat belt—and kissed her again.

"Stop that!"

"No." He shut the door and circled the hood. After he got behind the wheel, connected his own seat belt, and started the car, he said, "Now."

Gaby looked at the gift bag, thinking he meant for her to open it.

Instead, he said, "I'm sorry."

She just looked at him.

"Very sorry. I know you think I was making fun of your assertions that evil exists, but I wasn't."

"Whatever."

"Gaby." He leaned over and, again, caught her chin. "This morning, I got called to a foster home where the children were kept in cages. Then this afternoon, I had to investigate a shooting at a convenience store. The robber had the cash, was almost out the door, but turned back at the last second and shot the cashier in the head—just for the hell of it. She was a mother of a toddler and she died."

"I'm sorry."

Luther nodded. "I know evil exists, Gaby. I know it's out there, in unimaginable proportions, twisted in ways that I don't want to think about but can't deny. There are depraved, corrupt, ugly crimes committed every day, against men, women, and children. The lack of morals, or any sane description, devastates me, but I still have to deal with it."

Gaby had nothing to say to all that. "You didn't believe me."

"Actually, that's not it." He put the car in gear and pulled away. "I was just frustrated. You know, for a change, I wanted to see you have as much intensity directed at me as you always have focused on pursuing some evil incarnate."

Rage simmered. "You were . . . *jealous?*"

"A real kicker, huh?"

"That's pathetic!"

He worked his jaw. "Tell me about it."

Damn it. Gaby twisted to stare out the window. Scenery passed in a blur. Her thoughts cramped. Her heart ached. "I'm sorry."

"I have no idea if you mean that or not." How could he know when she jumped around so much?

Reaching for his thigh, Gaby said, "Luther? I am sorry. But I can't help who I am."

"Sure you can." His hand covered hers, keeping it on his thigh, flattening her palm there. "Let me in, Gaby. That'd be a start."

No, it'd be an end. To him.

She couldn't tell him so. She'd hurt him enough already. Once she settled things here, when the evil was destroyed, she'd slip out in the quiet of the night.

That'd be best for everyone.

Gaby pulled her hand away. "Do you want me to open this gift or not?"

"Yeah, go ahead."

She pulled the bag open and peeked inside—and saw a small rectangular machine with wires coming out of it. "It plays music, right?"

"Yeah. It's a digital audio player."

She lifted it out. "I've seen people walking around with these plugged into their ears."

"I took a chance," Luther said, "and saved a bunch of songs into the memory for you. I hope you like them."

Speechless, Gaby just looked at it. Then, unable to help herself, she fiddled around with it until she got it on and could listen. Rambunctious beats vibrated through the machine with incredible power. "Wow."

"You like?"

She found a natural rhythm and bobbed her head to the music. "Yeah, I do."

He smiled. "There's another gift in there, too."

"More?"

"Go on. Let me know what you think."

Unnerved by his generosity, Gaby again rummaged in the bag, digging below the pretty tissue paper. Her hand found a box and she lifted it out.

"Don't get pissed," Luther said. "Let me explain first, okay?"

Hearing that got her irritated right off. "What did you do?"

"Nothing. And it's not symbolic. Just . . . something that I thought would look right on you."

Oh God. He hadn't. He couldn't have. Gaby opened the box and found that, in fact, he had.

"A necklace?"

"A choker. The black leather is very you," Luther teased.

Her brows pinched down. "There's a silver cross."

"Not to ward off evil, I swear. Just because it's pretty." He reached over and trailed a finger down her cheek. "It reminds me of you."

Gaby went speechless.

"The leather choker is edgy and sexy. But the cross is so small and delicate—and regardless of your feelings on the matter, it represents good."

Gaby could only stare at him. "And somehow that matches your image of *me*?"

"Yeah." He kept glancing between her and the road. "Do you like it?"

Actually . . . "It is pretty, I guess. But not too pretty."

"It was made by a local craftsman to my specification. So there isn't another one like it anywhere."

Great. That'd mean if she wore it, it'd be as identifying as a scar or noticeable tattoo.

And maybe that had been Luther's purpose all along.

But for right now, Gaby wanted to pretend otherwise, she wanted to believe that he'd given her both gifts because somewhere in the depth of his soul, he actually liked and understood her. "Thank you."

"Will you wear it?"

Shrugging, Gaby wrapped the leather around her throat and connected the link in back. She tucked her hair behind her ears and turned to face Luther. "Well? What do you think?"

His gaze caressed her. "I think it looks even sexier on you than I imagined."

"Yeah, well I think you must've been too long without or something, because you've got sex on the brain big-time."

"Me? I'm not the one who was ogling a hooker giving a blowjob in a parked car."

Gaby went rigid—until she realized Luther was teasing. Then she relaxed again. "It was educational."

"But also revolting?"

"Pretty much." She idly ran her fingers along the music player dials. "It wasn't at all as nice as when you'd described it."

"Right." Luther cleared his throat. "Time to change the subject again."

"Or you'll get hard?"

"Exactly." Luther pulled up to the curb and put the car in park. He took a few seconds to compose himself, then turned off the engine and pulled out the keys. "We're here."

Gaby looked out the window. They were in front of the theater.

Granted, it was a cheapie, run-down theater—which suited her, but still . . .

"They only play old movies, and this is one I really like."

"The Big Easy," Gaby read on the lighted display. "Never heard of it."

"Cop show. Well, about dirty cops. But Ellen Barkin is a favorite of mine. She's super-sexy in this role."

Gaby scowled over that disclosure. "I've never been to the theater."

Glancing her way, Luther opened his seat belt. "I figured if you hadn't watched much TV, you probably hadn't taken in movies either. This place is low key and relaxed, but they have fresh popcorn and a variety of candy and colas, so I thought we'd start with it. If you like the experience, we can try stadium seating at a nicer place with a first-run movie next time."

Next time.

Luther made an awful lot of assumptions. But then, she'd admitted so much to him, how could he not?

"This place is fine." Or at least, better than the alternative he'd just described. She wasn't the type of woman who fit into "nicer" places.

Gaby started to open her door, but Luther got there before she could.

Though she didn't need it, he helped her out and took the music player from her. "You clip it onto your jeans like this."

Heat and age had curled the denim waistband so that it rolled out away from her skin. Going under her shirt, Luther slipped his fingers inside the waistband to attach the player. His skin was warm, his touch firm, and suddenly Gaby realized he was looking at her.

She didn't meet his gaze, but chose instead to watch his fingers. He drew his hands up, opening his palms against the bare flesh of her waist. His big thumbs nearly met over her navel.

"You are so slender."

"You mean skinny," she said, noting the thickness of his wrists, the sprinkling of hair on his arms.

"Mort said you haven't eaten."

"Mort needs to mind his own damn business."

Her surliness must have broken the mood for him. He shook his head and said, "Come on." Luther pulled one hand away, but left the other there in a casual embrace against her bare skin as he led her into the theater. "They serve burgers, too. We'll both get one."

To Gaby's surprise, her stomach growled, making Luther chuckle. "I guess I'm hungry after all."

"That's what I thought."

They went straight to the concession stand. Above the scent of popping corn, it smelled of grease and salt and onions. Gaby's mouth watered. She was suddenly so hungry, she didn't even argue when Luther paid for their bounty by himself.

Laden with burgers, fries, drinks, popcorn, and candy, they made their way to their seats. Only two other couples were inside, and the lights were already low, the previews already playing.

"This is kind of creepy," Gaby whispered as she paused in the dark, unsure where to go.

"Relax. Eat. Enjoy." Luther chose seats for them in the back, in a corner. As Gaby got settled, being careful not to spill anything, he whispered, "This is the make-out corner."

The flickering screen lit his face, showing his wolfish smile. "Really?"

He laughed. "I thought that'd get your interest. In fact, I wouldn't be surprised if lust hadn't been consummated here a few times."

Eyeing the folding seats, Gaby asked, "Is that even possible?"

"Very. It just takes a little ingenuity."

"And you have loads of ingenuity?"

"Right now, yeah. But I want you to enjoy the movie and the food, so we'll put off this discussion for another time."

Just like Luther to get her curiosity roused, then shut down. "But—"

He kissed her. "Shhh. Watch the movie." He settled his arm around her and, as if he'd read her thoughts, added in a whisper close to her ear, "After the movie, I promise, we'll pick up on the conversation again."

Oh. Well then. She supposed that'd be okay. "I'm holding you to that." With that declaration made, Gaby settled back in her seat, propped her feet on the seat back in front of her, and absorbed the unique experience of watching a movie on the big screen.

Chapter 16

When the credits began to roll, Gaby roused herself from her lethargic pose and mellow mood. Wow. Never had she felt so peaceful, so . . . outside herself and her annoying insights. Who knew a little dose of unreality could be so relaxing?

Theater lights flickered on, pushing away the darkness. She turned to Luther only to find him studying her. "What?"

Rather than share her mellow disposition, an earthy appetite intensified his hard-edged allure. "I like seeing you like this."

"This?"

He looked at her mouth. "Soft."

That got her back up. "I'm not. Ever."

"Yeah you are, Gaby," he insisted, and his gaze dropped somewhere below her chin and above her knees. "In lots of places."

Gaby snorted. "Now you just sound corny." But he didn't. Not really.

Luther smiled, ready to say something—and his cell phone buzzed in his pocket. Resigned, he settled back. "Damn, I'm sorry. But even off duty, I need to take this."

While he lifted out the phone, Gaby stood and let her seat fold. "No problem."

Into the phone, he said, "Hello?" He listened, frowned, and a second later, his gaze settled on Gaby again.

"Hang on, Ann." Covering the mouthpiece, he searched Gaby's face. "I need to take this in private."

So he could talk to *Ann*. Gaby's lip curled. "Yeah. Right." She made no attempt to hide her scorn. "I need some fresh air now, anyway." Shoving past him, she said, "I'll be hanging out front."

"You won't wander off?"

Like a halfwit? Or a child? "If I decide to leave, I'll tell you first." As she walked away, she heard Luther snarl something, then go back to his conversation on the phone.

Grumbling her way through the theater lobby, Gaby shoved open the front doors and stepped out into the drowning humidity.

She paced.

Up one side of the sidewalk and then back again. Disgusted with herself, she dropped down to sit on the dirty curb and stared at her feet.

Jealous.

That's what she was. And stupid. *Real* stupid.

Why should she give a damn if the detective liked Ann? It wasn't as if the two of them had any future together, anyway. And no one in her right mind would expect Luther Cross to play in celibacy. Not long.

Gaby was deep into her own misery when from somewhere to her left, a small voice said, "Hi."

Jerking her head around so fast that she almost gave herself whiplash, Gaby eyed the girl—the one she'd told Mort she wanted to see—standing on the sidewalk behind her.

"You!" Gaby couldn't credit such a coincidence. Hell, she didn't believe it. No way.

What did it mean?

Overly cautious, the girl inched closer. "You remember me?"

"Course I do." Cleaned up and without the blood and tears, something recognizable remained. It was in her eyes, some world-weary cynicism too deep for one of her young years.

What stumped Gaby most was the soft yellow aura enveloping her in a loving embrace. The color of mental ability and great purpose seemed out of place on one so . . . misguided. The girl probably had no idea yet of the important role she'd play in life.

Hopefully she'd realize it before it was too late.

Today, she wore a super-short denim skirt and a pale pink T-shirt that hugged her body too closely, showing off details better left undiscovered.

With an eerie foreboding, Gaby gave the girl a questioning look.

The high, chunky wooden heels of her sandals clunked on the sidewalk as she shifted. "You live around here?"

Thoughts moiling, Gaby chose a deliberate, casual pose, relaxing her spine, propping her elbows on her knees. "Not too far away. You?"

"Not really." The girl eyed the spot beside Gaby. "You mind if I join ya? My feet are killin' me."

"It's a free country."

"Not really, it ain't." The girl sidled up and carefully lowered herself to the curb. "Not for girls like me."

"Like you?"

"Yeah, you know. A whore. Alone and poor and stuff." She stretched out her legs and wiggled her dusty toes. "I've been walkin' and walkin' for hours, it seems."

She sat so close that Gaby inhaled the stale odor of overused cologne, sweat, and sex. Nose wrinkling, Gaby eased away a few inches. "What's your name?"

"Bliss."

That had Gaby's eyes rolling. "You going to tell me that's your real name?"

"No." Bliss picked at a tiny scab on her knee. "But it's pretty, don'tcha think?"

"I suppose." Gaby also supposed she wouldn't get the truth from the girl, so she didn't bother trying. What she called herself didn't really matter. Not in the bigger scheme of things.

What did she want? "I'm Gaby."

Bliss nodded, let out a long sigh. Attempting an overt friendliness, she shook back her hair, folded her hands in her lap, and smiled at Gaby. "I usually hang out with Rose, but I haven't seen her for a couple days now."

"Rose?"

"Another hooker."

The smile shrank away.

The idle hands grew fidgety again.

"She's my friend. My only friend, I guess. I was lookin' for her down this way, and that's when I saw you."

So much worry hung in Bliss's words, Gaby had to ask. "Where did your friend, Rose, go?"

Rounded shoulders lifted. "I dunno." She stared away. "I'm thinkin' maybe she got tired of me hangin' around."

Sympathy wrestled with Gaby's natural sense of caution. Something wasn't right, but she couldn't put her finger on it. "I doubt that's it."

"Well, she used to come lookin' for me at nights, almost like a momma would."

Bliss's bottom lip quivered, but Gaby sensed it wasn't so much with sadness as with fear.

"Sometimes," Bliss whispered, "if'n she wasn't workin' she'd even let me stay with her."

"Rose has a house?"

Bliss gave her a look of incredulity. "No."

"An apartment then?"

Arms wrapped herself, Bliss shook her head—and couldn't meet Gaby's gaze. "Most of us on the street jus' look for a place out of the weather, where cops won't trip over us. Rose found a place in the woods."

"In the woods?"

"Yeah. Me and her sometimes stayed there, in this old abandoned place. That's all."

Old abandoned place. The pieces—the conspiracy—began to click together. "Where, Bliss?"

Something in Gaby's tone made Bliss withdraw. "We didn't break in or nothin'."

"Where?"

At Gaby's stern voice, Bliss jumped and looked at her with accusation and hurt and . . . more fear. "It's an old hospital or something."

Oh God.

"It stinks real bad, and it's sort of scary." Bliss swallowed hard. "Do you believe in ghosts?"

How could she not? She'd destroyed many of them. "Of course." Gaby looked back at the theater door, but there was no sign of Luther. "Listen to me, Bliss. You should stay out of those woods, and you should definitely stay away from that hospital."

"But . . ."

"It's scary because disordered, rancorous spirits possess it."

Bliss's eyes went round. "Spirits?"

Nodding, Gaby said, "Not just spirits from the deceased either. The average person has such a fairy-tale perception of evil. They think energized emissions come only from those who have passed."

"You mean from dead people?"

"Exactly. But that's not the case. Not always." Gaby visualized the isolation hospital, the way it had made her feel, and she almost shivered. "Definitely not the case with that place."

"You're scaring me, Gaby."

"Good." Maybe she'd heed Gaby's warning and stay away from the hospital. "Dead, alive, sick, tormented, and tortured spirits stir the air all around that place. It's wicked, and treacherous."

In awe and worry, Bliss stared at her. "You've been there?"

"Yeah." Gaby had to make the girl understand. "Malevolent discarnates overrun that hospital and the grounds around it. Not just the dead, Bliss. But spirits of deranged people, desperately unhappy people whose circumstances have adversely affected their behavior."

Bliss whispered, "So you're sayin' there's live people there who'd wanna hurt me?"

How could the girl be so stupid? "Exactly. They might not be consciously evil. They could be confused, desperate, unaware of how their actions hurt others. But that makes them no less dangerous for someone like you." For someone like Gaby, it was a whole different story. "Promise me you won't go there again."

"I . . . I never wanted to go there in the first place. And now without Rose . . ." She chewed her lips. "But that's what I was gonna say to you—what if somethin' happened to Rose? What if she's there and hurt and I'm too chicken-shit to check on her?" Big tears spilled over Bliss's painted lashes, leaving muddy tracks on her cheeks. "What if them spirits have her is why I ain't seen her?"

It amazed Gaby that one person could look so pitiful and pathetic. Against her better judgment, with warning bells going off all through her system, Gaby said, "Don't start sniveling on me, okay? I'll go there to look for Rose."

Relief nearly melted Bliss over the curb. "You'd do that? Really?" She wiped at her eyes—and in the process removed some of her makeup, too. "When?"

That's when Gaby noticed the lingering bruises. The girl had not had an easy life. Maybe that's why, despite her wariness, Gaby felt an affinity to her. "Right now, if you want me to."

"Now?"

"Yeah." Luther could damn well talk all night to Ann, since that seemed his intention anyway.

"But . . ." Again looking away, Bliss shook her head. "If you go right now, and Rose ain't hurt, she wouldn't be there."

"No?" Gaby's eyes narrowed. "Where would she be then?"

Bliss drew away a little. "Um . . . Could be she's just mad at me or somethin' and maybe that's why she's not around."

Gaby saw the deception in every line of Bliss's body. "So now you think she's unhurt?"

"I dunno. Maybe. I'm just sayin', if she's not hurt, this time of night she would be workin'."

The cloud of conspiracy thickened—but that didn't de-ter Gaby. For whatever reason, she felt she needed to fol-low Bliss's lead, to carry out the plan. "Okay, Bliss. So if you don't want me to check on Rose now, then when should I?"

"I . . . I dunno." Nearly choking on the words, Bliss turned away. She fretted with the fringe off the end of her denim skirt. Misery weighed her down. "Oh God, I'm so sorry."

Gaby tilted her head. "You apologizing to me or Him?"

"What?" Bliss floundered in confusion. "No, I . . . You was so nice to me, and you already helped enough."

"But?"

Firming her resolve, Bliss drew a deep breath and blurted, "I shouldn't be dumping all this on you. I know that. But I . . ."

Don't have a choice, Gaby silently finished for her. Someone had coerced the girl, likely with threats either to her, or to a friend . . . perhaps Rose.

For once, Gaby put aside her suspicions and reached out to take Bliss's hand. "It's all right." And she meant it. Everything would be all right. Even a conspiracy. "Tell me when I should go."

Eyes squeezed shut, Bliss whispered, "She'd be most likely to be there tomorrow night." She drew a broken, shuddering breath, and whispered very low, "Will you please be careful?"

"I always am."

At that firm statement, Bliss opened her eyes again. She looked at Gaby, and some of her upset abated. "You will, won'tcha? You'll be real careful and everything really will be okay."

"Yeah." It'd be fine for Gaby, and hopefully for Bliss. But for the restless spirits—from both the dead and the tormented—hell would make some claims.

With a new calm about her, Bliss tried a small smile. "There's a lot of buildings by the old hospital. You need to go to the one with graffiti on the walls. That's the place. Rose might be in there, on the first floor."

"So specific." Gaby shook her head at the easily thwarted plan. Definitely a scheme. And not a very bright one. "Any particular time tomorrow?"

"After dark, but before midnight."

"That's when you and Rose would hang out there?"

"Yeah." Appearing more relaxed, Bliss said, "I remember how you fought that guy in the alley. You was like a superhero or a ninja or maybe both." She gazed at Gaby with adoring eyes. "I never seen nothin' like it."

"I know."

"You saved me, so you should be able to save yourself, huh?"

A verbal slipup, that. "Yeah, I can save myself." Taking a chance, Gaby said, "I'm sorry I couldn't save Rose, though."

Bliss started to nod, then caught herself with a sharply indrawn breath. She reared back in fear and shock, looking around the sidewalk. "I gotta go. I shouldn't have sat here talkin' so long."

"It's all right." They both stood, and Gaby said, "Go on. But Bliss?"

"Yeah?"

"Be careful tonight, okay? Stay out of the shadows and alleys. Stay where there are people."

"I will." Bliss turned—and ran into Luther.

He caught her arms, but looked beyond her to Gaby. "Making friends?"

Well hell. For a minute there, Gaby had forgotten all about him. "Bliss and I are already acquainted."

"Bliss, huh?" Luther's expression sharpened and he looked at the girl with new interest. "Is that so?"

Seeing Luther sent Bliss into a terror and she bolted

away in a run made more graceless by those hideous sandals.

Frowning, Gaby watched her disappear around a corner; utilizing her crazy intuition, she knew Bliss would be okay. She dismissed any worries and instead put her mind to figuring out the treachery that had been awkwardly presented.

"Let me guess."

Gaby recalled Luther's presence. "Don't bother. She's the girl I helped the other night."

"The girl who was there when you stabbed her attacker."

"One and the same."

"And somehow, she just ran into you here?"

"Actually," Gaby said on her way to his car, "I think she was looking for me."

Luther beat her to the door and opened it for her. "To thank you?"

"Not exactly." She seated herself, reached back to adjust the knife in the sheath so it didn't gouge her spine, and then waited while Luther studied her.

"What exactly?"

Impassive and unprovoked, Gaby stared up at him. "What did Ann want?"

He sighed—and slammed her door. When he got behind the wheel and had the engine humming, he said, "I can't tell you."

"Ah." Gaby propped her feet on the dash. "So it was something all sugary sweet and intimate, huh? I understand." She was probably better off not knowing. "That's not the sort of a thing a man like you shares, I guess."

"Actually, it was business."

"Sure it was." With any luck, she'd annoy him as much annoyed her.

"Ann is a detective, too, if you'll recall." He jerked the car into drive. "She had some information for me, and no, I'm not telling you what it is because I don't want you involved."

Gaby shook her head at his absurdity. At this point, there was no way for her to be uninvolved—but Luther wouldn't accept that. "You know, Luther, for a little while there I stupidly thought that we'd be able to work together. I see now that I was wrong." She put her head back and relaxed. "You don't trust me and I sure as hell don't trust you."

"You don't, huh?" He curled the fingers of his right hand over her slim thigh and, steering one-handed, pulled out into traffic.

"Well . . ." Awareness of his touch, how hot he felt, how electric, moderated her tone. "Maybe I'd trust you with some things."

"I figured." With a gentle pat, Luther withdrew.

Jerk. "But not *business*."

Hands flexing on the wheel, Luther said, "Look, it's police work and has nothing to do with you."

"Bullshit. It has to do with that doctor at the hospital, or those cancerous monsters, otherwise it wouldn't matter if you told me. And if that's the case, it's very much my business."

He glared an accusation at her.

"Yeah, too bad I'm not an idiot, huh?" Gaby folded her arms. "All right. Let me take a stab at guessing."

Visibly frustrated, Luther growled, "Don't bother." He flexed his hands again, then gritted out, "Ms. Davies's body is missing."

Gaby's feet hit the floorboard in shock. "You're shitting me."

Now his hands squeezed the steering wheel tight enough to crush it. "I wish, but no. Somewhere between the hospital and the crematorium, she vanished."

"Crematorium?"

"Apparently that's how she wanted things."

"But now her body is gone." Gaby's thoughts scrambled at the enormity of such a thing. "How could something like that happen?"

"With cover-ups, I'm guessing. A poor old woman with no family and no friends . . . who would normally notice?" Luther glanced at her. "Except you."

Uh-oh. Luther had that leery, take-apart-her-psyche look again. He didn't appear angry so much as . . . curious.

And curiosity about her was never a good thing.

"Lucky guess on my part, that's all. The minute I heard Dr. Marton talking about the patients, and heard what the nurses and Dr. Chiles thought of him, I figured something was up. Any fool would have put it together."

"No, Gaby." Luther reached for her hand. "You have a gift, a special intuition and a deeper perception that few people possess."

Luther had a way of making compliments sound like accusations, and vice versa, to the point that Gaby never quite knew how to take him. "If you say so."

"It scares the hell out of me because you've also got a stubborn streak and a save-the-world attitude." He gave one shake of his head. "It's going to get you into trouble one of these days."

Busy mulling over the entangled complexities of a dead body missing from the cancer ward, Gaby barely listened. It would be damn hard to smuggle out a corpse. Surely, there had to be endless paperwork and . . .

What if Ms. Davies wasn't dead at all? What if she'd only gone into a coma? Had the doctor forged results, maybe even with specialized drugs? Would Ms. Davies be-
the next ghoulish demon, covered in those awful

Or had she died, and the doctor only hoped to use the cells from her cancer-eaten body?

Gaby's thoughts churned in a hundred different ways. Without realizing it, she withdrew her knife; the weight of it in her hand helped her think and steadied her resolve.

Perhaps the doctor knew that people were on to him, and he felt cornered. Gaby didn't have a single doubt that Bliss's request for her to go to the isolation hospital played into these new developments.

Now all she had to do was figure out why.

Did the doctor hope to set her up as the culprit?

Did he hope to use her to make Luther back off—as if she had that type of influence on him? Ha!

Or did he only hope to force Gaby off his trail so he could more easily deal with Luther . . . which would mean it was Luther who was ultimately in danger?

"Put that knife away. If I hit the brakes for any reason, you're liable to stab yourself."

"Or you?" Gaby looked at his strong, proud profile, and made up her mind.

Fuck waiting until tomorrow, or until God sent her.

She'd go to the hospital tonight. She'd catch the foul doctor and circumvent his plans and somehow, some way, she'd keep Detective Luther Cross safe.

With that decision, a small, piercing pain penetrated her soul. Ah. It hurt horribly—and felt good.

God was with her on this after all.

Biting back any signs of discomfort, she whispered to Luther, "Don't worry, I've yet to have an accident with my knife." But she did reach back and slide it into the sheath—out of sight, but close to hand.

"Gaby?" Luther cupped a hand around the back of her neck. "What's wrong?"

"Nothing." *Everything.* The pain didn't expand, but it

niggled on her unease, a hard reminder that her time was never truly her own. At any moment, in any situation, when she might least expect or most want it, she could be called upon to destroy.

That fact made any conventional relationship inconceivable. Caring about Luther meant protecting him from the evil of the earth. Nothing more.

"You look . . . upset."

Gaby eased a hand over her midsection, where the burning reminder of her purpose throbbed. She shook her head. "I'm fine."

Luther snorted. "You know, Gaby, it makes me very uneasy when you take your thoughts private."

It made *her* uneasy that he seemed to know her so well and felt free to touch her with so much familiarity. "I was thinking."

"That's what worries me."

"Worrying is for old women," she snapped. She turned her head toward him. "What are you going to do now?"

He gave her a quick glance. "That's what you were stewing on for so long? Not what you'd do, but what I'll do?"

Gaby stared right at him, giving him no reason to surmise duplicity on her part. "Why should I do anything? You're the cop, aren't you?"

His eyes narrowed, and he released her. "Funny that you'd only remember it now."

Knowing Luther's plans was crucial. If he had any clue about the isolation hospital in the woods, she'd be hard pressed to keep him away. But given what she planned to do, what she *had* to do, running into Luther would be catastrophic. If he witnessed her in action, if he saw how easily she took life, he'd lock her away.

And without her to help balance things, evil would have sovereignty.

She couldn't risk that.

"Make no mistake, Luther." The steady clutch of discomfort roughened her voice. "If I see corruption in progress, I will take care of it."

"Here we go."

Gaby spoke over his long groan. "But I'm not going to play sleuth and do all your work for you. Earn your pay, damn it. Find that missing corpse."

"I plan to."

"Good. And once you do, you'll also figure out how Dr. Marton managed all this."

Neither or them denied that Dr. Marton had to be involved. There'd be no point now.

"I'll talk to him."

"Fine. But until then," Gaby stressed, "I don't think there's much I can do." She raised a brow. "Now is there?"

Chapter 17

Luther didn't buy a single second of Gaby's act. She was good, but he'd already figured out that when Gaby seemed most sincere, she had ulterior motives. This time her motive was to dupe him into thinking she intended to stay uninvolved.

He wasn't that stupid.

Especially not after seeing how she held that knife—with intent to use it.

Familiar, tender, with love and barely restrained eagerness.

She had plans to use her knife, and soon. He had no doubt.

Gaby was a woman who *had* to act. By whatever strange force possessed her—and he had a feeling it possessed her right now—she had skill and amazing ability, and *not* using those attributes would be as contrary to her as not breathing would be to him.

She remained silent, maybe even . . . stoic, on the remainder of the drive. He didn't like it. She had a pinched look about her that she tried hard to disguise, but he knew her too well.

How he knew her so well, Luther couldn't say, but almost from the onset he'd been keenly attuned to her. Right now she was separate from him, drawn into herself by some odd suffering that he couldn't comprehend.

Even after he parked and got out, she didn't budge a single eyelash. At least, Luther noted with a smile, she'd conceded to his courteous tendencies.

But then, given how she started when he opened the door, he decided she'd only been too involved in her own ruminations to give him a second thought.

Gabrielle Cody had the uncanny ability to put him entirely out of her mind.

If only he could do the same with her.

Eyes vague with an indefinable emotion, she got out of the car and started past him.

Realizing that she didn't even plan to say good night, Luther stood there in amazement.

At the last second, Gaby caught herself and, with her back to him, paused. She looked over her shoulder and, *really* seeing him again, gave him a thorough once-over. She came back.

Solemn and sincere, she stared at him. "The movie was great." A distinct lack of enthusiasm belied the sentiment.

"I'm glad you enjoyed it, Gaby."

Her gaze went to his mouth. "Thanks for the digital audio player, too, and the food, and . . . everything." She licked her lips, and in that instant, a veil of pain lifted from her expression.

She wrapped her arms around his neck and planted a wet one right on his mouth. What she lacked in finesse, she definitely made up for with enthusiasm.

Luther's hands automatically went to her waist. Drawn in by her, he turned his head a bit for a better fit and dragged her closer.

Standing in front of her apartment, he was very aware of the people milling around them on the sidewalk and the likelihood of Mort stepping out at any minute.

At least, for about two seconds he was that aware.

When Gaby licked over his lips, he opened for her—and lost all sense of time and place.

Luckily, she had more willpower.

Pushing back, she stared at him. "What do you plan to do now?"

Luther's thoughts tried to pull together without success. "About?"

Her eyelids twitched; her pain had returned. "The body." Typical of Gaby when she wanted to hide something, she jutted out her hip in attitude and quirked her mouth. "The corpse."

Seeing her like this, so determined to bear her woes alone, made a missing corpse almost inconsequential to Luther. Concern brought his brows together. "I'll take care of it."

"How? Where will you start? Are you going back to the hospital tonight?"

An ugly suspicion tamped down on his lust. Hands still on her waist, Luther back-stepped her against his car and leaned in to impose his will. "Did you kiss me just to get information from me?"

Her droll look of annoyance *almost* amused him. "So now you're accusing me of being a femme fatale? What are you, an idiot?" A very fine trembling coursed through her body. "Do you even realize how stupid that sounds?"

To halt the rapid-fire insults, Luther smashed two fingers over her mouth. "All right. Then why did you kiss me?"

She slapped his hand away. "Because I like kissing you. If you didn't want me to, you should have spoken up and said so."

Luther wasn't sure, but she sounded convincing enough. "I like kissing you, too. But you have a lot to learn about the etiquette of kissing."

The insult infuriated her beyond measure. "Fine. I'll try to get some lessons in before I bother kissing you again."

Luther knew she said it to hit a nerve.

He knew she baited him.

And still, his temper struck a high point. "We already had this discussion, Gaby." Struggling to keep his voice low and moderate, Luther stepped back from her. "Anything you want to learn, you'll learn from me."

She shoved her face in close to his. "I'll practice anywhere, with anyone I choose."

The thought of her with another man rattled him so fiercely that he might have lost it there and then. But as Gaby spoke, she went through that peculiar transformation again.

The skin around her eyes tightened; the hue of her irises grew brighter, her pupils bigger. Beneath the pale skin of her throat, frantic energy palpated.

Her scent was stronger, more captivating.

Though the actual physicality of her body didn't change, her strength was more defined to the naked eye.

In the usual course of things, Gaby looked like a ragtag, bedraggled beanpole of a girl.

At this moment, Luther saw an Amazon able to take on the world.

To gentle her, calm her, he brushed the backs of his fingers along that wild pulse beat in her throat. "You're very soft, Gaby."

The razor-sharp essence thawed. Her eyes focused; her lips compressed. "You're such an ass."

Glad to have her back, Luther smiled. "Yeah, I know."

"You need to find that missing body."

"Yeah." Running a hand through his hair, Luther decided it was past time to get back on track. He glanced at his watch. "Ann is meeting me at the hospital in a few minutes."

Gaby's expression went flat. "Well, whoopee for you. I'm sure you two will have a grand old time."

It felt odd to fix an emotion like jealousy to a woman like Gaby.

Odd, and exhilarating.

"We'll be working, Gaby. I already told you, there's nothing personal between us."

"Like I care."

"You care." Where Gaby was concerned, Luther felt certain of very little, but that much he knew. He kissed her again before she could dispute his claim. "I can do my job more efficiently if I know you'll stay out of trouble tonight."

She stared him in the eyes and said, "I always stay out of trouble."

That steadfast gaze gave him pause. If she had hoped to convince him, she accomplished just the opposite.

"Now." Gaby shoved him back. "Stop dawdling and go do whatever it is cops do to solve heinous crimes before more heinous crimes happen."

Turning to lean on the car, Luther crossed his arms and watched her retreat. He saw the discomfort in her usual graceful gait, the rigid way she held her shoulders. "Want me to come by later and tell you what I find?"

"Tell me in the morning." She kept on walking, over the sidewalk, up from the front steps, and to the door. She dug out a key. "It's late, and I'm tired."

Now he knew she lied. Gaby wouldn't admit to a weakness of any kind, not even exhaustion. "I'll be keeping an eye on you, Gaby."

"From the hospital?" She stepped inside and turned toward him to say, "Good luck with that."

The door shut with finality, and Luther took only two seconds to make up his mind. Finding a corpse and solving a crime was important. He wouldn't neglect his obligations and duty. But she was right—he couldn't very well watch her from so far away.

And she definitely needed supervision. She needed protection.

Whether she wanted to admit it or not.

Retrieving his cell phone, Luther put in a call to Ann.

She answered on the first ring. "Detective Kennedy."

Luther circled the hood of his car and got in. "It's Luther. Where are you?"

"At the hospital. Why?"

"Something's come up—"

"You're telling me." Ann's voice rose with agitation. "I tracked down the paperwork on our missing remains. Are you sitting down?"

"Do I need to be?"

"Oh yeah. Brace yourself, because I just know you're going to love what I've found."

Dread filled Luther. "Let's hear it."

"The signature authorizing a cremation was forged. Seems that's not what our Ms. Davies wanted at all."

The dread turned to anger and disbelief. "Shit."

"Yeah. A nurse broke down and told me some things she'd seen and heard, so I checked. This is definitely not the same signature. I already sent two uniforms over to the crematorium to talk to the staff. In another day or two, they could have claimed she was already cremated, and who would know different? Ashes are ashes, right?"

"It'd be an easy cover-up—with someone working at the crematorium."

"Exactly. Someone there had to be in on this."

"That'd make sense. The doc forges the name, someone else pretends to get the body . . ." Sickened by such perverse deception and corruption, Luther rubbed his forehead. "So the big question now is: where's the body?"

"I don't know that yet, but I did talk to Dr. Marton." Ann gave a heavy pause. "Luther, he's not the one who forged the signature."

Not Dr. Marton? So Gaby was wrong about that. "You sure?"

"Positive. Not only did I rule out Marton, but I'm putting my bets on someone else entirely."

Something in Ann's tone clicked. Luther straightened in his seat. "Wait a minute. Are you saying . . ." His brain almost cramped with the possibility. "Dr. *Chiles* did this?"

Disgusted, Ann said, "That's right, big boy. The sweet, little, soft spoken *female* doctor is as sick as they come."

"Holy shit." But . . . it made sense, in a twisted, shot-to-hell way. No one suspected her. She was so far from obvious that she'd get by with murder—literally—and no one would look at her twice. "Goddamn it!"

"Yup." Satisfied with his reaction, Ann said, "Now all we have to do is find her."

"She's not at the hospital?"

"And not at her home address. The good doctor is AWOL."

Luther looked at the front door of Gaby's apartment building. He recalled the altered state of her appearance, the rigidity of her posture.

He put the car in gear. "I know how to find her."

"You do?"

"Yeah. I'll get back with you." Going on a hunch, he disconnected the call and pulled away from the curb. If Gaby knew he waited on her, she wouldn't budge from the apartment. He'd show a little patience, share a little belief.

And Gaby would lead him to the doctor.

❧

Breath hitching painfully, Gaby barely got in the door before Mort was there.

Oblivious to her state, he smiled and asked, "How was your date?"

Striding past Mort, all but blinded by her purpose, she headed toward the basement steps. "It wasn't a date."

"It wasn't?"

Unlike anything she'd ever experienced before, a terrible premonition hung over Gaby. She felt the summons, clean and pure, and ripe with pain.

Yet a sense of doom veiled her. Writing it off as the interference of too many other people, Gaby shook her head.

She knew better than to get involved. "Leave me alone, Mort."

Of course, he followed her.

Damn it, she did not have the time or patience to chat with him tonight. "Okay, fine, it was a date."

Halfway down the stairs, she realized Mort was right behind her, and she turned.

Mort almost fell into her.

Hands fisting and brows pinched, Gaby glared at him. "Go back, Mort."

His easy camaraderie faded to nervous energy. "Back . . . where?"

"Upstairs. Away from me. *Out of my way.*"

"But . . . Why?" He looked her over with grave trepidation. "What are you doing, Gaby? What's happened?"

"For crying out loud." Gaby rubbed her tired eyes and tried to decide how to send him packing. She'd been stupid to let him get so close, to let him think he could question her and tag along at will. The inner turmoil built, reminding her that she had a job to do. "Look, I'm going out, and no, you don't need to know where. It doesn't concern you."

Sparse brows rose high, showing bloodshot blue eyes half concealed under his shaggy brown hair. "Which means you think it's too dangerous for me?"

"I don't think it, Mort. I *know* it."

"Oh." Visibly tamping down on his fear, he straightened his scrawny frame. The amateur tattoo on his shoulder looked even more absurd with his attempt at bravery. "I'm going with you anyway. You might need backup."

"No, I won't." She flattened a hand on his bony chest and gave him a decisive shove.

He stumbled, almost fell on the steps, but caught himself. "Gaby?"

Belief in her purpose cauterized any regret she felt for attacking him. "I managed to live twenty-one years without your help, Mort. I think I'll be fine one more night."

"God only knows how you've managed."

"Yeah," Gaby agreed, "He does."

"Oh." Mort gave a sickly frown—and turned to pleading. "Let me go with you, Gaby. Please? Even with divine intervention, you're not invincible."

Fool. Gaby looked heavenward. "Forgive his ignorance. He doesn't realize Your influence."

Giving credence to that claim, the internalized smoldering

of power heightened, making her faster, more agile, and Gaby leaped down the remainder of the stairs with ease.

"You're staying here, Mort, and that's that. Don't argue with me, and don't even think about trying to follow me." She gave him one quick glance. "I guarantee you'll regret it."

"Wait." The rapid thumping of Mort's descent on the stairs echoed behind her. He dogged her heels as she went to the laundry room to judge the distance to the small casement window that someone had recently used to sneak in. She'd fit, but just barely.

For once, her slight build was a blessing.

Dredging up an image of Dr. Marton, she surmised that he must have hired someone to vandalize them. The big doctor never would have squeezed his bulk through such a small opening.

While Gaby dragged over a broken chair and hoisted herself up to reach the lock, Mort asked, "What are you doing?"

"Taking a back way out. Regardless of what I always say, Luther isn't an idiot—and neither am I. I won't underestimate him."

Trying to see her face, Mort circled to the side of her. "What does Luther have to do with this?"

Gaby opened the newly installed lock and shoved the window wide. "If I try to leave through the front door, he'll follow me."

"Why?"

"Because he doesn't trust me, that's why." The dominant perimeters stretched, inflating her abilities, making her teem with energy.

Setting her every nerve on fire.

Soon she'd be sick with the potency of it—but she welcomed the physical intrusion, knowing that she'd made the right choice and that God would be with her on all she did this night. He'd guide her, and as she'd told Mort, he'd keep her safe. In turn, she'd keep Luther safe, and hopefully Bliss and Morty. Because of her, they'd be able to continue in their secure little world.

It was the others, the evil involved, who had reason to fear. Not Gaby.

"Once I'm out, lock this and leave it locked. I mean it, Mort."

"I don't want to be alone here, Gaby." Hands shaking and voice weak, he admitted, "I'm scared."

Busy judging the size of that window, Gaby said, "Be a man, damn it."

"Why don't you be a friend?"

Stunned at the outburst, Gaby turned and caught Mort in her sharp-eyed glare.

He put a hand to his head. "Jesus, Gaby. While you're off hunting down one monster, another could be hunting for you. *Here*." He held out his hands in entreaty. "What if one of those things shows up and I'm the only one around? I can't fight like you. I'm not as brave as you. I don't—"

Pushed by urgency, Gaby leaped off the chair and grabbed Mort's shoulders. While evil threatened, she knew better than to concern herself with one individual.

But this was Mort.

And he was . . . a friend.

She had to find the most expedient way to placate him. "I promise you'll be fine. I know these things, Mort, remember? But if it makes you feel better, there's a gun in my room. You can hold on to it until I get back."

A rush of color leached from his pallid face. "A . . . a gun?"

"I keep it tucked away in a special box in my bedsprings.

Go on up and get it. It's already loaded, and the safety is off, so be careful."

He shrank back. "But . . . I've never touched a gun."

Damn him for holding her up. "You aim and shoot. That's all there is to it. A couple of bullets will stop anything, even monsters. Just try not to hurt yourself, okay?"

"Maybe you should take it with you?"

"No." Again, Gaby bounded up onto the chair. "It makes too much noise, especially in the woods."

"Woods?"

Her vision fluctuated, going inward. Only with an effort did she clear it. "I'm out of time, Mort. If you want to help, go out front and see if Luther is still hanging around. If he is, make sure he doesn't trail me."

Sounding more sick by the moment, Mort asked, "How am I supposed to do that?"

"Talk to him. Keep him busy. Pretend I went upstairs to bed."

"You want me to *lie* to him?"

He made it sound like corrupting the innocent would be the worst of her crimes. "Fine. Don't help. But at least back off and let me do what we both know I can do!" To keep from having it snag on the narrow sill, Gaby removed the knife and leather sheath and held both in one hand. "I'll be back before you know it."

"Right." Misery etched every line in Mort's face. "Bloody and dazed and sick."

"Maybe. Now shut the window behind me." Weapon in hand, scraping her arms, nape, and spine in the process, Gaby wiggled out. Luckily, Mort kept the back lane mostly cleared, so there weren't any broken bottles to cut her on her clumsy climb from the window.

The window dropped shut behind her, and she heard the latch snap into place.

Churning motivation kindled through her veins, pushing her, urging her to haste. With only moonlight to guide her, Gaby went to the alley that connected the lane to the street, and peeked out. Streetlamps left a yellow glow on the hot pavement and concrete.

Making note of ordinary things outside God's command wasn't easy, but she managed to scan the area for Luther. She saw no one, but she wasn't one to trust mere eyesight anyway. Just because she didn't see Luther didn't mean he wasn't there.

Before the twisting ache took complete control, Gaby needed to make some headway. She needed to put a lot of distance between her and anyone who might detain her.

Ducking back out of sight, she reattached her sheath and with the familiar nudge of her blade at her back, crept two blocks down along the back lane. Moving in near silence, she went right past a druggie who didn't notice her and sidled by two thugs in deep conversation.

Once she'd left the apartment building behind, she cut toward the street. Staying in the shadows, she broke into a fluid run. It was dangerous, being here in the open where someone could try to interfere. But with each second that ticked by, the exigencies of the moment sharpened.

Events took place—with the doctor, with Luther . . . perhaps with her. Under His influence, Gaby could only decipher her purpose, not the why of it.

The pain became a ravenous craving, gnawing on her soul, obliterating all things peripheral. Surroundings faded away to nothingness. They held no import, not when God had need of her service.

And yet . . . a tiny worm of awareness remained, squiggling through the agony.

Please, she pleaded in small blips of sentient awareness, *keep Luther safe.*

Watch over Morty.
Guard Bliss.

Not physically with her but still right *there*, in her thoughts and spirit where she couldn't forget about them, these people afflicted her mind. She could literally see Mort, so beaten down and sad that she'd left him behind.

And Luther, ripe with suspicion and an overpowering protectiveness.

And poor Bliss, scared and young and alone—trusting her . . .

Go away, Gaby silently screamed to those emotional phantoms. She had a job to do, a job they couldn't understand, things they couldn't fathom.

The warring of her duty against her emotion made her ill. Too many people concerned her. Too many people had gotten past her shields, dividing her attention, causing her to fight the pull, weakening it and her.

To block them from her mind, Gaby concentrated on the agony, visualizing it as a live thing, red-hot and fierce within her.

She wouldn't stumble; no never that. She'd just suffer—and keep going.

Without thoughts of her *friends* to lead her into deadly errors.

Losing all concept of real time, she reached the face of the looming hospital structure. The moon cowered behind thick gray clouds. Distant streetlamps couldn't illuminate through the humid air. An aura of monstrous proportions bloated from the area, pickled with black holes indicating imbalance, muddy with evil, gray with depression.

For those who saw auras, the warning couldn't be clearer.

For those who fought evil, it didn't matter.

Single-minded in her purpose, without looking around

to check for witnesses, Gaby forged beyond the fog of con-tamination and plunged into the black woods. A gust of wind surged behind her, bowing trees, parting shrubs, cre-ating a bold ingress to her goal.

She blended with the shadows, moved with the night sounds. Undetectable. Agitated but inconversable. As much a spirit as those restless apparitions swirling round her in a maddened frenzy.

Oblivious to the thorny twigs that snagged her skin and the jagged stones that dug into her exposed toes, Gaby prowled deeper.

At the corners of her consciousness, images of both Luther and Morty tried to intrude.

No. She snuffed them with ruthless determination and pushed ahead. Farther and farther into the woods.

She would do what she must, and thoughts of them would *not* hinder her. Yet the more she tried to barricade them from her mind, the greater her agony became. A few shaky steps later, the effort of blocking them took out her knees, and she stumbled.

Confused, Gaby crawled upright and took two more steps.

Her lungs squeezed, making her gasp for each breath. She strangled, unable to go on.

What the fuck was this?

The agony tore into her, more ruthless than anything she'd ever experienced. She doubled over, stunned, disordered—and then she heard it.

Laughter. Moaning. From the doctor and the victims.

And worse: lumbering footsteps from her left. Eyes closing, Gaby curled in on herself. She didn't have to see the intruder to know who it was. Opening herself, she felt him, saw him, *knew* him.

Morty.

Oh God, no.

Now it made sense. She couldn't block him, because he wasn't just a troubling thought. The idiot had followed her after all.

And now, he very well might die.

Chapter 18

Morty's footsteps halted, and he whispered loudly, "Gaby?"

Collapsed on her side, moist dirt on her cheek and a multilegged bug nearing her ear, Gaby wet her lips. Her eyes burned and her heart ached for the possibilities ahead.

She had no one but herself to blame. She'd been greedy, wanting what she couldn't have. Father Mullond had told her many times that friendship was beyond her. It put her and others at risk. She had God's duty, and that should have been enough.

Idiot. Selfish, greedy fool.

But castigating herself would solve nothing. She had to put the pain aside and find some logic in this absurd situation.

Summoning great strength, Gaby struggled into a sitting position. The torment was so unbearable that she decided she'd kill Morty herself if he survived this. Through teeth clenched in pain, she said, "Shut the fuck up, Mort."

He went quiet—and crashed toward her. "Thank God."

Doing what few could, Gaby compartmentalized the pain and got to her feet. Her fingers dug into Mort's arm, hard enough to leave bruises that would linger for weeks.

"You will go back," she ordered. "Right now."

"No. I can't." Both his hands wrapped around her wrist, but he couldn't pull away her steely grip. "Gaby, please. I wouldn't be able to find my way out if I tried."

They were too close to the target. Morty might not hear it, but the sonance of inflicted misery clamored against her eardrums in a deafening roar.

The suffering of others made her ill.

She had a choice to make, and she had to choose the others. Mort would be on his own.

"Suit yourself," she said, and by sheer strength of will, she got her legs moving. Though she stumbled along like a zombie, Morty failed to keep up with her, and that suited Gaby fine.

She reached the isolation hospital with Morty trailing several yards behind. Eyes flinching, Gaby withdrew her knife and studied the graffiti-covered walls.

Bad premonitions vibrated from that structure.

In such close proximity, her highly attuned ears captured the perspicuous torment. Gaby found a jagged opening in the edifice by way of a boarded-up window. Termites had eaten through the broken wood slats. A rusted nail pulled free.

Holding her knife hilt in her teeth, sweat trickling down her temples, Gaby hoisted herself up to the ledge and looked inside. Oblivion greeted her. A great crepuscule of misery.

Then, as she stared with unwavering patience, a flicker
of light in the distance caught her attention. Gaby used
care as she brought a foot up to the ledge and levered herself into a sitting position on the treacherous sill.

A flashlight would have been a blessing, but she didn't
dare, even if she had one. She would see what she needed
to see, as God meant her to see it.

That's how it had always been.

Turning so her back faced the room, she slowly, inch by
inch, eased down into the chamber. When she dangled by
her fingertips and could still feel nothing beneath her, she
gave in to trust and dropped.

Breath held, she fell for a few seconds and then landed a
few feet lower with jarring impact. Her elbow collided with
a hard edge, but she felt no added pain. Something toppled,
metal clashed, and a cacophony of sound echoed garishly
throughout the room.

Gaby froze, but just as quickly turned to assess the
damage.

Nothing moved. No one stirred.

The faint light was gone.

To use her intuitive sight, she had to have something
to see.

Giving her eyes time to adjust to her tenebrous surroundings, her heart time to stop pounding, she waited.

As she quieted, another impression of Luther formed in
her mind. Big and strong. Honest and good. Rather than
discard the image, Gaby studied it, and saw woods surrounding him, a woman at his side.

Flashlights. Followers. Weapons.

The images of Luther possibly had significant meaning.
If Morty had followed her, Luther might have followed
him. He could be very close by.

Not that it could stop her.

Gaby opened her mind to her duty and knew what to do, where to go. As the blind might, she felt in front of her with each step and slowly dragged her feet to avoid stepping on anything sharp.

Shadows, made more vague by her perception of evil, indicated larger obstacles. Metal shelves. Tables. Objects cluttered the rotted floor, making progress sluggish. Somewhere outside, she heard Morty again whispering her name, and Gaby prayed she'd finish before he found her.

A light glimmered for an instant before snuffing out.

Ah. A tease. A taunt.

The doctor didn't realize that God guided her through such ridiculous stunts. True surroundings seldom entered into her navigation. She moved by premonition and divine persuasion.

Grasping the knife tightly in her hand, Gaby went toward the light with anticipation.

Like a trail of bread crumbs, the nictitating illumination drew her out of the large room and down a broad corridor. Gaby's every step wrought a screech of protest from warped, moldered flooring. Like thready tentacles, cobwebs reached out to her face, sticking to her hair, tangling in her eyelashes.

A thick haze of dust choked her nostrils.

There, at the end of the corridor, a narrow line of light near the floor indicated an illuminated room beyond the door.

Gaby saw only a trap.

Whoever had led her here did not want her to reach that room.

Feeling behind and to the right of her, she verified clearance, flattened herself to the wall, and waited for proof of her suspicions.

Seconds later, a rush of wind passed close to her face as someone tried to attack her with a thick, blunt weapon.

Perfect.

So fluid it was imperceptible, Gaby countered the missed attack with a rapid slash of her knife. She kept the thrust agile, clean, meaning to wound, but without throwing herself off balance.

Her aim was perfect.

The blade sank home in spongy flesh, caught for a single breath of time against muscle and sinew, and then sliced a slick path before breaking free.

The deep gouge spilled forth a flood of blood, filling the air with the acrid scent of death. It spurted into the air, over Gaby and the walls and into those annoying cobwebs.

Shock sucked the air from her victim, then gave strength to a horrified, high-pitched scream that spurred hair-raising wails from others close by.

The corridor exploded with weak howls and pain-filled shrieks, overlaid with the thumping of heavy furniture and metallic clashes reminiscent of the raucous, fearful frenzy of animals caged in a zoo.

Doing her best to tune out the disturbing caterwauling, Gaby sidled down the wall several feet and went stock-still.

She trained her ears on the quieter sounds, the whisper of a small movement and the hushed rush of painful breathing.

The approach of evil.

Energy moved past her to the door where most of the noise emerged. As it pushed open, light spilled into the corridor.

Gaby opened her eyes and, with God's guidance, she faced the bogeyman.

❦

Deep in the woods, mud clinging to his shoes, sweat and humidity gluing his shirt to his spine, Luther flicked the flashlight beam around the area. Swarms of mosquitoes followed

the light, hungry for new blood. As far as he could see, tree trunks loomed like endless specters in the dank night. Eerie silence, but for the sounds of crawling creatures, mocked him.

He had to admit he'd gotten lost. "Damn it, Mort," he whispered low, "where did you go?"

Beside him, Ann breathed heavily and for the fifth time asked, "Are you absolutely certain we're on the right track, Luther?"

"Yes." He wasn't, not anymore, but he said, "I saw him come this way. I'm sure of it."

"There's nothing here," she complained. "Only poison ivy, hungry insects, and—"

Horrific screams carried through the woods, piercing the silence, rustling the brittle leaves.

The fine hairs on Luther's nape rose.

Beside him, Ann whispered, "Dear God in heaven."

Gaby. Luther shoved Ann behind him. "Backup should be here soon. Call in, then wait."

"Forget it. You're not leaving me here alone." She tangled a fist in the back of his shirt.

Luther didn't argue with her. Holding the flashlight out front, he broke into a run. He tripped twice over twining roots, taking Ann down with him. On his way back up, he cut his elbow on something disgustingly wet.

"Go," Ann said, reassuring him in the least amount of words that she was okay.

"Keep up." Losing sight of Morty was his first mistake—an error that could prove fatal. He didn't want to put Ann at risk, too.

As she hustled along behind him, Luther heard her talking into her radio. In the center of the dense woods, the cells couldn't get reception.

Crashing through the underbrush, shoving aside spindly

tree limbs, he moved as fast as he dared. It no longer mattered if Mort knew he'd been followed. It no longer mattered if Gaby might be guilty.

Guilty or innocent, he wanted her alive.

In the distance, he heard the sirens of approaching cars. Almost at the same time, an awful stench, one he'd smelled before, choked him.

It was the smell of blood—and rotted flesh.

Something awful had happened here.

And somehow, Gaby was involved.

Expecting a monster of hideous proportions, Gaby instead witnessed the fearful limping of a wounded human, slumped against the wall, barely staying upright. Not a large, powerful man, but a woman.

A small woman.

Confusion kept Gaby immobile.

It didn't work like this. God showed her the heart of the demon, not the mortal body. The only time she'd ever seen beyond the haze of duty was . . . with Luther near her.

Oh God, oh God . . . Gaby looked behind her, but saw no one. If Luther did lurk nearby, she still had time.

Thank you, God.

Not yet daring to look into that room of torture, Gaby said to her victim, "You can't escape."

The woman turned her face, and all thought gelled.

Dr. Chiles.

The soft-spoken doctor. The defender of the indigent patients. The trusted one.

It suddenly made sense: The duplicity. The conniving. The ability to get close to Rose.

Only a slender woman would fit through the basement window of Morty's apartment building.

Dr. Chiles was both skilled enough to do deranged, sick, perverse experimentation on ailing cancer victims and inconspicuous enough with her gentle appearance to escape a brutal crime scene without drawing suspicion.

Furious with herself, Gaby cursed low. More than anyone else, she knew the unpredictability of evil. It didn't follow a pattern, didn't fit a profile.

She'd been sloppy. *Unforgivable.*

Ungluing her feet, Gaby tightened her hand on her knife and stepped away from the wall. "You deserve everything you get today."

"Freak!" the doctor railed at her, her voice barely audible above the commotion from the adjoining room. She pressed a hand hard to her side. "Look at what you've done, at all you've ruined! How will I continue my work? How will I find the cure?"

Her work. Teeth locked, Gaby glanced into the yawning space ahead. What she saw repulsed her.

Frankenstein's laboratory would look like a posh hotel in comparison to the makeshift lab the doctor had erected. Kerosene lanterns illuminated filthy glass jars overflowing with rotted flesh stacked on shelves, boxes, and crates.

Pilfered equipment, including instruments that could cut, saw, and clip, littered a section of sheet-covered floor.

Crawling with cockroaches, discarded food containers, blood-soaked rags, and soiled clothing cluttered each corner.

A half-dozen crude beds, made from cots, gurneys, and splintered boards, showed signs of unbelievable cruelty. Gaby made note of the thick straps, the raw rope and wires meant to restrain the bodies, and her skin crawled.

Only two of the beds were empty.

"You sick bitch."

Blood pulsed and gurgled from below the doctor's left

breast, drenching the clichéd white coat, the pale blue scrubs, in sticky crimson. "How dare you insult me? Some day soon my work will produce a cure, and then the world will hail me."

Gaby shook her head. "You will never work again." Numb from her heart to her brain, she trailed after the doctor, metering her pace the same, stalking her. It wasn't easy, not with her perception of the desolated people around her, but she kept her focus on the doctor. "Tonight you die."

Doctor Chiles stumbled forward into the room and dragged herself between two rickety beds occupied by patients of indiscriminate age, in various stages of cancerous decay. At the intrusion, the wretched souls roused enough to lament their fates.

Their movements emphasized the doctor's debauched experiments. Exposed, bloody tumors riddled with pulsing veins, rough scabs, and blackened lesions, adhered loosely to sagging, puckered flesh. Faces, bodies, limbs—the cancer grew over all parts of the bodies.

Clutching her side in awful pain, Dr. Chiles demanded, "Look at them." As she spoke, she continued to inch away, keeping a distance between herself and Gaby. "They're the scourge of our earth, a waste of humanity. For years, they defiled their lives and the lives of those around them."

"I know." Gaby saw it all, the contaminated pasts and iniquitous souls. "Right here, right now, it doesn't matter."

"They're all alone," Dr. Chiles insisted. "No one cares what happens to them."

"I care."

Pain turned the doctor's lips white. "Damn you, I've given them purpose. Through me, their lives will have meaning."

Beside Gaby, a man with sunken eyes mostly hidden by great globules of cultivated growths gave a pitiful moan.

Gray, paper-thin skin lay over protruding bones. Without words, he pleaded.

He wouldn't live much longer, but every second brought him immeasurable agony.

At Gaby's other side, a hairless woman jerked and flailed in futile rage. With each movement, a monstrous sac on her midsection recoiled with a life of its own.

Turning a slow circle, Gaby saw more of the same—until her gaze landed on the pile in the corner.

Decomposing bodies, overrun with maggots.

Failed experiments.

Patients whose usefulness had run out.

Knowing she'd allowed this to happen, angry tears burned Gaby's eyes. She wanted to kill the doctor now, this instant.

But as she breathed in the stench of decay and desperation, absorbed the misery in the frantic auras, their anguish became her own. The insurmountable burden bowed her shoulders and wrenched her heart.

She needed to kill them. All of them.

But for the first time, God made sure she saw things clearly . . . even through her blurring tears. They were all evil, and all human—capable of great suffering.

Gaby sensed the doctor moving toward her, along with other bodies. She recognized the danger, felt the encompassing evil.

Ready to fulfill her duty, she poised herself—and a gunshot rang out. The misfired bullet hit the wall, sending out a spray of splintered wood and plaster dust.

Shaken from her discipline, Gaby spun around and there stood Morty, shoulders back, chin up, arms straight out with the gun gripped tightly.

He took aim again and Gaby glanced behind her to see the doctor advancing, her lip curled in rage, her eyes hot with hatred. In her blood-soaked hand, she hefted a long surgical blade as lethal as Gaby's own knife.

The room echoed with the blast of another resounding shot. The doctor's body jerked at the bullet's impact, then crumpled to the ground, felled by a gunshot wound to the side of the face. No longer recognizable, Dr. Chiles now resembled the monster Gaby had anticipated.

Morty crept up beside her. "Oh God, Gaby. She's dead, isn't she?"

"Looks like." In the gray ugliness of the room, a blue glow floated around Mort. On the outermost reaches of the aura, the blue was quiet and calm, but closest to Morty, nearest to his heart, it shone rich and deep, indicative of a man who'd found his work in life.

Gaby couldn't quite credit Mort's transformation.

"Oh God," he said again. Trembling, he lowered his hands and gazed around the room in horror. "I'm sorry, Gaby."

"For shooting her? Don't be." Gaby had no regrets there. But now for the rest of them . . .

"No, I meant . . ." He swallowed hard. "Luther's not far behind me. Right before I came in here, I heard him in the woods. He's not alone."

Gaby tried to order her thoughts, but it wasn't easy. She had to contend with her ability and duty, and her own human emotions.

"He must have followed me," Mort rushed to say, "and there's no way he didn't hear those shots. He'll be in here any second."

"Which is why I avoid guns." Drawing in stale, odorous air, she forced herself to think. Luther's proximity no doubt had much to do with her altered state. His singular effect on her threw off her balance, robbed her of a much-needed edge.

She honestly didn't know if that was good or bad.

Either way, it was all too much, too discrepant from the bizarre reality to which she'd grown accustomed. Her stomach revolted and she clapped a hand over her mouth to keep from puking.

Mort's voice tottered with fear, further bewildering her. "Gaby!" Looking beyond her, he stumbled back.

She followed his line of vision and saw two of the poor creatures, armed with crude weaponry probably used by the doctor to inflict her experiments, now descending on them. Rubber tubing trailed from one stooped soul, while remnants of torture discolored the other.

They both had the same bulbous fingertips and toothless, slathering mouths she'd seen before.

The doctor must have cut them loose before she attacked.

Vociferating in excitement and panic, they lumbered forward, starting a frenzy with the others who didn't understand. The noise grew deafening.

Disheartening.

In that moment, Gaby made up her mind. They all needed to die. Thanks to the doctor, they were barely human anymore. Their black souls, now disoriented with sickness, frightened by chaos, and maddened from pain, made them dangerous—especially to Morty. Besides, anything other than death would only cause them more cruelty.

Grabbing up the surgical tool from the doctor's limp hand, Gaby handed it to Mort. "Cut them all free."

"But . . . !"

"Do it, Mort. But be careful. Stay out of reach." The order had barely left her mouth before the first monstrosity fell against her, awkwardly stabbing. Gaby sidestepped, turned, and sliced cleanly across the throat, cutting the carotid artery. She shoved the pitiable creature aside.

The other reached out, and Gaby sank her knife into its

heart, twisted, and dragged it out again. The body dropped hard to the ground.

One by one, she dispatched the tormented souls.

Without God's intervention.

Without His purer vision.

She saw them all for what they were, and though she had a paladin's power, she acted out of her own conscience, not divine instruction.

One of the more weakened patients offered no more than garbled pleas—for a cessation of suffering.

Gaby made his death quick and painless by cutting off life support. She severed IV tubes and disconnected an oxygen tank.

"Luther will be here soon." She sensed it. But by the time he and his fellow officers ordered medical care, the bodies would be at peace.

"Go," Morty whispered to her, his voice barely audible over the now blaring sirens. "Find a back way out. If Luther catches you here . . ."

"He'll arrest me," Gaby finished for him. She had always understood that. "What about you?"

From a distance, Luther shouted, "Gaby! Where are you?"

"Go," Morty begged. He waved the gun at her. "There's a door at the back of the room. Go through there. Find a way out. I'll stall him."

Still she hesitated, unable to make the decision—unable to abandon him.

Morty hauled her close and gave her one bumbling kiss, startling her senseless. His aura burned bright with determination. "You're important to the world, Gaby. You have a purpose. You have to be free to do what you can." His crooked smile wavered. "And finally, I think I found my purpose. For once, I get to be the hero. Now *go*."

"Gaby!" Luther's voice echoed down the corridor. The beam of a bright flashlight hit the walls.

He was only a few yards away.

Gaby turned and fled. On her way across the room, she spotted a fresh corpse, unmarred with disease. Given the bright, suggestive clothing, it had to be the prostitute Rose.

Poor Bliss.

Gaby found the door and went through it with no idea where it led. She trusted God to see her safely outside. As the door shut behind her, impenetrable darkness closed in.

She crawled forward, feeling her way . . .

And that's when she heard the doctor speak. "You let her do this."

Gaby's heart dropped. Dr. Chiles wasn't dead!

Luther shouted, "*No, Mort.* Drop the gun. Now."

"I can't."

The doctor laughed.

And a final shot rang out.

Unable to bear it, Gaby turned back, frantically retracing her steps. If Luther wanted to apprehend her, she'd somehow talk him out of it. Or she'd find a way to evade him.

But she had to know if Morty was safe. He'd come to help her because he cared; she couldn't just abandon him.

Reaching the door she'd gone through, she opened it a mere crack and saw Luther bent over a supine body.

Morty.

He wasn't moving.

A scream crawled up her throat, but before Gaby could get the sound out, several things seemed to happen at once.

She saw the doctor drag herself upright against a rickety table, her mouth twisted in wicked delight. She held Mort's gun.

Luther pushed to his feet and faced her.

The badly wounded doctor stumbled, and a kerosene lantern crashed into one of the oxygen tanks.

An explosion rocked the building, shooting flames everywhere.

The door blasted shut on Gaby. She tried, but it wouldn't budge an inch. Something must have collapsed against it, blocking it. She listened hard, but all she heard was the snap and crackle of hungry flames devouring the carnage.

"No!" Gaby pounded her fists on the door, but it didn't matter. No one acknowledged her calls, and the door didn't dislodge. Smoke seeped into her darkened room, bringing with it the caustic scent of burning wood, cloth, and . . . flesh.

Gaby tried kicking the door with her feet, but the smoke grew thicker, burning her eyes and throat, reminding her that despite being a freak, she was still all too human. She finally had to move away.

Heart pounding hard, silent prayers running amok, Gaby crawled and crawled until she found a hole in an outer wall that led to the swamp.

She stumbled out, fell onto her back in the prickly weeds, and gulped in great gasping breaths. When she could breathe again, she faced the destruction. The flames didn't seem to spread, but with how that room had exploded . . . could anyone make it out of there alive?

Gaby didn't realize she was crying until the sirens began winding down and she heard her own sobs. The weakness so enraged her that she shook a fist at God.

"This is why I can't be friends with people? This is it? Is this my fucking lesson?"

Her raw voice competed with the sounds of chaos, echoing in hollow dismay over the surface of the swamp, emphasizing the futility in all that she did, all that she'd dared to do.

More emergency personnel arrived. Police, firefighters,

EMTs. More voices. Enough lights to brighten the woods and send eerie, dancing shadows everywhere.

Drawn to concealment against her will, Gaby got to her feet and moved out of the open, choosing a position behind a copse of trees where she could watch the busy swarm of police and medics, and still escape if anyone spotted her.

The hot tears continued to fall unheeded down her cheeks as she hunkered down, praying to see Luther or Mort in one of the bright emergency beams trained on the building. So much pain filled her that she wanted to curse and wail. She wanted to scream out her anger.

But doing so would accomplish nothing more than her capture. She'd screwed up enough already—no need to add to it.

Doing her best to tamp down emotion and heighten awareness, Gaby waited as professionals got the fire under control. Soon, the thick smoke subsided and only choking odor billowed out the windows and a busted door.

Please, she prayed.

Seconds later, her heart thumped in relief as a tall, familiar form emerged.

Fingers locked together at the back of his neck, Luther stepped away from the destruction. The female detective, Ann, stood close beside him.

"I don't fucking believe this," Luther cursed.

Appearing dazed, Ann put a hand to her stomach. "They're all dead, Luther. I don't . . . I don't even know what they are. Human?"

"Fucking experiments." Luther dropped his hands and punched the damaged door hard enough to break knuckles.

Glued to the sight of him, Gaby winced in sympathy for his pain, both physical and emotional.

Cuddled up to him, Ann pleaded, "Don't be a caveman, please. I'm too shook up to take it."

"Sorry." Luther flexed his hand. "It's just . . . I know the guy who killed them all."

Gaby's stomach hollowed out. Surely, Luther didn't believe that Morty had done the deed? That was too absurd.

As Gaby's thoughts tumbled, Ann hugged herself up to Luther. "Why do you suppose he did it?"

Slinging his arm around her and pulling her close, Luther said, "God only knows, Ann. God only knows."

Gaby turned her back on them and buried her face against her knees. Yeah, God knew. But He wasn't about to share with the likes of them.

If only she'd gotten that damn door open, if only she hadn't left Morty in the first place, then . . . Luther would have locked her up.

For the sake of humanity, it was better this way.

But then why the hell did it hurt so much?

With nothing else to do, she used a rough tree trunk to pull herself to her feet and, in the near-silent way of wraiths, exited the woods. She had to disappear, and if she didn't hurry, Luther would catch her in the act of packing up the tools she used to write and illustrate her graphic novels.

Nothing else mattered. Not anymore.

Feeling an awful twinge in his heart, Luther pressed a fist to his chest.

Ann grabbed him. "Are you all right?"

"Yeah." But he wasn't. It felt like someone had just ripped out his soul. He'd thought for sure that Gaby would be here, in the middle of the awful destruction.

But so far, there'd been no sign of her.

Duty demanded that he couldn't leave yet, but damn it,

he *needed* to find her. He wasn't sure why, but it felt crucial.

As paramedics carried Mort out on a gurney, Luther had them pause. "One second."

"We need to move."

"Yeah, I know." Luther touched Mort's shoulder. "Mort, where's Gaby?"

Faint and filled with pain, Morty whispered, "Luther?"

"Yeah, it's me. Was Gaby here with you? Is she hurt? Where is she?"

Reddened from smoke and blurry with pain, Mort opened his eyes and looked at Luther. "No."

Frustration threatened to implode. "No *what*?"

Mort pressed his lips together. Flames had singed parts of his hair. A hastily bandaged wound in his side still oozed blood. Various scrapes, bruises, and burns discolored his fair skin. "Gaby's not here, Luther," he said. "She was never here." And then he passed out.

The paramedics hurried on their way.

Sensing a betrayal, Luther watched as Mort was loaded into the ambulance, and he stood there as it drove away, stood there even as the lights disappeared from sight.

Morty had appeared too sick and hurt to lie.

But then, maybe he was too sick and hurt *not* to lie.

Luther needed to figure out which it might be.

Epilogue

Head pounding and irritation level at an all-time high, **Luther** strode down the hospital corridor. His thoughts joggled left and right, but always there, dead center, was a need to see Gaby.

She'd gone and disappeared on him, and he was pissed as hell.

When he pushed open the hospital door to Morty Vance's room, he found Ann sitting on the side of the bed, one of Mort's big-knuckled hands in both of hers.

Un-fucking-believable. But he had to admit, ever since the night of that awful debacle a week ago, Mort was different.

The nurses saw it, and Ann evidently did, too.

In the normal course of things, Ann was too independent to accept any gentlemanly favors. She went out of her way to prove herself an equal to the male detectives.

Yet today, she'd asked Luther to drop her off near the

hospital entrance before sending him off to park the car. She was that anxious to see Morty.

The entire world had turned upside down.

Ann ignored his entrance, but Morty said, "Hey, Luther."

Reclining in bed, his hair freshly washed, his face cleanly shaved, and a crisp hospital gown the only concealment to his scrawny bod, Mort seemed . . . more of a man than Luther remembered.

"Am I interrupting?"

Ann let out a sigh. "Instead of being an ass, why don't you keep Morty company while I go get him something to eat?"

"There's nothing I'd rather do." Luther waited until Ann had circled the bed, then said, "I'll be right back, Mort. I need a quick word with Ann first."

"Sure thing, Luther."

Damn it, he even sounded more confident. Once in the hall, Luther stared down at Ann. "Please don't tell me you're interested in him."

Smug, Ann smiled and examined a nail. "Why would I tell you anything at all? My private life is none of your business."

"Jesus."

Ann shrugged. "There's definitely something about him."

Because he'd felt the same way about Gaby, Luther let it go. "Is he talking much this morning?"

Ann's smile became a warning frown. "Don't you dare forget that Mort almost died and is just now recovering from all he went through. He doesn't remember many of the details from that night, and you badgering him won't change that."

"And now you're a mother hen." Luther rolled his eyes. "Go get the food while I entertain Sir Lancelot."

As she walked away, Ann said, "Sarcasm is not an attractive trait in a man."

Luther waved that off. After days without sleep, a nonstop headache and a feeling of grave loss, being attractive dropped way down on his list of priorities.

The second he stepped back into the room, Morty said, "I haven't seen her, Luther. I swear. I wish I had."

Unconvinced, Luther sidestepped that to ask, "How are you, Mort?"

Leery, Mort frowned at him. "The docs say I should get out of here soon. My head is fine now. If that explosion hadn't sent debris into my guts, giving me an infection, I wouldn't have been here this long." He leveled his brows. "And I really don't know where Gaby is."

"Okay." Taking the chair beside the bed, Luther said, "But you'd tell me if you did?"

His eyes narrowed. "Not if you wanted to arrest her. Gaby didn't do anything wrong."

"I didn't say she did." As annoying as it was to be without answers, Luther applauded Mort's defense of Gaby. She deserved a few defenders in her life. "In fact, against my instincts, I'm beginning to believe you that she wasn't even there that night."

Mort's eyes widened. "You are?"

Not entirely, but he said, "I located that little hooker friend of hers—Bliss."

"The girl Gaby saved from being abused."

"That's the one. Bliss had an interesting story to tell me. She claims Dr. Chiles threatened to kill her, just as she'd killed Rose, another hooker, if Bliss didn't trick Gaby into coming to the isolation hospital. The thing is, Gaby wasn't supposed to go until the next night, when the doctor planned to ambush her."

"You mean kill her."

"Probably." The idiot doctor hadn't realized whom she was up against, to think Gaby would be that dumb. "Far as Bliss knows, Gaby planned to do just that, even promised that she would. But then she went missing, and you went to the abandoned hospital instead." Luther leaned forward, lowering his voice. "And you found the doctor and killed her."

Putting both hands to his head, Mort closed his eyes. "I still can't believe what I saw there. I only went because Gaby seemed cautious of the place. She said the woods were filled with malevolent spirits."

"She had that much right."

"When I couldn't find her, I went there to look for her."

"I'd just dropped her off, Mort."

"I didn't know that." He rubbed at his temples. "I wanted to protect her from whatever was there, but I'm a coward, so I took the gun—which I'd bought off the street from some guy I haven't seen since."

Dryly, because he didn't quite believe that either, Luther said, "Yeah, I have your statement on my desk."

Mort shook his head. "That crazy doctor would have maimed me, Luther, just as she'd done to those other people."

"Probably."

"Even after I shot her, she still tried to come after me. She hit me with that long-handled saw. And she was strong, let me tell you."

"I saw. She'd practically bled to death before she collapsed. If she'd been just a little stronger, I don't think you'd be here today."

Mort shuddered. "And those poor patients of hers . . ." He squeezed his eyes tighter. "They were so deranged from Dr. Chiles's torture that they didn't know what they were doing. I had to defend myself from the ones that came after me."

"Brain cancer is a horrible thing," Luther said, citing

what professionals had told him. "It can obliterate a kind personality, and instead bring out very hostile behavior." Sitting back, Luther stretched out his legs and kept a close watch on Mort's reaction. "But some of those people were too far gone to move, much less physically assault anyone."

"I know." Mort nodded and opened his eyes. "The doctor killed them. You saw that awful scalpel she had. It was insane the way she started slashing and slashing—"

Luther still had a few nightmares himself, so he interrupted Mort's morbid retelling. "In all the time you knew her, Gaby never mentioned any place she might go?"

"No." His voice softened with sadness. "Until recently, Gaby never told me much of anything. I wish I did know where she was. I'd go to her and tell her . . . I'm still her friend."

"Yeah." Luther rubbed his tired eyes. He wanted to tell her something similar himself, only with a little more passion. "If you ever do hear from her, tell her I want to see her, okay?" He glanced toward the door to ensure their privacy. "Off the record, Mort. Tell her I just want to talk to her, to know she's okay. Nothing else."

"Okay." He eyed Luther. "If I see her."

As Luther stood, he noticed the large, thick envelope on the bedside table. "A present?"

Excitement brightened Mort's countenance. "A new *Servant* manuscript. Ann found it when she picked up my mail for me."

Suspicion sparked, and it had nothing to do with Ann's additional signs of infatuation. Luther recalled the similarities in Gaby's behavior and the lead character of the *Servant* novel. If she modeled herself after the heroine, it might be a way to track her.

Of course, it could just be that he was getting desperate. But still . . . "You've already read it?"

"Most of it." Though he winced, Mort sat up a little straighter. "It's incredible. Do you want to read it when I'm done?"

"Yeah. I do. Soon as you finish with it, let me know."

Ann walked back in carrying a tray of fresh fruit and a warm waffle.

As a visual nudge, Luther glanced at his watch. Now that he'd spoken to Mort, they both had other things to do.

"Don't start pacing," she said. "I'm ready to go, too."

She gave Mort the food, kissed his forehead, and after whispering something in his ear, left with Luther.

"That was nauseating," he told her.

"Get used to it."

"Really?" Luther could barely credit such a thing. Morty and Ann? He shuddered. "You're hitting me at a bad time, Ann. I'm not sure I can take it."

"You're just stressed. You've worked hard tying up the loose ends, getting that creep at the crematorium to confess. But he did just that, even detailing how the doctor paid him to look the other way. You need to take a day off, relax a little. Sleep. And eat."

"Yeah, I'll get right on all that—tomorrow." Today, he wanted to follow a few improbable leads. If he didn't track Gaby down soon, he had a feeling he'd never find her.

And that possibility was unacceptable.

❦

Unfortunately, the weeks went by and still Luther had no clue where to find Gaby. Mort continued to deny any contact with her, and after staking out his place, Luther had to believe him. The *Servant* novel, while addictive, hadn't provided any new clues. In fact, it had depressed the hell out of him because the lead character had suffered a setback and as a result, would live her life in lonely, detached isolation.

If Gaby allowed the graphic novel to influence her, that plot turn didn't bode well for him.

After another long stressful day, he was about to pack up and head home for the night when a bruised and battered man walked in. He made a beeline for Luther.

Feeling more than a little uncharitable, Luther asked, "Got run over by a truck?"

"No, some little bitch over on Fifth and Elm did a number on me."

That put Luther back in his seat. The man sported a black eye, a bleeding nose, bruises on his cheek and chin, and a hand pressed to his ribs. "You say *she* was *little*?" With a nod of his head, Luther indicated the man's bludgeoned posture. "And she did all that to you?"

Hot color flushed beneath the black and blue marks. "She was skinny, but tall. Maybe as tall as you. Fast and strong and mean as hell."

Tall. Skinny. Mean.

Could it be? Hope slowly brought Luther to his feet. "Dark hair?"

"Yeah. Has someone else been in to complain about her, too?"

Luther waved that off and scowled at the man in accusation. "Why'd she maul you?"

"Hell if I know! She took offense at something I did."

"To her?"

He propped himself against Luther's desk and shook his head. "No, to some old whore trying to rope me in."

None of it seemed plausible—which seemed *exactly* like Gaby. "Rope you in how?"

In a quandary now, the man did a verbal stumble. "She . . . made an offer. I wasn't going to take her up on it. I don't need to pay for sex. But I told her she was charging too much anyway."

"Right." In other words, the man had tried to short-change a prostitute on an agreed-upon amount. "You insulted a hooker, and for that a female bystander beat the shit out of you?"

More color rose in his face. His teeth clenched. "I think she was a whore, too."

Rage seeped in. *"What?"*

"She was hanging out with a few of them, being all chatty and friendly-like. Then boom." His fist hit the desk. "She threatened me."

Surely, the man wouldn't be that stupid. "And then you took a swing at a woman?"

Guilt had him backing down off his tirade. "I wasn't really going to hit her! I swear. But before I knew it, she was all over me. Kicking, slugging it out like a dude. All without making a sound. I swear, I think she was letting off steam."

Every nerve in Luther's body twitched. "You say she's over by Fifth and Elm?"

"She was. But that was damn near an hour ago." He touched his swollen eye. "You going after her?"

"Damn right." Luther grabbed up his car keys, his wallet, then he paused. It sounded like Gaby, but then again, it didn't. "Was she dressed like a hooker?"

"Not like any I've ever seen. But why else would she be hanging out with them?"

Thank God. He couldn't quite imagine Gaby in flaunt mode. "What'd she have on?"

"Sloppy clothes. Loose sandals. Oh, and a choker necklace."

Luther's heart pounded hard. Would Gaby still be wearing his gift? "Describe it."

With a shrug, the man said, "Black leather, I think. With a little silver cross in the middle."

"Ann!"

At Luther's shout, the man jumped a foot and Ann came running. She looked worried. "What?"

"Finish with this guy, will you?"

"Sure, but why?"

Like he had time to explain! "I'm going out."

"All right, fine, but . . . Luther! Slow down."

"No time."

"You can answer a single question, damn it." Ann caught his arm and pulled him to the side. "Now, what's going on? Are you okay? Where are you going?"

He tucked his wallet away, straightened his tie. "That's three questions, Ann."

"Answer one of them, damn you!"

"I'm fine." A smile broke over his face. "I'm going to get someone who got away."

"A suspect?"

"No. She's not . . . that." Gaby was too smart to stay in the area if she thought he'd have any reason at all to arrest her. Either she was innocent, or she knew he couldn't pin anything on her. At the moment, either suited him just fine.

Ann didn't appreciate his rush. "This is insane. Do you need backup?"

He actually grinned, his first real grin in a long while. "No, but *she* might when I get my hands on her." On impulse, whether Mort liked it or not, he pulled Ann in close and gave her a sound smacker right on her mulish mouth. "Hold down the fort, sweetheart. I'll be back when I can."

On his way out the door, Luther vowed, "You won't escape me again, Gabrielle Cody. Not a second time."

And now a special preview of the next book
in the chilling new series by L. L. Foster.

SERVANT: The Acceptance

Coming soon from Berkley!

Standing deep in the shadows of a tall brick building to avoid the glow of a streetlamp, Detective Luther Cross clenched his teeth together. Off duty, but determined, he stared down the sidewalk a good ten yards ahead. His eyes burned and his fury built. Even from that distance, with the moon high in the sky casting eerie shadows over the bleak surroundings, he recognized her.

Gabrielle Cody.

The bane of his existence.

The source of nightmares—and scorching hot erotic dreams.

Her long, thin legs, sleek and toned with muscles, shown beneath a denim miniskirt. Black-leather ankle boots replaced her familiar flip-flop sandals, and a loose tank top revealed the outline of the sheath at her back.

Her short, dark hair now had vivid purple streaks throughout.

She'd disguised herself in her idea of a whore's garb, but Luther would know that stance, feel that cocky attitude, no matter her outward appearance.

For weeks he'd hunted her, lost sleep over her, worried and ruminated and raged . . . and there she stood, appearing as aloof and untouchable as ever.

Alone.

Deliberately distant.

Taunting him without even trying.

Unsure exactly what he'd say or do, Luther started forward. With her keen perception of her surroundings, Gaby might have picked up on his approach. Very little ever got by her.

But at that moment, a young, lanky boy, maybe twelve or thirteen, came out of an alley. Blond, well-groomed, he didn't seem shy or reserved. Dressed in clean jeans and a buttoned-up shirt, he bore no resemblance to the homeless or desperate runaways that often crowded the streets. He stared toward the building that Gaby protected, sizing it up for some purpose that Luther couldn't fathom.

Gaby focused on him.

And when Gaby focused, it was something awesome to see.

She went rigid, straightening away from the building then immediately relaxing in the deceptive way appropriate to true warriors.

Not a good sign.

Gaby could attack without warning, fight with lethal skill, and her motives remained more elusive than not.

Luther knew this, and accepted it.

But why did the boy interest her?

Forgetting his own disgruntlement for the moment, Luther picked up his pace to reach her, to protect the kid—but not in enough time.

The boy saw him and bolted.

Gaby wasted no time chasing after him.

Shit.

They darted around a corner, disappeared into the darkness of the night, and Luther, not being an idiot, slowed and pulled his gun. He wouldn't shoot Gaby, but then again, he wouldn't walk into a trap either.

He wanted her, but he didn't trust her. Not anymore.

Now using caution, he crept into the narrow, dank alley and willed his eyes to adjust. At the far end, he saw movement and crept farther inside. Finally he found Gaby, that lethal blade of hers in her hand, slowly opening a broken door.

Heart pounding, Luther steadied his hands, and his thoughts. "Not another step, Gaby."

Other than a slight stiffening of her neck, she made no acknowledgment of him.

All her intense scrutiny remained on whatever she saw beyond the door. Even from the back, in the murky gloom of the odorous alley, Luther noted the changes in her features, the tightening and subtle morphing that signaled her sense of threat.

"Gaby."

She didn't look toward him, and at first, Luther was uncertain if she'd even heard him. He caught his breath, eased closer, and said again, "Gaby, listen to me."

By small degrees, she exposed her awareness of him. It showed in the subtle relaxing of her shoulders, the easing of her tension.

Without altering her attention, she warned, "It's not a good time, Luther."

Just hearing her voice reassured and pleased him. His pulse slowed. "That's too bad." He flexed his fingers around the gun. "Put the knife down and your arms up."

As she mulled over his order, her jaw worked. She eased back the tiniest bit—

Suddenly a clatter came from inside the abandoned building, and Gaby, realizing her prey had found an alternate way out, slammed the door hard.

"Son of a bitch." She rounded on Luther in a rage. "You let him get away!"

Semi-used to her and her odd manners and coarse language, Luther feigned a negligent attitude and asked, "Him who?" Now that she faced him, he saw that some strange emotion still gripped her. She looked like Gaby, but then again, she didn't.

Storming toward him, the knife still out and her pale eyes glittering, Gaby curled her lip. "Now that you blundered in, there's no way for us to know, is there?"

"That's close enough," he warned.

Disregarding that, she came right up to him, nose to nose. "Is it?"

Jesus, he'd missed her ballsy bravado and brash disregard for common civility. He wanted to crush her close, wanted to tell her . . . what?

In their current position, the barrel of his gun pressed into her sternum. "Put. The knife. Away."

Blue eyes sparking, Gaby scrutinized him. "Ah, what's the matter? You afraid of me, Luther?"

Her snicker deliberately provoked—but she did reach behind herself and sheath the knife. The purple highlights in her hair caught scant scraps of moonlight. The thrill of the moment had tightened her nipples, now showing beneath her thin tank top. A light sheen of sweat touched her skin.

"I won't gut you, cop." Her slim brows came down, and she added a low, "Not without reason."

The second the knife didn't pose a threat, Luther grabbed both her wrists and slammed her up against the brick wall. The gun he still held pressed into her flesh, but he couldn't temper himself, couldn't take the time to holster it or reason with her or . . . anything.

Chest to chest, anger simmering between them, he sought words that would somehow convey all he felt—the resentment and relief, the concern and . . . so much more.

Gaby looked at his mouth. "How'd you find me, anyway? I've been quiet. I've been *good*." Her gaze came up to his, challenging him and firing his blood. "I figured on never seeing you again. But here you are."

God, she sounded the same, as if nothing had happened, as if people hadn't died and monsters hadn't existed. He sounded hoarse as he pointed out, "You've been knocking around johns."

Quiet satisfaction chased away the last remnants of her odd transformation, showing him the Gaby he'd grown to know so well. "Only when they deserved it, Luther." She relaxed against the wall, uncaring of how he held her, unconcerned with any threat he might pose. "Only when they deserved it."

God almighty, would he ever understand her? Would she slip away from him again? Would she forever make him crazy with conflicting emotions?

"Why, Gaby?" There were so many unknowns. A million of them. Hopefully, she caught all that the simple question encompassed.

COMING FEBRUARY 2008

LORI FOSTER

HARD TO HANDLE

SBC fighter Harley Handleman has an outlook on life as hard as his muscular body. Fate has dealt him a sucker punch—and a one-two, at that. First, there were his failed attempts at the title belt. Then, Harley's mother lost her own fight with breast cancer, leaving him with no family but his trainer, Uncle Satch.

But now, Anastasia Kelley walks back into his life....

penguin.com
AD-014787